Million Reasons

Also by Lisa Herrington

The Renaissance Lake Series

The Fix

Fall Again

Million Reasons

Standalone Books

One Starry Night

Million Reasons

Lisa Herrington

Writerly House Publishing

MILLION REASONS

Published by Writerly House Publishing
www.WriterlyHouse.com
www.LisaHerrington.com
This is a work of fiction. Characters, names, places, and events are products of the author's imagination. Any similarity to events or places, or real persons, living or dead, is purely coincidental.

ISBN: 978-0-9990626-2-3

10 9 8 7 6 5 4 3 2 1

For G. G. & J.

Chapter One

The quaint town of Maisonville was considered a haven for most retirees and young adults alike. Surrounded by water from a river on one side and a large lake on the other, there were endless options for those who loved the outdoors.

The small town was a suburb of New Orleans, and a long 24-mile bridge over water separated the two. Many believed it was just far enough for residents to partake in crowded city festivals and enjoy the peaceful sanctuary that was Maisonville.

Olivia Dufrene would argue about how peaceful the town was or whether it should be called a sanctuary after her long day at work. She slid down onto the stool behind the lunch counter in the diner where she'd been a waitress for six years. It was the first time she'd stopped since seven that morning, and she couldn't believe it was Wednesday and not Saturday.

The weekend would bring an even larger crowd, and the diner would be packed beyond reason. It was south Louisiana, and October brought the first reasonable temperatures since spring, and everyone loved to visit the town during that time.

Miss Lynn, who owned the diner, put her arm around Olivia. "I promise to get us more help soon."

They had been short-handed for seven months since their

friend and previous waitress, Sydney Bell, had left to work with her now husband, Ryan Gentry. They remodeled old homes and were another example of why Maisonville was popular. It was nicknamed Renaissance Lake because everyone believed there was a little magic to the town. It was said that when you moved to Maisonville, you were given a chance to begin again at life, a career, a friendship, or maybe even romance.

"It's fine. I need the hours, Miss Lynn," Olivia said. "Of course, right now, I could use a foot massage."

"I think I know someone who would be up for the job." Miss Lynn grinned as she teased Olivia about her late-night caller.

"Hell— O kitty," Olivia said, covering her curse word as her young son walked through the diner door. Lucas was in second grade, and his school bus let him out in front of the diner each day.

"Mom!" Lucas began to scold her.

"I didn't say it, Lucas. I said, hello, kitty," Olivia turned and rolled her eyes at Miss Lynn. She'd tried to stop cursing for months, and it was a lot harder than she'd thought it would be.

During his summer break, Lucas helped his mother put away the clean dishes and accidentally dropped a bowl onto the tile floor, breaking it. He promptly yelled, "Shit," which made Olivia cringe. She explained how crude it was for people to curse and then promised to stop doing it herself. They took an old canister and labeled it as "The Swear Jar," and if she or Lucas said a bad word, they had to put a dollar in it.

She was already up to twenty dollars, and that was only from what he'd caught her saying. Focus, Olivia, she thought to herself and then promptly burned her hand on the empty coffee pot sitting on the hotplate. "Sugar-Honey-Iced-Tea!" she yelled before rushing to the sink to run her hand under cold water.

Miss Lynn hurried over to examine the damage, but Olivia told her she was okay.

"Good save," Miss Lynn said. She was tickled over Olivia's substitutions for her bad language and ever surprised at what she came up with on the fly. She winked at the younger woman and then cleared a space at the counter for Lucas to start his homework.

That was their afternoon routine during the school year. Every afternoon, Lucas would come in and do his homework while Miss Lynn made him a snack. She loved to dote on the seven-year-old and had felt like he was a grandson since the day Olivia walked through the diner door with him on her hip.

It was six years ago when Lucas was only a year old, and Olivia was twenty-two. It was right before closing, and the dinner crowd had thinned out when the raven-haired beauty with cobalt blue eyes hurried into the diner. She was clearly shaken and trying to hide it. She sat at the bar and simply asked for a glass of water so she could make a bottle. Miss Lynn saw that she didn't have on any shoes and sat down at the bar with Olivia offering to hold Lucas while she mixed up the formula for him.

By the time the last customer had left, Miss Lynn had found a pair of sandals for Olivia and offered her a room for the night. By morning, she'd given Olivia a job and allowed her to bring baby Lucas with her until they could find childcare nearby.

It was the beginning of a lovely friendship that turned more familial by the day.

Olivia sat next to Lucas as he worked out his math problems and then kissed him on the forehead before she began setting up for the dinner crowd.

Some days Olivia took Lucas home to play outside after school, and on others, he would stay at the diner until Olivia got off.

Miss Lynn enjoyed sitting with him to color until they got busy. Once the diner began to fill up, she or Olivia would get Lucas set up in the back room where he could watch television or look at books. At seven or seven-thirty, Olivia got off, and they headed home.

At their small duplex, Olivia rushed Lucas through his bath

time and then laid in bed with him to read. He loved reading and insisted on five of his favorite books every night.

Thankful that she hadn't fallen asleep, she quietly padded out of the room and left the slightest crack in the door so she could peer in on him later.

She had towels to fold and another load of laundry to finish before washing the dinner dishes. She checked her wall calendar and saw the reminder to check Lucas' bookbag for his folder and papers that she needed to sign.

Rushing through a quick shower, she headed to the laundry room so she could finish her chores and eventually get into bed. She checked the clock on the kitchen wall and smiled that it was nine o'clock.

ALEXAVIER REGALIA WAS in his last term as Mayor of New Orleans. He had a little more than a year left on his second term and had spent most of his time helping modernize city hall. He'd changed the landscape for local government, making them more efficient and better able to serve the public.

He was an overachiever and one of the most beloved mayors in the city's recent history. He truly understood how to increase the quality of life for residents and worked tirelessly to clean up crime and give some affordable housing and even healthcare options for its citizens.

Alexavier had grown up in the heart of the city and had strong Italian roots that could be traced back for generations. He'd lost his wife to cancer early in his first term, and after a year of mourning, he slowly began to date.

The beloved mayor was seen with local beauties like Miss Louisiana, the local favorite evening news anchor, and various single doctors, lawyers, and real estate agents. He never seemed serious with anyone, but he was social and kept local gossip buzzing about him.

However, while he continued to keep up appearances at all the local festivals, farmer's markets, high school theater shows, 10k running events, and various high school football games, Alexavier had been quietly but seriously focused on only one woman.

He'd met beautiful Olivia almost six months earlier at a friend's cook-out in Maisonville, but she had yet to let him take her out on a proper date. Instead, they slowly began to chat over texts and late-night phone calls.

For a couple of months, he'd sent texts to her, or she'd text him a funny meme, but she wouldn't go out with him. He'd figured it was because she had a young son, but he'd offered to take them both to the zoo or the aquarium. Still, she declined, making excuses about work or other obligations.

July and August brought their own excuses, but the texting turned into a few late-night calls.

It gave him hope.

Then in September, things turned even more promising. He'd begun to call her almost nightly. They would laugh and talk for an hour or longer about her day at work or his. Sometimes, they discussed music and the lyrics of their favorite songs. She liked to read smut, as she called it, and she would brazenly tell him about those stories. Those phone calls were hot, and he knew she was teasing him but also affected by the naughty conversations. But still, she wouldn't have lunch or dinner with him.

He'd driven across the lake once a week for months to Maisonville to have lunch at the diner where she worked, just to see her. It took forty minutes one way to get there, but it was worth it to speak to her in person.

He loved her laugh but to see her do it in person was even better. She had a great sense of humor. She also had a big heart, and he watched her on more than one occasion give someone a sandwich or cup of coffee because they forgot their wallet or didn't have enough. Alexavier and Olivia clicked on many different levels, and the attraction between them was mutual. He could see it in her eyes, her beautiful blue eyes. Still, she wouldn't let him take her out to dinner or even allow him to cook dinner for her.

He wasn't going to give up. It was October and a fantastic time to enjoy the city and all the fun it offered. He would find a way to talk her into spending a day or night out together.

Alexavier finished eating a leftover bowl of spaghetti for dinner and then propped up his feet on the coffee table in his living room. He wondered what Olivia and Lucas had eaten for dinner and smiled that all boys liked spaghetti and meatballs.

A notification ring came from his phone and made him laugh. It was nine PM and later than he'd thought, but he could almost set his watch by Olivia Dufrene.

Chapter Two

If Olivia didn't hear from Alexavier by nine, she always sent a text. He liked how she checked on him. But he also noticed that she was a strong, confident woman that would wait for him to call her.

He immediately dialed her number.

"Hey," she said, and he could hear how tired she was over the phone. Her voice was a little lower and huskier at night but especially when she was exhausted.

"Hi, beautiful. Are you in bed?"

"Not yet. I have a load of Lucas' clothes to finish, and then I'm falling face-first into my pillow."

"It's Wednesday, couldn't that wait until the weekend?"

"I'm working all weekend. Besides, Lucas and his friends have decided rolling down the hill on the playground and into some leaves would be a great way to spend recess this week. His clothes are filthy."

"Aaah, boys. Got to love them."

"I love that one, but he's never getting any brothers or sisters. I need all my energy solely to keep up with him," she laughed.

"That's not funny, Olivia."

"I wasn't trying to be funny. I was being honest," she said, trying to figure out why he sounded serious all of a sudden.

"You honestly don't want any more children?"

So that was what bothered him? "I'm not sure, Alex. Being a single mom isn't exactly a walk in the park," she said, and he heard her opening and closing her washing machine and then the dryer.

"I'm not proposing you go it alone, and you know it."

She smirked. "I think you're teasing me. You don't seem like the type of man who wants kids. You do know they cramp your dating lifestyle."

"Is that why you won't go out with me?"

"I didn't say I wouldn't go out with you."

"Yes, you have. Every time I've asked, you've made up an excuse."

"Um, those were all legit."

"Tell me the truth, Olivia. Do you not want to be seen with me?"

Alexavier had made a gross error in judgment six months ago before meeting Olivia. Someone he'd mistakenly trusted as a close friend had used that trust against him. Mathew Nunan had been a successful attorney and scheming criminal that distracted Alexavier with investment deals.

Mathew had also convinced Alexavier that one of Matt's law partners, Reagan Gentry, desperately wanted him. He'd constantly pushed Alexavier to be aggressive with her because it turned her on. Alexavier was lonely and open to flirting with the attractive woman and, in the end, figured out the lie almost too late.

At the same time, Nunan bribed two city council members to get a health facility voted into the city, where he had a substantial vested interest. They'd almost gotten away with it if it weren't for Reagan Gentry, her best friend, Amber, and the man she truly wanted, Seth Young, coming to the rescue.

Unfortunately, several people died before it was over and plenty of information about the ordeal made national news. Alexavier was sure that six months later, Olivia was still too embarrassed to go out with him.

Olivia laid down in her bed and pulled the covers up to her neck. "It's not that I don't want to be seen with you. I simply don't want to be in any newspapers or magazines— especially as the nameless face you're sampling that week."

Did she think she would be one of many? He'd tried like hell to figure out why she wouldn't go out with him, and while there were other reasons it could have been, he decided it was the embarrassing and tragic event from six months prior.

Could it be something so simple? It had been a long time since he'd had privacy, and he'd forgotten how important it was to others.

"Olivia, I haven't been out with anyone since we met."

"I know. I mean, Miss Lynn reads all the gossip, and she's informed me that you haven't been photographed with anyone lately." Olivia wasn't about to tell him that it thrilled her not to see him with anyone else.

"I'm glad Miss Lynn is keeping an eye out."

Olivia laughed at that. "There isn't much she doesn't know. Miss Lynn's like a British tabloid when it comes to gossip. She knows everything about everyone. People follow her around the diner and spill every secret they've ever had so that she'll tell them what to do. I've seen it. It's kind of amazing."

Alexavier laughed about Miss Lynn. He'd noticed her in action at the diner himself. She handed out advice with slices of her homemade pies.

Olivia yawned.

"You're exhausted, Olivia. I should let you get to sleep. Are you in bed?"

He couldn't see her, but she was smiling.

"In bed, and lights are turned off," she said.

"What are you wearing?" he asked, using his deep voice and making her laugh. She always asked him that whenever he said he was in bed. She was such a tease.

"Shorts and a sweatshirt. It's very sexy."

He thought she was sexy in everything that she wore. "No doubt, it's sexy."

"Come over and see for yourself," she said, knowing he wouldn't.

Such. A. Tease.

"Do you know how much I wish I were there?" he asked, making her stomach tighten. "But you know, I'm not that kind of man. You at least have to let me feed you dinner once," he said.

He'd made every mistake possible when listening to his so-called friend give him advice the last time. He hadn't trusted his own instincts. Although Olivia was saying the words to him directly, he had to go with his gut.

She would never see them as more than a fling if he slept with her secretly. He felt a connection with Olivia from the beginning, but over the past few months had felt even closer as he'd genuinely gotten to know her. He wanted it to be more.

He grinned, thinking about all the Italian women in his family, young and old, that would jump on him if he dated a single mother and didn't do right by her and her son. And they would find out. They always found out everything before it showed up in the papers.

"I can find a way to keep our date private. Just give me some time to think about it," he said.

"I don't get you, Alexavier. I've invited you into my bed more than once, and all you seem to want to do is feed me." Olivia didn't try to hide the disappointment in her voice. She was frustrated at the gorgeous man on the phone. They'd talked about everything during their late-night calls and even had some sexually charged conversations that left her hot and bothered, but still, he hadn't accepted her offer of hot sex with no strings.

"It's my mother's fault," he laughed. "I'm Italian, and we woo you with food. It's in my DNA."

"Talk about making up excuses," she said. "If you don't want in my bed, then you could tell me. I'll still talk to you."

Alexavier shook his head. She was the most frustrating woman he'd met in a long time. "I'll call you tomorrow with a plan for our date, and we will discuss it then. Deal?"

"If you say so, Alex. Good night."

"Sweet dreams, Olivia," he said and then went to take a shower.

§

OLIVIA WAS UP EARLY, washing the dishes she'd left in the sink, and then made breakfast for Lucas.

She was still a little tired, but she always spent a few minutes with him over breakfast before she had to send him away to school all day. He was the light of her life and the reason she'd constantly tried to be a better human.

It was that goal that got her moving early every day. She scrambled the last two eggs from the refrigerator for Lucas and hurried him to the breakfast table. They had twelve minutes before he had to be out the door to catch the school bus.

"I don't like eggs," he grumbled as he ate a few bites. He knew his mother worked hard to provide food for them, and he rarely complained. But it was 6:45 in the morning, he was still sleepy, and it slipped out.

"I know, buddy. I promise to buy you some of that chocolate milk you like when I get paid. Here's some more ketchup," Olivia said as she kissed his forehead and ran to get his schoolbag.

She sat there with him while he finished the eggs, and she opened the mail from the day before. "Mother—," she paused as Lucas sternly looked at her. "Trucker. Mother trucker. Mother trucker," she said as she opened a letter from her bank.

"Sorry, Lucas. I wasn't going to say the other one," she said, smiling at him. Her ex-boyfriend and Lucas' dad, Brent, had bounced another check to her for child support. It was the second one in a row. Her bank had charged her a twenty-dollar fee for it.

Damn-Damn-Damn

"Darn," she said and smiled at Lucas. "It's okay, buddy. It's only bills," she said to her son so he wouldn't worry. She held herself together until his school bus drove away, and then she hurried back into her duplex before saying more expletives.

She'd done everything she could to make ends meet. She lived in the cheapest rental house in town and still drove her first car which was over ten years old. She also monitored their electricity and water usage to the dollar and didn't buy a single item at the grocery store unless it was on sale, or she had a coupon. The only exception was Hershey's chocolate syrup for Lucas' milk. Once a month, she splurged on that syrup, only for him. He was seven, and chocolate milk shouldn't be a luxury.

She knew Brent wasn't reliable, but he was bouncing more checks lately, making it harder for her to budget the necessities. They'd agreeably split up and went online to figure out what was customary when sharing custody of a child. He'd even agreed to pay her a hundred dollars more than the recommended amount based on his income.

None of that mattered.

All that agreeing had gotten her nowhere. She never went more than a few months without having at least one of the checks returned for insufficient funds. Two in a row was ridiculous. It was challenging to take care of Lucas with what she made as a waitress, but the tips were good, and with the child support, it was enough to get them by. It didn't matter that Olivia hadn't had a new item of clothing in two years. She didn't need much as long as Lucas had everything he needed. She worked double shifts to ensure he was set, including a new coat for winter. He was growing like a weed and needed new clothes and shoes often.

Grabbing her cell phone off the counter, she rushed out to get to the diner. Miss Lynn had already given her extra hours to help compensate for the lost money. But on her way there, she would call Brent and give him a good cussing.

She shook her head. It was too early to say the things she was about to say to Brent, and she scolded herself. Besides, she would go broke if she didn't break the bad habit soon.

She pulled into the parking lot at work and threw her phone into her purse. She should have expected that Brent wouldn't answer. He always avoided her when he owed child support. He had no clue how much it cost to take care of a child full time.

Olivia pulled her long hair into a ponytail holder and straightened her shoulders. She would earn enough tips by the end of the day to at least buy a few groceries. There was no need to get upset when she had the means to take care of the situation. She was strong and capable. Of course, no banker had better sit in her section, or she might have a little talk with them about their whole ridiculous-fees-against-their-own-customers nonsense.

She smirked at how much fun it would be to torment one of the buttoned-up managers from the bank when her phone rang. She wouldn't have to take out her frustration on one of the local bankers after all because she was about to yell it out with her ex, Brent.

Chapter Three

Olivia sat her purse behind the counter and thanked Miss Lynn for the cup of coffee she had waiting for her. Then she held the phone out so she could show her that Brent was on the line and scooted out the back door of the diner so she could talk to him.

She was exhausted trying to hide things from her son, and damn if Brent wasn't making her life more difficult.

"Mornin' Liv, I know why you called. Listen, It's not my fault. I have been working like crazy and have three big jobs going at once. I lost track of the deposits and mistakenly bought more supplies before I had payments. You know how bad I am at finances, and fuck if I didn't know until your call that I bounced a check. I'm doing good, woman. I'm hitting it big time, and I promise I'll make it up to you and the little man soon."

She'd heard all his excuses before, and he'd never once made up any lost child support money. "You sound high, Brent. You always sound like that when you've stayed up all night."

"Liv, don't worry about me. I've got it under control. You have to run with the wolves all night if you want to make the big deals. I'm telling you, things are turning around for me. I'm going to make a ton of loot off these jobs. Look, darlin', I promise I'll get you something by the end of next week to hold you over until they pay out."

He always made it sound like he was doing her a favor instead of paying what he owed for his son's care. "You know he needs groceries every day, right? He's outgrown all his clothes, and I had to buy all new school uniforms, plus shoes, underwear, and a raincoat this month. You can't keep putting him off, Brent. He's a living human being. He needs a father."

"That's a low blow, Liv, and you know it."

"No. What's low is you not keeping your word. You don't come to see him, and you don't send child support like we agreed. I have had it."

"What is that supposed to mean?"

She threatened to take him to court and have them handle the child support, and he promised her again he would send some money by the end of next week. He didn't need to know that she couldn't afford an attorney. He would do anything not to have his wages or taxes garnered, and so she used that threat whenever she needed.

It used to work on him, but things had changed in the last year. He talked more lovey-dovey to Olivia over the phone, which drove her crazy. He also went longer and longer without seeing Lucas, and that hurt Lucas' feelings which crushed her. She spent loads of time playing with Lucas outside to try and make up for all the physical time he didn't get with his father.

"Mother trucker!" Olivia stared at her phone. In the middle of her threatening to take Brent to court, the line went dead. The minute it happened, she knew it was off for good until she could pay the bill.

Brent was full of bullshit. Bull-shark, she reminded herself. He wouldn't send her money soon because he was probably gambling again.

He'd had a little bit of a problem when they first dated, but it quickly grew out of control once she'd gotten pregnant. It was one of the reasons she took Lucas and moved across the lake. She didn't like the way Brent acted when he lost really big or even when he won. It was a drug for him, and he couldn't control his behavior.

She also didn't like the people he borrowed money from when he gambled. Every bottom feeder in the city swarmed around him when he played cards. She wasn't about to raise her baby boy around that crowd. It wasn't safe.

She didn't have a family anymore, but her childhood had been decent. She had a sister eight years older than her, Beth, and she was good to Olivia when she was a kid. She'd braided her hair and dressed her up in the cutest dresses. Their family was religious, and they'd attended church whenever the doors were open. It was a good place to grow up until it wasn't, and it taught her to at least give her son a fighting chance in the complicated world.

Brent rarely came through for Lucas, but she would find a way to provide for him. Brent's money didn't matter. Of course, she didn't want to be late on her rent. She had until Monday to pay it in full, or there would be a hundred-dollar late fee. She had most of it, and she'd already made arrangements to work all weekend to try and earn the rest. Still, it was going to be close.

She shoved her phone into her pocket as she walked back into the diner. It was a cheap phone, on a month-to-month prepaid plan, and the only luxury she had that she could give up in desperate times.

When she walked back inside, Miss Lynn had all the tables ready for the morning customers and handed Olivia an apron and a fresh cup of coffee.

It was evident that Olivia was a little upset, but she rarely discussed her ex-boyfriend, and Miss Lynn didn't force the conversation. Initially, she would prompt Olivia over her ex or her family, but the young woman seemed to tuck all the negativity away as she put all of her energy into Lucas.

Miss Lynn would do anything to help Olivia, but outside of letting her make Lucas a snack or give him puzzles and coloring books, she always told Miss Lynn that she had everything under control.

It was unnerving sometimes watching Olivia juggle things on her own when most people in her situation would break. But it was also inspiring watching her work hard every day for a better life for herself and her son.

She was a wonderful mother and gave everything she had into being a mom. Still, Miss Lynn wished the young woman would find some happiness and wondered what it would take for her to accept a little something for herself.

ALEXAVIER GOT HOME LATER than usual and heated some homemade ravioli that his auntie made for him. He'd missed the weekly family dinner that happened to be on Tuesday that week and at Auntie Francesca's house because he'd had an evening event for work. When he'd gotten home, a cooler was sitting on his porch with enough ravioli for three people.

One day he would treat Olivia and Lucas to his family's cooking. He ate at the kitchen counter and then showered. He decided to watch some football he had saved on the DVR until nine.

He'd had a rough day and couldn't wait to hear Olivia's voice. Most days were busy as the city mayor, but he enjoyed it. After seven years, he'd become accustomed to the crazy schedule that could turn on a dime. However, when city workers were injured, he took it personally and felt for the families involved.

It started going to hell around one that afternoon when the first fire was reported, and by four o'clock, there had been three large fires that resulted in six injured firefighters and some construction workers. The police chief called him while the fire departments battled the blazes. The fires had been set deliberately. Alexavier visited each site and then headed to the hospital to speak with the injured men and their families.

It wasn't business as usual, and once he walked into his house, he was thankful to have time alone to decompress. At least he needed time alone since he couldn't be with Olivia. As soon as he'd received the worst news, he wanted to talk with her. She had a way of making him relax that he hadn't experienced in a long time, if ever. She was strong and funny, and he liked her more than he'd admitted. He didn't want to scare her off, but he was beginning to need her in his life more.

Alexavier rechecked the clock, and it was 8:15. Olivia had a schedule she kept solid for Lucas, and he didn't want to interrupt their evening time. He would wait until nine.

He'd laid awake most of the night before deciding on a plan to take her and Lucas out and keep it private. As long as the press thought he was going to be somewhere else, he would be able to sneak away and be with them. It was a simple plan, but he looked forward to it more than just about anything else he was doing, especially after dealing with the day's tragedies.

Settling in, he planned to watch the recorded game until their usual time to talk but accidentally fell asleep.

Alexavier jerked awake on the couch and immediately checked the large iron clock on the wall. It was after eleven, and he'd fallen asleep sitting up on the couch. He hadn't done that in a long time, knowing it was from the stress.

He picked up his phone to double-check that he hadn't missed Olivia's text.

Nope.

She hadn't texted him. He quickly called her but got a recording telling him her number was no longer valid.

Alexavier immediately stood up. What the hell? He tried to remember their conversation the night before. Had he upset her without knowing it?

He paced the floor and then tried her number again. Still, the recording came on that it wasn't a valid number.

Why did it have to sound so ominous? It couldn't have sounded worse if the operator had said, "Olivia Dufrene has changed her number so that you won't bother her anymore, Mr. Mayor."

He ran his hands through his hair several times and rechecked the clock. It was too late to head across the lake and check on her. She was probably asleep.

He paced the floor a while longer, tried the number one more time, and then turned off the television and went to bed, keeping his phone close to him all night. Hoping she'd changed the number for another reason and would call and talk to him.

Chapter Four

Lucas was happy that it was Friday. He would get to feed the class iguana because it was finally his turn. He also had his favorite chocolate milk for breakfast.

Olivia loved seeing her son so happy, and it helped ease the crappy way her day had started. She'd run out of coffee the day before and couldn't afford it and the chocolate syrup at the same time. She'd made a little grocery money, but she didn't have extra to spare for her favorite drink too.

After seeing Lucas off on the school bus, she hurried to the diner. She had three long days ahead of her with extra work hours and needed to pull herself together. She could do whatever it took to provide for her son.

Miss Lynn smiled at Olivia when she walked in and held up a steaming cup of coffee for her. She drank it black with one sugar, and Miss Lynn had it ready and waiting.

"You're the best, Miss Lynn," she said. "You do know that you save my life with caffeine, right? Thank you." She smiled and then thought about Lucas and how happy he was to have chocolate milk. She could wait to buy herself coffee. Especially since sweet Miss Lynn always had some for her.

"You're welcome, honey. I love that I can do something to

help start your day off in the right direction. It's the least I can do since you're going to pick up all those extra shifts this weekend. I've gotta do something to keep you going," Miss Lynn winked at the young woman she'd thought of more like a daughter than an employee.

It was going to be a busy day and an even busier weekend than they'd had in a while. There was a wooden boat festival scheduled for that weekend, and it brought tons of tourists but also all the locals out to celebrate too.

Miss Lynn would get one of the kitchen guys to help on the floor if she needed them, but she had to find someone else soon for the waitressing job.

She knew Olivia needed the money, though, and with the holidays around the corner, she would see to it that the young woman had all the hours she could stand. She would also try and help with a few things for Lucas, but it would have to be covert.

Olivia wouldn't take charity and always insisted on working hard for everything she got. Miss Lynn knew how to get around her, though. She saw to it that Olivia got all the large groups to wait on, specifically the local workers. They liked pretty Olivia and tipped her well.

A line began to form outside, and they opened a few minutes early to ease the crowd. Time flew by in a blur, and before they knew it, breakfast orders ended, and lunch began.

They hadn't picked up the syrup condiments that were still out on most of the tables. Olivia rushed around, piling them into a bin so she could hide them behind the counter. She knew Miss Lynn cared a lot about the presentation, and syrup wasn't supposed to be out during the lunch shift.

"I've already made a hundred and sixty dollars in tips," Olivia whispered as she picked up the full coffee pot and headed to refill cups. She walked around the diner smiling and playing the perfect waitress. She was a woman on a mission, and she gave the best customer service she could so she could reach her goal.

"Don't I get a cup," she heard a rich baritone voice say behind her, and she didn't have to turn around to know it was Alexavier Regalia. Her pulse picked up a beat, and her stomach fluttered, making her feel like a schoolgirl with a crush. How did he do that to her?

She pulled her shoulders back and plastered a sultry smile on her face as she slowly turned around. "We need to find you a seat first, Alex. Then I'll pour you a cup of whatever you want to drink," she said, winking at him.

Alexavier liked when she called him Alex. No one had done that since he became the Mayor of New Orleans. It felt intimate. He followed Olivia, watching her hips sway as she guided him to a private booth near a corner of the diner. When she flipped over the thick porcelain cup so she could pour him some coffee, he reached out and touched her hand.

She jumped at his warm touch, and he intertwined his fingers with hers. "Thank you for the coffee, Olivia."

Swallowing hard to wet her dry throat, she nodded, avoiding his stare for a moment. She had to get a hold of herself. She could handle a little attention from a powerful man. She could handle anything.

"Of course, Alex. What can I get for you?" she asked, manufacturing that smile again.

He shot one back at her, but it didn't reach his mahogany eyes. She could stare into his eyes forever, but she knew that wasn't going to happen.

Their late-night phone calls had proven he strangely paid too close attention to her. Given only the smallest details or comments about her life sent him into investigator mode. No matter how many times she redirected the conversation, he would steer them right back to those details she'd carefully avoided. It was unnerving.

He had a reputation, and she'd so wanted it to be true. Some surface get-to-know-you conversation and a few nights of hot sex would have been great, but the gossip around the mayor's dating practices seemed to be a lie.

She'd straight up told him what she wanted, and he didn't seem the least bit interested in a fleeting moment of great sex. Instead, he acted like he wanted something serious with her. Their late-night phone calls made it feel real.

None of it mattered because she didn't have a phone anymore. Still, there was some crazy attraction between them, and whenever Alexavier came to the diner, she had to work at not looking desperate.

He stared at her until she handed him a menu.

"I'll take the lunch special and a few minutes of your time if you can spare it?" he asked, locked onto her blue eyes.

Olivia usually would have a sassy retort to that kind of remark, she received flirtatious requests regularly, but she didn't have it in her to be ugly to Alexavier.

She'd missed talking to him, and although it was only one night, it felt like the end of whatever they were doing. After all, it would be weeks, if not months, before she could afford to turn her phone back on, and by then, he would surely lose interest. She'd grown to really like him, but all good things came to an end.

He cleared his throat as he looked at her, and she realized she was standing there staring back after he'd given her his order. She quickly nodded and then turned to go tell the kitchen what he wanted.

Miss Lynn smiled at Olivia when she walked behind the counter to put the empty coffee pot down and grabbed the full iced tea pitcher. She gently placed her worn hand over Olivia's. "I can refill the tea glasses," she said. "Isn't that the mayor sitting in your station? Go sit with him for a few minutes."

Alexavier had frequented the diner ever since Miss Lynn and Olivia met him at Ryan and Sydney Gentry's new house. They'd had a cookout, and he sat between the two ladies. Before that day, he'd never eaten at the diner in Maisonville, and suddenly he was a weekly patron. She'd tried to nudge Olivia toward him, but it hadn't worked yet.

Miss Lynn held the tea pitcher, but it took a second before she recognized the look on Olivia's face. She was nervous. She never looked nervous.

"You look beautiful," Miss Lynn said and then reached around Olivia's head to gently remove the large tortoise-colored hair clip she had attached around all her beautiful hair. She ran a hand over her cheek and gave her an affirming look. "Beautiful. Go and sit with him for a few moments. I'm sure Alexavier was shaken from the fires yesterday. I've got your tables until you return."

"Fire?" Olivia hadn't watched the news.

"There were three different ones set yesterday in the city. He looked upset when they interviewed him. Several firefighters got hurt."

Olivia nodded and went to the window to wait for Alexavier's food. She usually watched a snippet of the news either at ten or first thing in the morning. Alexavier was a sweet man and took his job seriously. He was probably upset over the tragedy and wondered why she hadn't mentioned it.

The cook slid a plate toward her, and she took a deep breath. Alexavier was one of the most handsome men she'd ever met, but there was something else about him that drew her to him. It didn't make sense. She was a single mother and a waitress. She knew it couldn't go anywhere beyond the flirting, but some days were harder than others to accept that fact.

She had to get over herself. She could sit with Alex while he ate lunch and talk about current events, even if it was the beginning of goodbye.

Couldn't she?

Chapter Five

Alexavier looked around the hip little diner that had become his weekly habit and considered how special it was to the town of Maisonville. It was named The Main Street Grocery but wasn't on Main Street and wasn't a grocery. He'd have to find out the mystery behind that someday.

Still, it was a favorite spot for locals and visitors because Miss Lynn provided meals that made everyone feel at home. That is, as long as someone at their home could cook some of the best southern classics around. She was famous for her meatloaf, chicken and dumplings, fried chicken and sausage jambalaya, red beans and rice, and muffulettas. Blue-collar and white-collar workers loved the place, and social lines crossed daily as many patrons ate at the bar together, talking about local high school sports teams or their families.

It was one of the things that Alexavier loved most about the place and why he couldn't understand Olivia being uncomfortable sitting with him when he stopped in for lunch. She'd even told him once that it looked strange for a regular waitress like her to sit with the Mayor of New Orleans. He'd tried everything he could to make her understand that she was not ordinary. He'd even told her he came to the diner just to see her, and he wouldn't do that for over twenty weeks in a row if she weren't special. But when that didn't work, he explained that he was an ordinary man that also happened to be the mayor of a great city.

At least he got a great laugh out of her for that one. But still, she always hesitated and stalled as long as she could before joining him. He watched as she pulled everything together for his meal and finally had a seat across from him.

"Thank you," he said as he dipped his homemade fries into some ranch dressing meant for his side salad.

He smiled as he looked over at her.

"Ever tried it?" he asked.

When she shook her head, he found the perfect fry and dipped it into the tangy dressing for her. Then he sat back and watched her eat it.

She nodded and smiled.

"Strangely amazing, right?" he asked as he ate two more.

When Alexavier finished his chicken, he wiped his mouth with a napkin and sat back in his seat to look at her.

She hadn't said more than two words since she set his plate in front of him.

"How are you, Olivia?" he asked.

"Great. You?" She watched him measuring her words and body language, as she did the same to him. "I heard there were some suspicious fires in the city yesterday?"

His face darkened. "Yes. It was terrible. Several people were hurt, and one passed away this morning."

"I'm sorry."

"Me too. He'd been with the fire department for fifteen years."

"Kids?"

Alexavier nodded. She looked as upset as he did over the incident, and he hadn't wanted to upset her.

"If we can catch whoever is responsible, that will help the family find some closure."

"So, it was definitely arson?"

"Yes. All three fires."

Olivia wrapped her arms around her waist, and Alexavier wished he could wrap his arms around her too.

"I'm surprised you were able to get away for lunch."

He watched her closely as she avoided his stare. It wasn't her usual behavior, even though she took her time to sit with him. Once she joined him, she would usually tease and joke with him smugly.

"Nothing would have kept me away today."

She finally looked at him.

"I came here today to figure out why you don't want to talk to me anymore?"

"It's not that," she whispered.

"I thought things were good between us, Olivia? I look forward to hearing your voice at the end of the day. I'd accepted that it would take some time to earn your trust." He watched as her eyes slid away from him. He didn't understand what could have happened. "Did I say or do something wrong? If you wanted me to stop calling, you could have told me. I would have respected your wishes. You didn't have to change your number?"

Was he hurt? Olivia wasn't sure, but it felt that way. It tugged at her heart which was the only reason she admitted, "No. My phone is turned off temporarily." As soon as the words were out, she instantly stopped talking.

Shit. Shit. Shit. Olivia couldn't believe she had told that to Alexavier.

"Turned off?" he asked like he didn't understand. "Temporarily?"

Olivia couldn't backtrack. She knew he wouldn't let it go, and she had to make it seem alright. She could take care of things. She'd always done that. "Yup. Not a biggie. I had some unexpected bills and have to wait until payday before I have it turned back on. You know I'm a waitress, right?" She plastered that I'm fine, don't question me look on her face that usually worked with everyone.

It worked with everyone but Alexavier Regalia.

"Why didn't you tell me? I have some extra money put back, Olivia," he said, and she saw him straighten his shoulders.

Was he really relieved? It didn't matter. He had money, but she didn't. She wouldn't be able to talk to him for a while.

"As if," she said without elaborating.

"What does that mean?" Alexavier asked, looking directly at her, and she felt the heat of his stare.

"I can take care of myself and Lucas, thank you very much." She crossed her arms in front of her, and he knew he'd insulted her.

"I know that. You've done a great job."

Olivia rolled her eyes at how understanding he looked. How did she get herself into those situations? She wanted Alexavier in her bed, but she didn't need him lurking around in her business and certainly not inside her head or heart.

Still, she explained. "I was with Lucas' dad, Brent, for a short while after Lucas was born, and he couldn't keep all his bills paid. Not much has changed with him in the last seven years. Sometimes his child support is there, and sometimes it's not. But a kid always has to eat and have a roof over his head. I sometimes need to wait on little luxuries like coffee or my cell phone."

It hurt to hear her sound so alone. She'd only mentioned her family once and how they'd moved to Florida years ago. She didn't have anyone to help her with her son or anything else when things got tough. She just hadn't told him why.

They sat there looking at each other for a moment. Neither one knew how to move forward, but their attraction vibrated the air. Olivia thought about how warm his touch would be on her skin. Alexavier's hand twitched, wanting to feel her. Both sat perfectly still, longing for the other to give the go-ahead.

It didn't happen.

Olivia, with all her natural or manufactured confidence,

couldn't bring herself to tell him how much she wanted to spend real time with him. And Alexavier, with all his internal strength and external power, didn't admit how happy it would make him to be with her.

Finally, he drank the rest of his iced tea, and Olivia jumped up to get his check. He put cash inside the black bill holder as he stood beside her.

Then he leaned in close enough for her to feel his body heat. It made her shiver. "Thank you for keeping me company during lunch. As always, it was a pleasure to see you," he said.

She couldn't be sure, but it felt like something he might say to a coworker. It made her heart sink as he stepped back and said goodbye. Why did it make her want to weep? She didn't cry. Olivia had been through so much crap, and something so unimportant as a gorgeous, powerful man that was out of her league walking away was going to make her a blubbery mess?

She whispered, "Goodbye," then turned and headed for the kitchen.

Miss Lynn watched the entire exchange. The restaurant had slowly emptied while Olivia sat with Alexavier. There were only a few customers still eating, and they were almost done, so Miss Lynn cleaned the front counter. She couldn't help watching Olivia and the mayor because they made such a beautiful couple. He with his dark hair and eyes. He could have been in a commercial advertising Italy with his solid, Italian looks. Olivia was a stunning woman with ivory skin, glowing blue eyes, and a mane of hair that belonged in hair product ads. She saw the hurt on both their faces as they parted, and she had to know why.

She hurried to Olivia and caught her quickly wiping her eyes with her apron. When she turned around, she pretended as if nothing was wrong. Miss Lynn knew better. She reached her hand out to hold Olivia's. "What happened, honey?"

Olivia shook her head and smiled. "Oh, you know me. I'm only serious about one little man, and he's due to get out of school in a couple of hours, so I need to finish wiping down those tables and refilling the condiments."

It was true. Olivia had dated around but hadn't gotten serious with anyone since Lucas was born. Lynn babysat for her occasionally so she could go out, and she'd even stopped doing that almost a year ago. It seemed like Olivia truly cared about Alexavier Regalia. But now, she'd even pushed him away. There was no use in trying to console her because she would pretend it was all silly and a waste of time.

The end of an almost great relationship hung in the air for the rest of the afternoon. The diner was quiet and for Miss Lynn and Olivia, time dragged on until Lucas got off the bus.

Lucas was a ray of sunshine for everyone. He bounced through the door, excited to show off his homework folder. He'd been the helper of the week and had gotten five gold stars for his hard work. He'd also made an A on his spelling test and a 100 on his math test. But his most significant moment was when he fed Iggy the class Iguana. The teacher had allowed him to take Iggy out of the aquarium and hold him during reading time. It made Lucas' week.

After an hour, Olivia hurried him home so she could grab his jacket and a sweatshirt for herself because the evening weather had turned unseasonably cold. She had to drop Lucas off at Sydney's house so she could work the dinner shift, but before that, she took him bike riding for half an hour. Her boy needed a lot of physical exercise, and she was going to make sure he had an opportunity to get his energy out before dinner. Miss Lynn had always told her that it was the quality of the time they spent together and not the quantity that mattered most. Miss Lynn had raised a wonderful large family, and her advice was always valuable.

Olivia and Lucas had a great time together before she dropped him at the Gentry's house, and it gave her the boost she needed to get through the dinner shift.

By the time she'd picked Lucas up, it was almost ten-thirty, and she was extra sleepy.

Thankfully, Sydney's oldest son Daryl had read Lucas his standard stack of books before bedtime, and she could put Lucas straight to bed.

It was midnight when she finally laid her head down and thought about Alexavier. It was only the second night that she hadn't talked to him before bed, but it felt like forever. She missed him, and he'd made all the effort to come to the diner for lunch to see her. It was the most effort anyone had made for her in a long time. And she should have told him that she'd missed talking to him too. Even if the relationship couldn't go anywhere, he was a fascinating man, and she loved to hear him talk about his life and his job. Why didn't she tell him she missed their late-night conversations?

She knew why. She always sabotaged her love life. She would never believe anyone would stick around with her for any amount of time. Her parents taught her that when her father took early retirement before she graduated high school and then they left her.

She never heard from them, and as they traveled all over the country in their RV, they never came to see her or meet her son. She wouldn't even know that much if her sister, Beth, hadn't told her. Beth lived in Nashville, but she also didn't come around. Beth had gone away for college and never returned. She called Olivia maybe once a year, but they hadn't spoken in almost three years now.

Olivia found the energy to sit up and turn her bedside light off. When she laid her head down again, she refused to think about her family.

She'd been alone for a long time, and she would be fine.

Olivia distracted herself by imagining Lucas with the classroom Iguana. He was so animated as he told Miss Lynn all about it. Alexavier would have loved that story. Alexavier had a sincere way about him. Sure, he dressed better than anyone she knew, but he wasn't pretentious. He was hot in his dark suit and red tie at lunch. He was always the most attractive man in the room, and she was drawn to him in ways she couldn't explain and several that she could.

She pulled her blanket up tighter around her body. It might have been the last time Alexavier came to the diner for lunch, but she could still dream about him.

Chapter Six

Saturday morning Olivia rushed around the house trying to find her shoes and some warmer clothes for Lucas. She was dropping him off at Ryan and Sydney's house again. Thank goodness that Sydney and Ryan loved her kid.

Olivia missed working with Sydney, but she was a great friend and always offered to help her out on the weekends when she needed to work by keeping Lucas. He would play with Sydney's four boys, or if they were with their dad, then Ryan and Sydney would shower Lucas with lots of attention. It meant the world to Olivia.

She grabbed Lucas' coat, zipping him into it before she opened the door, and the wind blew across her. It was the first cold snap of the season and about a month early. She was thankful she'd bought Lucas a new coat already. She had her eyes half-closed as they watered from the heavy wind and barely caught herself before tripping over a large brown bag on her doorstep. She looked at it carefully, trying to see if it possibly belonged to the people next door to her in the duplex, but it had her name.

It was half-past seven, and they would be late if she stopped to look at the contents, but she couldn't help herself. Who had sent her a package?

She sat in her car while the engine warmed up and pulled out several nonperishable grocery items from the bag. Then she felt a rigid rectangular box in the bottom. It was a brand new I-phone. On the box, there was a post-it note taped with instructions on how to set it up and nothing else. She looked around her neighborhood to see if she recognized someone or a car with someone that could have dropped it off. She didn't see anyone. Lucas reached over and picked up the box of Oreo cookies.

"Not this morning, Lucas. You're going to Auntie Sydney and Uncle Ryan's house today. You can bring them with you and share them with the boys later. Okay?"

He smiled at his mom. He'd had chocolate milk two days in a row, and now he would get cookies too.

Olivia dropped him at the Gentry's house and then hurried into the diner. The bag had to be from Miss Lynn. She had told Olivia she didn't like her to be without a phone several times. She also wanted to give Lucas treats. Still, how did she know that they were low on groceries too? The cans of soup and loaf of bread with peanut butter and jelly would come in handy for the month. The macaroni and cheese was as much her favorite as it was her son's. She didn't like charity, but she was grateful. She would have to thank Miss Lynn and then explain that she could handle things.

Miss Lynn was interviewing someone when Olivia got there. By the looks of things, it wasn't going well, and Olivia smiled that she would get to continue working doubles a while longer. She hustled around the room and opened the door to let the breakfast crowd inside.

The diner was busy as expected all morning, with every table full and almost every chair. It wasn't until after lunch that Olivia could talk to Miss Lynn about the bag of groceries and the new cell phone.

"Honey, I have wanted to do that for years when I saw you struggling. But I didn't want to insult or upset you. I wish I'd gone ahead and done it. But I swear, it wasn't me."

Olivia looked confused. She'd seen Sydney that morning, but there was no way she could have known how difficult things had been for her. Unless Lucas said something? Of course, Sydney would have found a diplomatic way to tell Olivia that she knew she needed help, and then she would have given her the phone in person. Wouldn't she?

Who could have sent all that stuff? Her mind flashed to Alexavier's smile. It couldn't have been him. His curt goodbye the day before meant things were over between them. She was sure of it. Besides, he was too busy to worry about buying cookies for her kid or staples like peanut butter. Sure, if it had only been a phone then she could see it. But no, it couldn't have been him. She shook her head. She'd secretly wished he would give her a gesture that there was some hope for the two of them, but the idea that he sent that stuff to her was preposterous.

It must have been Sydney.

Plus, she didn't believe in good guys or happy endings. She was a good time girl for a night or two, and that was all. Alexavier hadn't even taken her up on that offer. Truth be told, she hadn't gone out with anyone for a very long time. She'd seemed to outgrow all the Mr. Right-nows and spent more time alone than ever. Of course, she was busy with Lucas, but even when he visited his father for a weekend, she stayed home alone, catching up on housework or reading one of her romance books. Apparently, book boyfriends were her thing.

Book boyfriends. Olivia had read some of it to Alexavier and told him she liked to read smut. She laughed at herself. Smut was one of her favorite words, and Olivia needed to give it up too. She couldn't have Lucas sounding like a potty mouth.

She spent most of her busy day trying to come up with a replacement word. She wracked her vocabulary as she tried to find something that rhymed, but by the end of the day, she still had nothing.

Before Olivia left, she hugged Miss Lynn. Although tired, as usual, she'd had one of the best days at work in a while. The three hundred and fifty dollars in tips would be enough money to help cover the rent, and with the box of goodies to stretch their meals, Olivia and Lucas would be fine. She hurried to the Gentry's house and rang the doorbell only to hear the tune had been changed to car horns. Lucas loved cars. She rang it again and laughed.

Ryan answered the door and smiled. "Everyone's out back sitting around the fireplace and roasting marshmallows for their hot chocolate."

Olivia made a face at Ryan, and he shrugged. "Don't ask me. I don't like fire-roasted marshmallows in my hot chocolate. Sydney made that madness up, and all the boys think it's great."

He laughed as he led her toward the backyard. The sweetness that always surrounded the newly wedded couple and their household made Olivia happy. She also loved watching Lucas act like a big boy whenever he hung with Sydney's older sons. Olivia rounded the house, ready to watch her child and the other boys burn sugar into charcoal. But when she turned the corner and walked into the yard, everyone was quiet. Alexavier was there and acting like he was hosting the event. He told a story, using his whole body to walk like a creature across the wooden deck. It must have been the punchline because all the boys laughed, and that's when Alexavier walked directly over to her.

"What are you doing here?" she asked.

"I wanted to tell you I was here, but you don't have your phone."

Olivia hadn't introduced Alexavier to her son yet, and now they'd spent the evening together with what Olivia liked to pretend was her extended family.

"I hope you're not mad at me. Ryan and I got to talking about one of his houses, and then they invited me over for dinner. I didn't realize Lucas was here. I didn't tell him about our relationship or anything."

"Relationship?" She was still surprised to see Alexavier. He had the five o'clock shadow that naturally grew perfectly every evening, and when he smiled at her, his dark eyes lit up. She acted like it didn't affect her.

She stepped around Alexavier and walked over to Lucas. "Hey, Buddy. You ready to go?"

"Aw, Mom. I haven't had but one marshmallow."

She saw all the boys putting giant-sized marshmallows on their skewers and tried not to laugh. One of them was the equivalent of four regular-sized ones. Still, she couldn't deny him the fun of an open fire on a cool night with good friends. She'd been on her feet for twelve hours, but a few more minutes wouldn't hurt.

"Go ahead. I'll wait," Olivia told Lucas and stepped back to give him some space. Whoever, most likely Ryan, thought giving each boy his own sharp metal skewer was a good idea must not have planned to stand nearby as they wielded the things in the air.

"Let me get you a drink," Ryan offered, and then Sydney motioned for her to sit down next to her. Alexavier waited for Olivia to sit and then had a seat nearby.

"Thanks for watching him, Sydney."

"Oh, sure. We love to have him, and the boys are good with him too. Ryan and the boys have been working on a tree house, and they taught Lucas how to use a hammer today. Evidently, he's proficient at it now, and they got most of the floorboards nailed in." Sydney pointed toward several giant oak trees, and Olivia could see the makings of a large tree house. With Ryan's building skills and how much he loved his stepsons, she could imagine that the tree house would be nicer than the duplex she and Lucas called home.

"How was the diner today?"

"Hectic. But I'm thankful for it. The festival helps a lot, and I made a ton today with all the extra tourists visiting."

Sydney worried about Olivia and Lucas. She'd had difficult times before but only had to worry about herself.

"If you need anything, Olivia, please ask. We're your friends, and we love you."

Olivia gave Sydney a big smile and nodded. "I know. I love all of you too. But I'm fine. We're fine." She leaned in and whispered to Sydney, "So, you didn't have anything to do with the package we got this morning?"

Sydney winked at her. "What package?"

It wasn't like Sydney to not give a straight answer, but Olivia was tired and figured that was her friends way of not admitting the truth. She had to make sure Sydney understood that she had everything under control. "I just had a great tip-day, tomorrow is only a half-day, and Lucas and I might just lay low and order a pizza." She knew she wouldn't order pizza, but she didn't want Sydney worrying about her.

Alexavier listened as Olivia talked to Sydney. He'd noticed early on in his conversations with her that Olivia wouldn't admit to needing any help from him. But he'd hoped she might accept it from her close friends. She didn't. He remembered a month or so earlier, she'd had a cold while Lucas was away visiting his dad. She sounded horrible and admitted to having a fever, but she still wouldn't let Alexavier bring her soup or any medicine. If he could go back, he would have done it anyway and simply left it at her door.

He could tell by her expression at lunch that she hadn't meant to admit her phone was turned off. She was struggling but wouldn't confess it to those closest to her. Earlier in the evening, Lucas had mentioned how happy he was to have chocolate milk again because they'd been out of chocolate and milk for a while. Sydney made him a big glass for dinner and helped him change the subject so he wouldn't tell too many of his mom's secrets. But Alexavier could see Sydney was worried about them too.

The boys roasted their marshmallows and ate whatever they didn't lose in the fire. Ryan and Alexavier talked a little more about two different properties he and Sydney were working on, with one down the street from their house. After thirty minutes, Olivia told Lucas it was time for them to go. She thanked the Gentry family again, and then Alexavier thanked them too so he could walk out at the same time.

He held the car door for Lucas to get in and helped him with his seat belt because it got twisted around his coat. Olivia stood behind Alexavier to make sure he could get it buckled correctly, and then he walked her around to her car door.

"I'm free tonight if you want to invite me over. I'll help put Lucas to bed, and then we could talk," he said.

Olivia was beaten from the day. She would love someone to read Lucas' bedtime stories before lights out. And the gorgeous Mayor was standing right there, capable and offering to do it.

She stared at his beautiful smile, knowing she should say no.

He leaned in as he opened her door for her. "Say, yes, Olivia. I'm standing right here in front of you, and I would really like it if, for once, you would just say yes."

Chapter Seven

Once home, Lucas was exhausted from his adventures in helping build a tree house. Bath time only took five minutes, and halfway through Alexavier reading the first book, Lucas fell asleep.

Alexavier looked over at Olivia, sitting at the foot of her son's bed. She shrugged her shoulders and then tucked the blankets around her little boy. She then kissed his forehead before walking out with Alexavier. They went into the small living room and sat together on the couch.

"I thought you said he had a five-book minimum?" Alexavier teased her.

"Who knew you were the kid whisperer?" she asked with a straight face. Then she added, "He has a great time with Sydney's boys. Ryan always has some sort of outside project, from washing the boat and gear to building benches and now a tree house. Lucas is one hundred percent boy and needs all of that stuff. He'll talk about it for a week."

"Does his father do a lot with him?"

Olivia paused for a moment, and Alexavier watched as she seemed to decide whether or not to answer the question. She was guarded when they talked over the telephone, but she would tell him much more than she would say in person. He knew a lot about her from those discussions that sometimes went on for hours. They talked about all sorts of things. However, Olivia didn't share much about her past.

Seeing her with her son and sitting with her in her house for the first time made him want to know everything.

"Brent isn't what you would call reliable. I guess he loves Lucas in his own way but doesn't have what it takes to be a full-time parent."

"Financially, emotionally, or physically? Alexavier asked. He had a cousin who married a man who was not good at marriage or being a father. He saw firsthand how difficult it was for her and her children. However, she did have the support of their large Italian family, and Olivia didn't have anyone.

"All the above."

Alexavier reached his hand out to hold Olivia's, and she looked at their fingers intertwined. What was she doing? It felt nice to have Alexavier there, but he couldn't stay.

He moved closer toward her. "Why haven't you turned on the new phone I sent you?"

Olivia closed her eyes. She was tired from work, and she didn't have the energy that it usually took to pretend to have everything together. She didn't want anyone, especially him, to see her vulnerable. He moved over closer to her and put his arm around her. When she opened her eyes, his face was close to hers. The understanding she saw there almost did her in. She didn't say a word because she couldn't trust her mouth.

"Olivia, it doesn't mean you owe me anything. It would make me feel better knowing you have it in case you need it. You and Lucas can't live here without a phone. Plus, I'm a little selfish and miss hearing your voice after a hard day at work."

Alexavier stood up and reached a handout for her. He helped her stand. She thought he was going to leave, but instead, he asked, "Where's your phone?"

She walked into the kitchen and pulled the unopened box from the brown bag. Alexavier didn't say anything when he saw everything he'd sent was still in the paper bag except the box of cookies. He quickly removed the plastic and got right to work setting up the device. It only took him a few minutes, and then he handed the phone to her. It was the nicest phone she had ever owned. She'd never had an iPhone and didn't exactly know how to use it.

"Thank you, Alex. But this is only temporary," she said, and he pulled her into his arms and hugged her.

"It's a gift. I want you to keep it. It cost almost nothing to add a phone to my service plan, and it's one less thing for you to worry about."

She nodded but didn't say anything. She knew she should give the expensive phone that cost more than her rent back to him. Instead, she tried to be gracious. Miss Lynn had her nervous about being home alone with Lucas without a way to call anyone in case of an emergency.

"You don't know how to use it, do you?" he asked sweetly.

When she shook her head, he kissed her on the lips. It was the first time she'd let her guard down around him. He didn't want to make a big deal out of it, and instead of commenting, he showed her the phone basics. It was easier than it looked, and once she had the hang of it, she wrapped her arms around him tightly and thanked him. "Since you're here, would you like to tuck me into bed?" she asked, trying to make the moment lighter. She knew he would decline.

"I would love nothing more, beautiful, but you know I have conditions," he said, giving her that smile that probably won him the mayor's office.

She melted a little more into his body. "I know, but you ate at the Gentry's house with Lucas, right?"

Alexavier leaned in and whispered, "That doesn't count, and you know it," before he pressed his lips onto hers and then kissed her thoroughly. When she parted her lips with a gasp, he invaded, and their tongues danced and explored until Olivia's whole body was on fire. It had been too long since she'd been with anyone, and she was incredibly attracted to him.

Alexavier's voice was thick, and she was happy he was also affected. "Perhaps I could take you and Lucas out to dinner tomorrow?"

"Lucas has the attention span of a gnat when taken out to eat. Have you ever eaten with a seven-year-old?"

"Well, I was once seven myself. Does that count?" he asked and then laughed at the face she made.

He held her hand as he walked to the door, but before Alexavier slipped out, he leaned in and whispered, "Call me?"

Olivia gave him that sultry smile he'd fallen for six months ago, and he kissed her again before forcing himself to leave.

By the time he made it back to his house in New Orleans, it was late. He debated on whether or not to call her but decided against it. He was still thinking about their heated kisses and how much he wanted to ravage her body right there on her impossibly small dining table. But he felt if he gave in and slept with her, then she would stop talking to him soon after. She'd practically admitted that was what she'd done for years, and he wanted to be more to her. The anticipation was getting to him.

He could see how exhausted she was from her long day at work. Saturdays in the fall were busy in the little town of Maisonville, and it seemed like there was always a street festival or extra-large farmers' market. He would've loved to have spent the night and then gotten up the next morning and cooked her pancakes for breakfast. He could have served her coffee in bed, and then the three of them could have eaten at that strange three-chair dining table.

She was probably asleep before he got off the long causeway bridge to his home. He plugged his phone in and turned off his bedside lamp, and then heard the alert on his phone. He had a message.

You make it home, alright? Olivia had texted him.

He couldn't stop smiling as he reread the message before answering her.

Yes. Lying in bed reading your text.

I'm in bed too.

Feel like talking?

I thought that was what we were doing.

She had so much sass, and he loved it. He immediately dialed her number.

Olivia picked it up on the first ring.

"What are you wearing," she asked, and his laugh had just enough huskiness to it that it caused her to shiver all over. What she would do to have him in her bed was sinful.

"Black boxer shorts. You?"

"Same," she said without missing a beat.

"That's not fair. I know you don't wear boxer shorts."

"Are you asking for pics now? I'm not sure I'm ready for that kind of commitment."

"What can I do to get you there?" he asked. He was a lot more serious about her than she even knew.

"I thought you were a good-time Charlie. You know that's what I am. I've told you before. I'm committed to one little man, and that's all I can do right now."

"You forget that I saw you at the Gentry's house tonight. You watched their family dynamics, and I know you loved it. I think it's something you could get used to in your life."

"Nope. Not me. I was there from the beginning, and Sydney and Ryan deserve that life. It's sweet to see them and the boys together. Especially after all the turmoil, she went through."

"Olivia, you're not going to change the subject so easily. You've told me their story already, and I agree that they deserve happiness. But, sweetheart, why do you think you don't deserve the same thing?"

There was silence on the other end of the phone, and he thought for a minute that she might hang up. "Olivia?"

"Yes?"

"Are you going to answer me?"

"I don't think I will. I mean, I don't think that because I'm happy for Sydney and Ryan, I necessarily have to have the same life to be happy. Besides, who says I'm not happy right now. I have my health. And I know I'm only a waitress, but I love my job and working for Miss Lynn. My son is an amazing kid, and he fills me up every day."

Alexavier knew he'd hit a nerve. She started the phone call off with a sexy comment, and now he'd gone and upset her by getting serious again. He needed to lighten up. "He's a great kid. And he's pretty funny too. Did you know he's a great campfire storyteller?"

"Um, a campfire storyteller?"

Alexavier laughed, thinking about Lucas telling his version of the scary story with a man who had a hook for a hand. He explained, "Lucas told us the story of the escaped mental patient with the hook for a hand. Instead of being a teenage couple parked at lover's lane making out in a car, he had the guy show up at a school on a stormy afternoon when all the kids were in the library. Did you know his library is in a separate building with a metal roof?"

"No. Then what happened?"

"Oh, he was animated. Lucas walked around the fire dragging his hand on the ground like the crazy man in his story. Screeching each time his hand slid across the ground. He explained how they could hear the screeching of the hook as it scraped across the roof. Then the teacher left to check out the sound, and when she returned, they found the hook stuck in all the hairspray on her bouffant hair. He had all of us captivated with the scary scraping sounds he made, and then he ended it with the funny hook stuck in the teacher's hair bit. He's clever."

Olivia liked to hear stories about her son, but she couldn't help but feel like she'd missed out on things when she worked every weekend. "I've never heard him tell a story like that. It is funny."

"I'm pretty sure he made it up for the older boys and maybe for Ryan and me. We told several stories to the kids."

"I saw you entertaining them when I got there. You really do like kids?"

"What's not to like?"

"I guess I figured that you don't have any, and your biological clock is getting on up there, so maybe you weren't interested."

"My late wife was diagnosed with cancer early in our marriage. It went into remission, but she said she wanted to wait until she was sure the medicine was out of her system for a few years. The cancer came back before then. She fought it the second time for two years before she passed away."

"I'm sorry."

"Me too. It wasn't meant to be. And I honestly have been busy with work and haven't heard anything from my biological clock, as you call it. You do know men can have children in their seventies and eighties."

"I'd like to see you throwing a football with kids in your seventies," she said.

"Maybe it will be our grandkids by then, but I do not doubt that I'll be active in my seventies and eighties."

She didn't miss how he referred to them being together for years. He was only flirting, and she knew it, but it was getting to her. She liked him, and he made it harder for her to tease and pretend she didn't care about him.

"I have plenty of energy to keep up with kids, especially funny seven-year-old boys that like to tell stories by the campfire. You know I'm looking at houses in Maisonville. I only have a short time left as mayor, and I plan to either have a second home, or who knows, I might move there full time."

Olivia had no idea he was interested in Maisonville. The town was a favorite of most people that visited. Still, after being the mayor of New Orleans, she couldn't imagine Alexavier being happy with the slower pace the suburbs provided. Besides, the town was known for being a place to start over again. It was even nicknamed Renaissance Lake by its residents. It was the reason Olivia moved there, and it had absolutely changed her life. Why would Alexavier need that?

"You sure this place would be exciting enough for you, Alex?"

"I'm not exactly looking for excitement. At least outside of the bedroom," he said in that deep lazy voice he used at night when they talked for hours.

"Really?" was all she could say. Why in the ever-loving hell wouldn't he sleep with her?

"You never answered me about dinner tomorrow. I know it's Sunday, and you usually work half a day. I'm sure Lucas has an early bedtime. But I could bring a picnic for us, and we could go to the lakefront with Lucas to eat, and then he could play?"

It was late, and Olivia was exhausted, but she needed to stand her ground. "It does sound nice, Alex. But I've already told you I don't want to be in the newspapers with New Orleans' most eligible bachelor." She had to keep saying no.

She'd enjoyed talking and flirting with him over the phone, but she wasn't the person for him. He was gorgeous and kind of famous, but he couldn't afford more bad gossip.

If her picture appeared in the paper or the social pages of the local magazine, then someone would recognize her. And if she dated the single hot mayor, she couldn't avoid the press. Her past would end up haunting them both.

Chapter Eight

Alexavier was ready for her excuse. "I know you don't want the invasion of your privacy. You told me that, and I've thought it through. I figured I could post on social media that I was going to the street fair tomorrow. The reporters would all plan to see me in New Orleans, and I could pick you and Lucas up instead. We could have the entire afternoon together. You won't have to do a thing. My mother cooks enough for an army on Sundays, and I'll go and pick us up some of her amazing food."

How could she say no to him again? He'd heard her reason for declining him before and thought seriously about how he could work through it. He just didn't know all of the reasons why. Still, she would like to spend more time with him, and she was sure that Lucas would too. It seemed she pawned him off on Sydney and Ryan more and more as she tried to make enough money to pay for everyday expenses.

"Alright. I have to open the diner in the morning and work the breakfast shift. And I'm not saying that we can stay a long time or that we're going to make a habit of this, but we can do an afternoon together," Olivia said and felt her stomach twist. Was she making a big mistake?

Alexavier could hear how nervous she was and while he didn't understand why, he was going to get to the bottom of it, after they finally had a date. "I'll text you tomorrow when I'm on my way, Olivia. Plan for noon," he said and then hurried to get off the phone before she tried to back out of it.

*。

ALEXAVIER'S MOM and aunt were in the kitchen with four of his cousins when he arrived. They had put together the most impressive picnic he'd ever seen, all while they grilled him over Olivia and her son.

They scolded him for not bringing her over for a fresh hot meal and then for not taking the beautiful woman out for a fancy dinner and dancing on their first date.

He tried to explain that Olivia wasn't like that, but they told him he was wrong and that all women want to be treated specially.

"Of course, I'm going to treat her like she's special, Mama. And her son," he said before sitting next to his uncle. Alexavier's parents had thirteen siblings between them and over sixty first cousins, and they all lived in the New Orleans area. That didn't count their spouses and then their children. He joked that he won the election both times with merely his own family voting.

Every Sunday, his mother and Auntie Francesca cooked dinner for their families, which was still a large group. But once a year, everyone got together for a family reunion. Alexavier had bought some property for the family with a large house and an even bigger barn. He had two of his cousins living there and keeping it up. They would set up tons of tables and clean the barn to have live music and dancing. Many of the older women would start cooking the Thursday before, and by Saturday, the whole family would show up to help. There was horseback riding, four-wheelers, fishing, horseshoes, and darts, and by dusk, everyone would end up at the barn for a huge dinner. He wanted to bring Olivia and Lucas to the next one.

He went into the living room and talked to his dad and a couple of his older cousins, who grilled him on some recent car break-ins, and he had to defend the city's police department because they were getting it handled. Cleaning up the crime was one of the best things he'd done as mayor, and the police department had almost doubled in size since his first term. Still, they loved to give him hell.

His cousin Theresa brought him homemade bread and sat down next to him. She was a single mother, and she wanted to give him some pointers on dating a woman like her. He smiled, trying to be respectful, and listened to her advice until her younger brother Antony came in and teased her. Cousin Theresa had five kids under the age of six, and she was the last person who could hand out dating advice. Antony taunted her and told her that she would have to live in a shoe if she didn't stop having kids. She then took off her shoe and threw it at him.

Alexavier figured that was his signal to get out of there. He jumped up and said goodbye to everyone and thanked his mother and auntie again for making the picnic for him. His mother walked him to the door, and he hugged and kissed her again. Alexavier was his parent's youngest, and he had a special bond with his mother and father.

He headed toward the long bridge that would take him to Olivia and Lucas and grinned as he thought about introducing them to his crazy family. Olivia didn't seem to like him butting into her business, and he wondered what she would think of all of them doing it regularly.

While stopped at a red light, he sent a quick text to Olivia to tell her he was on his way and then drove as fast as he could to get to her.

Olivia answered the door wearing jeans and a white long-sleeve shirt. Alexavier leaned in and kissed her on the cheek and then handed her a bouquet of cut flowers.

She blushed when she saw them, and that made him smile.

She was always so sure of herself, and the small gesture must have caught her off-guard.

Lucas walked in, and Alexavier said hello to him. "Hey man, you like cars?" he asked.

Lucas nodded and looked at the brown paper bag Alexavier was holding. "I thought this might be fun to use at the lakefront today," he said and handed over the bag with a large-sized remote-control sports car and controller.

"What do you say, Lucas?" Olivia said, prompting him.

"Thank you," he said as he stared at the car.

"It's not fragile. It's meant to go on the ground and spin around. Take it out and look at it. It's yours, buddy," he said.

Lucas looked at his mother, who nodded, and then he reached inside the bag and picked up the yellow sports car with red flames painted down the sides.

Alexavier got down on the floor and showed Lucas how to use the remote control to make the car move and turn. His entire face lit up as Alexavier gave him some pointers and handed the remote to him so he could do it himself.

Olivia whispered to Alexavier, "You didn't have to bring him an expensive toy. He's super happy about going to the park and having a picnic."

"Yes, I did. I want Lucas to have a great time today. This is about him as much as it is about us."

Olivia tried not to let him see how much that made her heart hurt. Alexavier was trying so hard, and no one had done that in a long time for her. She plastered a smile on her face and looked over at Lucas. "Hey, buddy. It's windy outside today. Go grab your coat," she said, and Lucas picked up the car to carry it with him while he ran to his bedroom.

While Lucas was out of the room, Alexavier kissed Olivia as he wrapped his arms around her, pulling her into his body. She instantly leaned into him. "You're going to need a coat too, beautiful," he said and then licked her bottom lip, making her breathe heavier.

"Okay," she whispered.

He'd only been there a few minutes, yet she seemed over-whelmed by his attention. Were the women in his family right? Olivia wouldn't know what to do when treated like she was special because she hadn't been treated that well before?

He watched Olivia grab a worn sweatshirt jacket that zipped up and looked too big for her. Lucas had a new coat lined with corduroy, brown gloves, and a hat. It was exactly like his cousin Theresa said, Olivia took care of Lucas but neglected things for herself. He didn't like seeing her in what he imagined was second-hand clothing. She deserved the best.

He pulled her hand into his as she told Lucas it was time to go, and then he led them both out to his car.

The lakefront park was beautiful. There was a new play set that included a tunnel and a climbing wall. Lucas was excited to have most of it to himself, and he immediately began to climb to the top.

Olivia started to run after him, but Alexavier held her hand. "Boys love freedom or at least the illusion of it. Help me set up the blanket in the sunshine, and I'll set up the picnic while he plays. We can see him clearly, and he can see us."

Olivia nodded but kept watching Lucas closely. "You know it's mostly been only Lucas and me, and I'm not used to letting him get too far away."

Alexavier kissed her on top of her head and handed her the blanket. "I promise I won't let him out of my sight," he said. "Plus, I'm a really fast runner."

Olivia laughed at the idea of Alexavier running after Lucas. She had a hard time seeing him as athletic when he was always so dressed up and put together. He was wearing athletic clothes, though, and a pair of expensive-looking sneakers. He was an incredible man, and she avoided his stare as she considered how many times he'd surprised her just that day.

He'd been romantic, suggesting a picnic and bringing every-

thing they needed to have a good time at the park. He definitely
had her attention.

Alexavier pulled her down on the blanket to sit next to him,
facing the playground. Lucas climbed on top of the jungle gym,
and she was nervous. "He's got it. Look at him go," Alexavier said.
He opened the picnic basket and pulled out a plastic-divided
tray. He took the top off the container, and there were various
cheeses, olives, and cold meats like pepperoni and hard salami. He
then took out a loaf of warm fresh bread wrapped in paper and a
thin towel.

He held the loaf up for her to smell it. "My cousin Theresa
made the bread this morning."

Olivia watched him as he tore a piece off for her to eat and
then for himself. He then pulled out a water bottle for her and
opened it.

"I'll be right back," he said, and then she watched him head
over to where Lucas was playing.

The next thing she knew, Alexavier was up on the play equip-
ment with Lucas, and they were pretending to steer a ship. There
was a large wheel on the top of the fort area and a periscope.
Lucas yelled that they were heading into a storm, and when she
saw him and Alexavier leaning way over to the left and then the
right like they were going to be thrown overboard, she shook her
head. Lucas laughed so hard that Olivia almost teared up at how
much fun he was having. She drank some of her water and wiped
her eyes. How was that guy so good with kids?

Alexavier carried Lucas under his arm over to the blanket and
then handed him a water bottle.

"Spaghetti and meatballs or pizza, my man?"

"You have spaghetti in that basket?" Lucas asked, surprised.

"You betcha."

Olivia and Lucas watched as Alexavier pulled out a flat ther-
mos-style bowl and opened it up. Steam came bellowing out, and
the aroma of garlic and meatballs wafted in the air.

Lucas sat up on his knees, looking over at the meatballs. "Thanks," he said as Alexavier handed him a fork.

"What else can I get you, beautiful?"

Olivia smiled at him. "I'm not picky. Whatever you don't want, I'll eat."

He leaned in closer to her. "That's not how this works. Today, I am waiting on you. You get to choose whatever you want. I have ravioli, more spaghetti, pizza, and I think some cheese stuffed manicotti."

Olivia shook her head. Who packed a hot picnic basket like that? "How did you get all of that in there?"

"It's the magic of an Italian mama and aunt," he said. "When I got there this morning, they had it ready to go except for the bread that Theresa had just taken out of the oven."

"Wow. Your family must really love you," she said and took another drink from her water bottle.

"That they do. But honestly, I think they did all of this for you and Lucas. As soon as they found out what it was for, they got to work. Auntie Francesca still had curlers in her hair, and I think she drove over to my parents' house like that when mama called her and told her I had a date."

Olivia laughed.

"So, what will it be?"

"The only thing I know is spaghetti and pizza. Maybe I can try the ravioli? I don't even know what manicotti looks like."

"Well then, I wouldn't be a good Italian son if I didn't educate you on our cuisine." He sat up on his knees like Lucas and pulled out four separate containers like Lucas had and unscrewed the lids.

Lucas' eyes were big as he watched the presentation of food that Alexavier laid out before them.

"The only thing you're missing is the wine," Olivia teased, and then he pulled out a bottle of red wine from the never-ending picnic basket.

"You're like Mary Poppins with that thing," she said, biting her lip, and he loved that he impressed her.

"I want to make sure you have what you need."

He handed a fork to her and then a container of food to try.

"Hey, Lucas. How's that spaghetti?"

"The best," he said and wiped his mouth with the back of his hand. He was a mess but looked happy.

"Why don't you try some ravioli?" he offered and then winked at Olivia. "I think we should share. We can each take a few bites from a container and then pass it to the next person."

"I'm pretty sure your mother didn't have that in mind when she packed this beautiful basket and those bowls."

"Oh, my mother and aunt are schemers. If they could have added a love potion to your water bottle, then I'm sure they would have."

Lucas giggled when he said 'Love potion,' which made Olivia laugh.

They did exactly what Alexavier suggested. Olivia and Lucas loved each dish, and when they had all the food they could hold, Alexavier pulled out dessert.

"You're going to make me fat," Olivia said as she took a bite of the homemade cannoli.

"I like thick women," Alexavier said, and Lucas fell over on the blanket laughing.

It was the single best afternoon Olivia could remember having in months, maybe years, possibly ever.

She did want a life similar to Ryan's and Sydney's, but she didn't dare let herself dream that it could happen. It was rare, and they were the only couple other than Miss Lynn and her husband, before he passed away, that she'd ever seen truly in love. Her parents loved each other, but it was hard to see beyond their judgmental ways.

Alexavier noticed that Olivia was quieter than he'd ever seen her. She and Lucas helped clean up the picnic, and they loaded everything into the trunk of his car.

He held Olivia's hand so they could walk the lakefront and let Lucas play with his electric car. They had to stop for a few minutes so that Alexavier could sit on the ground in front of Lucas. He patiently showed him again what each button was for and how to maneuver the car to do tricks. Lucas was thrilled to get to play with it as long as he wanted, and he headed out ahead of them.

They walked over a mile before turning around, and on the way back, Lucas accidentally sent the car over an embankment, and it began to slide down into a culvert filled with water. Alexavier quickly climbed over a metal railing until he could reach down and grab the car, saving it from going into the water and being ruined.

Lucas marveled at his ability to climb over the railing and then was shocked when Alexavier gave him back the car so he could play.

"It was an accident, little man, and could have happened to anyone. Just try to keep it out of the soft dirt," he said and then went back and held Olivia's hand.

"Thanks for being patient with him."

Alexavier nodded and then put his arm around her as they followed Lucas to the playground area again and played for a couple more hours. They finished by skipping rocks across the water before returning to the car.

It wasn't long before Alexavier pulled into the small, one-car driveway and ran around his car to open Olivia's door before getting the picnic items out of his trunk. Lucas played with his remote-control car for a few seconds while Olivia helped Alexavier. Suddenly, they heard a man's gruff voice and quickly turned around.

"Watch where you're going with that thing, kid," the stranger said, and instantly Alexavier was in front of Olivia and heading for Lucas.

Lucas stood on the sidewalk in front of their house but had run the little car past the neighbor's driveway, and a stranger dressed in all black stepped out from behind a parked car to pick up the little electric toy. Alexavier walked right up to him and held out his hand. He didn't say a word until the man handed the car over.

"We didn't see you standing there, friend."

The man looked at Alexavier and then recognized who he was. "No problem," he said before turning and running across the street to get into a gray town car. He didn't look over at them again but sped away.

"Did you know that man?" he asked, walking back over to Lucas and Olivia, who were now standing next to each other.

"I don't think he lives around here," Olivia said. "I know everyone on this street, and I've never seen him." She held the picnic blanket to her chest and looked at Alexavier. "Do you think he was a reporter?"

Alexavier shook his head. "He wasn't a reporter. I know everyone who writes for the paper and the television journalists. "

"He was at the park," Lucas said, holding onto his car and heading for the porch.

Alexavier looked at Olivia. The man was wearing black slacks and a black polo. He should have stuck out to them since there were only a few people at the lakefront, and they all had children.

"Where did you see him, Lucas?" Alexavier asked.

"He was sitting in his car while we ate our food, and then I saw him again when we got to the end of the trail," he said as if it wasn't a big deal.

"What was he doing out there, buddy?" Olivia asked.

Lucas shrugged his shoulders. "Nothing. Looking around."

Chapter Nine

Alexavier walked them into the house. He unpacked the food items while Olivia got Lucas into his bath. She left Lucas to play in the water for ten minutes and joined Alexavier in the kitchen.

"Are you certain you didn't know that man?" she asked.

"No. I didn't. But while you were in the bathroom with Lucas, I made a few calls to my security team. I gave them a description of the car and the license plate number."

"What? You saw all of that?"

Alexavier pulled her into his arms. "It comes with the territory. I've had concerns in the past and learned to be diligent from the beginning to keep those around me safe."

"So, you think he was here watching you?"

"I can't say for sure. I don't want to worry you. The guy was probably visiting one of your neighbors."

"A single woman rents a room from the Moore's at the end of the street, but if you think you needed to have him checked out, then I'm worried."

"I'm erring on the side of caution. Maybe the man was simply in the wrong place. He seemed surprised when he figured out who I was and that I was angry at him for being short with Lucas."

"I'm a waitress, and Lucas is seven. Who would be interested in us?" She knew who might be interested in them, but she refused to acknowledge they were still on the mob's radar.

He watched her worry settle in like an old friend, but she wasn't going to tell him why. He decided to try and distract her. He kissed her forehead and then asked where she kept the plates.

He then set the small table and pulled the heated pizza out of the oven.

"I didn't realize we hadn't touched this pizza, and I figured it would be good for dinner," he said.

Olivia poured water for Alexavier and herself and a glass of milk for Lucas. She then headed back to the bathroom to make sure that Lucas dried off before putting on his pajamas. He was impatient and usually came out with his pajamas stuck to his entire body.

They ate and talked at the small three-chair table, enjoying the incredible homemade pizza. Soon it was time to put Lucas to bed, and Alexavier asked if he could read to him.

Lucas liked Alexavier and was thrilled to have him read. Olivia stood in the doorway for a few minutes as Alexavier acted out Lucas' favorite book characters while Lucas read some of the books aloud.

He had never asked her to do that, and she laughed at her funny kid. Alexavier winked at her and then suggested she take her bath or relax. "I've got this," he told her and went back to growl like a monster for Lucas.

Thirty minutes later, Olivia showered and put on her pajama shorts and a thermal long-sleeve top. She checked on Lucas, who was sound asleep, and then walked into the kitchen and living room area to find Alexavier had poured her a glass of wine and put up her clean dishes.

It was a small duplex, but it had an open floor plan with the kitchen connected to the living room. It looked like Alexavier had straightened things up, and she was a little embarrassed.

"Sorry, I usually keep a neater place."

Alexavier walked right over to her and pulled her into his arms. "You haven't had a day off in weeks. I only wanted to help."

"But you don't have to do that. I'll get it done," Olivia said, wriggling out of his arms and heading to the kitchen to wash the few glasses in the sink.

Alexavier followed her and dried the glasses before putting them away. When she finished, he watched her wipe down the countertops and search for something else to do.

Finally, he reached for her hands, and she looked up at him. "Hey, I didn't mean to insult you. I thought I was helping out."

Olivia nodded, and Alexavier pulled her over to the couch before handing over the glass of wine he'd poured for her. "My cousin Theresa, who made the bread, is a single mother with five kids. She sat me down this morning and told me everything single moms have to do in a day and how difficult it is to get small tasks done. I didn't mean to overstep. I was simply trying to make things easier for you."

"Thank you, Alex. I know you meant well," she said, avoiding his stare.

He moved a little closer to her and laced his fingers with hers. She stared into his eyes like she was trying to figure him out. "You know, it would help if you didn't make everything seem super easy for you."

He kissed her forehead, nose, and then lips. "You're doing an amazing job, Olivia. Lucas is a great kid. He's happy and inquisitive. Funny and smart. You're a wonderful mom."

"I really try to be. He's a good kid, and I want to do right by him. Today was perfect for him."

"Just him?"

She smiled but didn't answer him.

Alexavier laughed at her, teasing him. "Well, if you aren't going to answer me, then I'll tell you that today was the best date I've ever had."

Olivia rolled her eyes, and Alexavier kissed her hard on the lips. "Ever," he said using his deep voice that made her stomach tighten.

She took a deep breath and stared at him. Finally, she said, "I had a great time today too."

Alexavier kissed her again several times. "Does that mean you'll go out with me again?"

"Yes," she whispered, and they made out like teenagers on the couch for an hour.

"Do you want to go to my bedroom?" she asked in the heat of their make-out session.

"I would really like to say yes, but I have an early meeting in the morning, and when I spend the night with you, I don't plan on getting any sleep."

"Promises, Promises."

Alexavier pulled her under him and kissed her until she couldn't doubt how much he wanted her.

It was late when he forced himself to go home. It was one of the hardest things he'd done in a while. Olivia had let down her guard, and he wanted to stay desperately.

He stood up, and she followed him into the kitchen. He put their wine glasses into the sink after rinsing them and then turned to kiss her again. "Mind if I check on Lucas before I go?" he asked, and she tried to hide the emotion that she felt.

"Go ahead," she whispered and walked behind him as he headed down the hallway and quietly opened Lucas' bedroom door. As usual, her son had kicked off his blanket. Without a sound, Alexavier crept into the room and tucked the covers back over Lucas. But when he quietly closed the door behind him, he saw tears in Olivia's eyes before she quickly turned away. Without a word, she walked ahead of him straight to the front door. He didn't know what to do, but he couldn't leave her like that, and she was standing there with the door open.

He pulled her back against the front of his body and wrapped both arms around her. His warmth surrounded her as he whispered to her, "Tell me what I did to upset you?"

"I'm just tired."

He turned her around so he could pull her body into his. She fit against him perfectly, like she was made for him. "I want to do the right things with you, Olivia. If you'll let me in, a little bit."

He felt her chest rise and fall with the deep breath she took. "Sometimes I feel sad for Lucas because he has no family but me. Brent's never around, and neither of us has a family. Seeing you be so good to Lucas reminded me what it would be like if he had more people looking out for him."

Alexavier closed his eyes and hugged her tighter. She had no idea how her words affected him. He would be there for her and Lucas if she would let him. He'd been trying for months.

He felt her shiver, and he leaned down and kissed the top of her head. He had to go. He had a seven o'clock meeting that he would surely miss if he stayed. His obligations didn't make leaving her any easier.

"Let me come back tomorrow night?"

Olivia nodded, and he kissed her hard on the mouth before he told her to lock the door behind him so he could make sure she didn't forget. She did forget to lock the doors sometimes but had gotten comfortable in Maisonville.

Looking out the window, she thought about the man from the sidewalk that had also been at the park. Her quiet street looked peaceful as usual, and she thought about how much she loved the little town.

Of course, making out with Alexavier had distracted her from what had happened earlier. She thought about the man again and then about the simple life she'd created for her and Lucas. That man must have been there watching Alexavier. He was probably with the press. No one had bothered her or Lucas since she moved to Maisonville. No way that man was there for her or her kid.

Alexavier was being over-cautious. She was sure of it.

Chapter Ten

Olivia woke up with slightly swollen lips from all the kissing she'd done the night before with Alexavier. He was a great kisser. Of course, she hadn't found anything that he wasn't great at doing.

She rolled her eyes and smiled again, thinking about how sweet of a man he was for playing with Lucas at the park and then at the house. She checked the time on her phone and then smiled to see a text that Alexavier sent at five in the morning.

"Good morning, Beautiful. I had a great time yesterday with you and Lucas. Have a great day. I'll see you tonight."

He was undeniably good at the dating thing.

She hurried into the bathroom and pulled her hair back into a ponytail as she headed to Lucas' room to wake him up for school. When she stepped into his bedroom, Lucas was already dressed and had the electric car out that Alexavier had given him.

"Good morning, buddy. Are you dressed for school, already?"

"I made my own cereal too."

"You've had breakfast already?" Olivia was confused. Lucas had never gotten out of bed without waking her up.

"Well, you're getting too big for me. Stop it," she said playfully and then carried his backpack into the kitchen.

She usually got dressed while Lucas asked for five more

minutes of sleep before he had to get dressed for school. They would rush around with her making breakfast, and then she'd see him off on the bus before she jumped into her car to do her mascara in the rearview mirror before driving to the diner.

It was Monday, and he'd thrown off her groove.

"Look, kiddo, I have to run and get dressed. Since you've already eaten and gotten ready, you can watch a cartoon this morning. They rarely had time for television during the week and never in the morning before school. He cheered and headed toward the couch with his car to find the remote.

Olivia hurried to get dressed. She threw on some jeans and a fitted black long sleeve top. She scrubbed her face, brushed her teeth, and then worried with her long hair again until she threw it back into a ponytail. The little makeup bag she carried had lip balm and mascara, which was her everyday work makeup.

When she walked back into the outer room, they had a few more minutes. "Hey bud, did you remember to brush your teeth?"

Lucas shook his head before running to brush his teeth with only a few minutes to spare.

Olivia praised him again for getting up on his own and making breakfast until she reached the door and found it unlocked.

"Lucas? What time did you get up this morning?"

"I dunno. You were still asleep."

"I know that but was the sun up or still down?"

Lucas looked at his mom without answering, and she knew what he'd done.

"You got up before sunrise and went outside to play with your new car. Didn't you?"

"Yes, ma'am," Lucas said, lowering his head. "It has headlights that turn on in the dark."

"Lucas, you can't go out without asking me. What if I woke up and you weren't in your room? Do you know how scared that would make me?"

"I only wanted to play with my car a little longer."

Olivia was super proud that she didn't lose her shit with Lucas. Shit, she meant shark. She'd promised herself that she wouldn't use the other 'SH' word anymore.

What the hell. It was Monday, and she meant every curse word she said in her head.

"Lucas. Give me the car. It's going into restriction for one day."

"But mom."

"Don't but mom me. You knew you weren't supposed to go outside without asking. If you thought it was okay, you would have come into my room and asked. Right?"

Lucas reluctantly nodded.

"One-day restriction for the car, and then you can have it back. We will talk about it some more when you get home. I love you. Go catch the bus, buddy."

She kissed him and then walked out on the porch to watch him.

As soon as the bus pulled away, Olivia couldn't help but look around the neighborhood again. No sign of the man from the day before. She waved to a neighbor across the street who had two girls that rode the same bus as Lucas before she walked back inside to grab her things and head to work.

Without scaring Lucas, she had to make him understand that it wasn't safe for him to go out without her. Of course, he didn't need to worry because she worried enough for everyone already.

Her ex-boyfriend's problems had haunted her for a long time, along with her own hometown issues. Thankfully, all of that was in the past because if danger were coming after her, it would have happened six years ago.

The more she considered the stranger from the park, the more she decided he must have been there for the mayor of New Orleans. She and Lucas lived a modest life, and Maisonville had been good to them. However, there were probably lots of people who wanted to follow the ever-popular Alexavier Regalia around. It just so happened to be the day she'd finally said yes to a date.

She grabbed her shoes and jacket and headed to the diner where Miss Lynn would have a cup of Joe waiting for her. She would also be ready to hear about Olivia's afternoon off, and when she found out that she spent all of it with Alexavier, Miss Lynn would lose her mind.

🙋

"Don't you dare set that table," Miss Lynn said as soon as Olivia told her that Alexavier was at Sydney and Ryan's house when she got there Saturday night. Her eyes were dancing with curiosity when Olivia added that she and Lucas spent Sunday afternoon and evening with him too.

Miss Lynn usually took Sundays off while Olivia worked the breakfast shift with help from the kitchen guys. The afternoon and dinner crowd ordered from the counter cafeteria-style until Miss Lynn could hire more help. They usually didn't see each other from Saturday night until Monday morning, and Miss Lynn was about to burst with excitement.

Olivia laughed and sat down at the bar to tell her sweet confidant everything that had happened.

Miss Lynn didn't interrupt or ask a single question until Olivia finished. They only had five more minutes until the restaurant opened for the day, but Miss Lynn wouldn't let her move while she asked questions and refilled Olivia's coffee cup.

"And he brought you flowers?" she asked.

"Yes. It was a mixed arrangement, but it also had six roses." Olivia leaned in and whispered, "No one has ever bought me flowers."

Miss Lynn hugged Olivia. "Never?" she asked. How could no one have ever bought that child any flowers?

Olivia shook her head. "Not even when I was in the hospital to have Lucas. Brent brought balloons."

Lynn had met Brent when he came to pick up Lucas. He always stared at Olivia, and it gave Lynn an uneasy feeling. She never told Olivia, but she didn't think he was entirely over the blue-eyed beauty. She also thought his quiet behavior was fake. There was something sneaky and dishonest about him, and she couldn't put her finger on it, but she didn't trust him. He certainly didn't know how to treat a woman like Olivia. She deserved hundreds of flowers for putting up with him.

Olivia confided in Miss Lynn that she and Alexavier had a hot make-out session on the couch, but when she asked him if he wanted to go into her bedroom, he declined. And it wasn't the first time that had happened. "What do you make of that? I mean, I've never met a guy that said he wanted to wait. He's got me in knots."

"Sounds to me like he cares about you, honey. He's trying to be respectful. You know he comes from a huge family. I think he's the youngest son, and I read that he has something like sixty or more first cousins."

"Shit. I mean, Shark." Olivia smiled as Miss Lynn laughed at her. She would have to put more money in the swear jar and try harder to stop cussing. "He is the youngest son and does have a huge Italian family."

Their conversation was interrupted by knocking on the front door, and Olivia jumped up. "I better go unlock it. They're going to think something is wrong with us in here."

"Well, you aren't getting out of this conversation so easily. When the breakfast crowd thins out, I'll get one of the boys from the kitchen to come and bus the tables so we can chat."

"I told you everything, Miss Lynn."

"I wasn't done yet," she said, winking at Olivia. "Now, let's get those condiments on the tables."

Olivia rushed around, trying to get them caught up for the morning. It didn't take long, and before she knew it, it was eleven.

The breakfast crowd was huge for a Monday, and so was the lunch crowd. The ladies didn't have a chance to talk again until later that afternoon. Miss Lynn was behind the bar making another container of sweet tea while Olivia picked up an order from the kitchen window. She told Olivia that she liked the mayor and thought they had made a beautiful couple.

Olivia shrugged her shoulders. "Honestly, I think he's a little out of my league," she said as she headed to drop off a piece of pie with vanilla ice cream.

Lynn watched her as she walked away. That was the first time she'd ever heard something like that from Olivia. She knew the young single mother didn't have it easy, but she always put on a brave face. Olivia pretended to be confident about everything.

The customer thanked Olivia for the pie, and she smiled at him and then turned toward the kitchen. She hadn't meant to admit her insecurities about Alexavier because it was also an admission of how much she liked him. And she did really like him. However, it couldn't go beyond their late-night confessions. She wanted the quiet life she'd made for herself and Lucas. Once Alexavier realized she wouldn't go to any formal events with him, then it would seal their fate. After all, it was part of his job, being seen all around town. She'd told him about not wanting to be in the paper or magazines, but he didn't know the truth. She wasn't a spot-light kind of girl. Lucas was too young to hear all the gossip that would occur if she and Alexavier went public. She'd been through something like that before as a teenager. She was infamous in her small town, and she wouldn't go back to that life for anyone. Not even the gorgeous mayor.

Business slowed by mid-afternoon when Lucas' bus let him off in front of the diner. He walked inside and sat at the bar, as usual, to do his homework. Miss Lynn brought him chocolate milk and a grilled cheese sandwich.

Olivia helped him with some math problems, and then Miss Lynn sat with him so he could read a story out loud to her. His reading skills were rocking, and his teacher said she could tell he'd been practicing more at home. He got five out of five stars on his timed readings and was in the top ten percent of his class. After completing his homework, Miss Lynn gave him some colored pencils. Lucas drew pictures of animals and then wrote facts about them on the bottom of the pages.

Olivia praised him and showed several of her regular customers his impressive artwork. He was an intelligent and talented boy, and everyone complimented his drawings.

It was already seven, and Olivia's shift ended in half an hour. She would need to hurry home to get Lucas in the bath and read more at bedtime. She liked that he was doing well in school and had to keep up the hard work.

She hadn't heard from Alexavier, and she tried not to overthink it. They'd had a great time, and he'd asked if he could come over again, but maybe he was busy. Besides, it had started raining a couple of hours earlier, and perhaps he didn't want to drive across the long bridge in the inclement weather?

Doubt crept into her mind as she thought about how maybe he'd changed his mind altogether. She ignored the fact that maybe she'd been right all along that they didn't fit together, but the idea kept swirling around in her head. It was why she'd been quiet all night, and Lucas and Miss Lynn both noticed. She tried to smile and talk a little more, but she couldn't keep it up. She explained she was a little tired, but every time the brass bell on the front door rang, she looked up expectantly and then turned around disappointed.

Miss Lynn felt the hurt on Olivia's face even though the young woman tried to hide it.

Before long, Miss Lynn and Lucas also began watching the door like Olivia. It was ridiculous, but none of them could help themselves. The bell would ring, they all would turn around, it would be someone other than the mayor, and then they each sighed in disappointment.

At 7:30, the bell rang again, and every single person in the diner turned around to stare at who walked through the door.

Chapter Eleven

Alexavier started his Monday as usual by waking at five in the morning and working out for an hour. He'd sent a text to Olivia first thing and couldn't get her off his mind no matter how hard he pushed and pulled his rowing machine or ran on his treadmill.

He had a breakfast meeting with some executives from the New Orleans Saints Football Team, and while it was engaging, he still wished to be wherever Olivia was instead.

His day didn't slow as he went from meeting to meeting and then into the office for messages and updates regarding the arson fires. There wasn't much news, and he thought if he worked a little harder, then he might get to skip out early, but the weather turned stormy. When severe rain hit the metro area, he personally followed up with the pumping stations and kept an eye on the streetcar shutdowns due to potential flooding. Those things were essential to the city, and it was important to him. Once the rain slowed and the danger passed, he could get updated by phone and finally left his office, worried that it was too late to make it to the diner before Olivia and Lucas went home and started their evening routine.

He drove faster than usual, straight to Olivia's house, but she and Lucas weren't there.

Next, he headed to the diner.

"Hey," he said, rushing in the door and seeing Olivia's beautiful face first.

"Hey," she answered on an exhale. She had a fistful of colored pencils that Lucas spread out all over the counter and floor underneath his chair.

Alexavier walked over and grabbed two stray blank pieces of paper from the floor. "Hey, little man. How are you doing?"

Lucas grinned at Alexavier, and then they shook hands, making some strange handshake moves Olivia had never seen Lucas do. They had a secret handshake?

"Great," Lucas said and then handed Alexavier a picture of a lion that he drew. "You can have that if you want."

"You drew it? Then, of course, I want it," he said and looked up to see Miss Lynn watching them.

He stepped closer to Miss Lynn and gave her a hug and a kiss on the cheek. "Good to see you," he said, making her smile bigger.

"Good to see you too, Alexavier."

"Did you guys eat?" he asked Lucas.

"I did. Mom never eats."

Alexavier looked at Olivia, and she looked sternly at her son for ratting her out.

"I'll make sure she eats," Alexavier told Lucas loud enough for Lynn and Olivia to hear.

"I can take care of myself. Thank you very much." Olivia didn't look at Alexavier as she handed Miss Lynn the pencils and extra paper before picking up Lucas's coat and backpack.

Alexavier took the bag from her hands, and Lucas took his coat. They waved to Miss Lynn and headed for the door together while Olivia stared at them. Why were they already acting like a team?

She told Miss Lynn she'd see her in the morning and followed the guys. Alexavier held the diner door open for her, and Lucas was talking his head off about his day and what he would like to do the next time they got to take the toy car out.

When Alexavier closed the door behind Olivia, he wrapped an arm around her and pulled her close. "How was your day, beautiful?"

Olivia wiped her face with her hands and then ran them over her ponytail. She felt worn out and knew she looked that way too. "Great."

Alexavier kissed the top of her head. "You're great."

Lucas laughed and made kissing noises. Alexavier chased him to the car. I'll follow you home," he said as he opened Lucas' door and then Olivia's.

She nodded but didn't say anything.

The drive to her house seemed to take much longer than usual. Alexavier considered how anxious Olivia seemed with him there. She was clearly used to doing things on her own, but he'd hoped their time together the day before had eased her mind. He didn't want to rush her and would do whatever it took to prove they had a more significant connection than the fling she'd suggested.

Olivia carefully pulled into her carport, and Alexavier parked closely behind her. She looked surprised when he opened her door and when she stood up, he pulled her in for a warm kiss as he wrapped his arms around her.

Suddenly, it began raining again, and the carport barely covered them. When Alexavier stepped back, Olivia's entire face was flushed, and he couldn't stop smiling.

"Alex," she whispered, and he loved the breathlessness in her voice. He'd missed her all day. He winked at her before hurrying around the car to help Lucas, who couldn't open his door because Olivia kept the child locks turned on.

They piled into the house, shaking off the rainwater, and while Olivia put her things down, he conspiratorially sidled up next to Lucas. "What's your mom's favorite food?"

"Chinese food. Stuff with rice or noodles, especially if it comes in a weird-looking box," he said.

Olivia laughed at her son. "You like fried rice and lomein noodles too, kid."

Lucas nodded and then told Alexavier he'd see him later because he had to take a shower.

"You don't take showers." Olivia stared at her son.

"I'm a big kid, mom. Baths are for babies."

"For your information, I still take baths," she told him.

"You're a girl," he said, rolling his eyes and heading for the hallway.

Olivia shook her head. Since when did her son become a teenager? "Baths are not only for girls," she yelled after Lucas.

He didn't answer her or turn around. Olivia excused herself from Alexavier and went to help Lucas adjust the hot water.

She seemed to be gone a long time, but Alex needed the extra time to find an open Chinese Restaurant. Things on that side of the lake closed early, especially on Mondays.

He poured Olivia a glass of wine, and when she returned to the room, he offered to help get Lucas settled.

She looked like she was thinking about it and then nodded. "Okay. If you keep an eye on him, then I'll run and take my shower. If that's okay?"

"Of course," he said, happy that she was acting more relaxed with him there.

When Lucas finished showering, Alexavier turned off the water and wiped up the water all over the floor and partially on one wall.

"Little dude, was the curtain closed?"

"It doesn't look like it." Lucas laughed.

"I almost had to swim to get to the faucet," Alexavier said, getting Lucas to make swimming motions out of the bathroom.

Lucas picked out books for them to read as Alexavier went to answer the door for the Chinese food delivery.

When he returned to Lucas' room, the kid had ten books beside him.

"All of those?" he asked.

Lucas nodded proudly. "They're my best books."

"I know, man, but I want to spend some time with your mom too. How about making that pile half that size? I'll read the other half tomorrow night."

"You're coming back tomorrow too?

"Do you want me to come back tomorrow?"

"Yes!" Lucas said.

Alexavier was beginning to love that kid. In fact, he was certain no one was more excited to see him when he walked into a room than Lucas. They picked out five books and put them in order of importance. Saving the best for last, they performed the first two they read. Lucas acted out the characters in the first book while Alexavier read, and then Lucas read so Alexavier could act out the characters. By the fourth book, Lucas could barely keep his eyes open, and halfway through the fifth book, he was out.

Alexavier tucked the blankets around him and turned off his bedside lamp. He then grabbed the takeout food to set it up on the coffee table. Pouring two glasses of water and wine, he sat on the couch right before Olivia walked into the room.

"You got him to sleep again," she said, and it was a statement instead of a question. "How was his shower?"

Alexavier patted the couch beside him for her to have a seat. "I'm not sure if he actually got rinsed off, but if the water on the bathroom floor was any indication, I think he had a good time."

"Oh, no." Olivia turned to go clean up the bathroom, but Alexavier stopped her.

"Lucas and I got it."

She stared at him for a moment before realizing what she was doing. "Thanks for that," Olivia said as she finally sat on the couch.

Her worried expression had Alexavier confused. Was she upset, or did she not want him there? He wasn't good at the guessing game, and honestly, he didn't want to play games with her. Reading a woman's mind was impossible. Did she think he was being too pushy? He naturally was a control freak but could tone it down for Olivia.

"Is everything okay?"

"Yes," was all she said.

He sat there looking at her.

Olivia sat back on the couch and stared at him. "I don't know what's wrong with me."

"Am I moving too fast?"

Olivia smirked. She'd gone out with most of the single guys in town, but it never meant anything to her. Why was she so screwed up over Alexavier?

"No," she finally answered.

"Would you like me to go?"

She shook her head.

"Perhaps, I should wait to see you again when Lucas is at his dad's house? I like him. I think he's a cool kid, but maybe you would feel better if he and I weren't buddies?"

Olivia shrugged her shoulders. Her ex-boyfriend, Brent, didn't know how to be a father. He wasn't consistently around, and they never knew when he would actually come and pick Lucas up for a visit. Seeing Alexavier with him upset her because he was a perfect example of everything that Lucas would never have with Brent.

Finally, she admitted, "I love how you are with Lucas. I wish he had that with his dad."

Alexavier leaned forward and kissed her. "My dad and uncles played with me as a kid. And there are a ton of children in my family. I don't know how to be any different around them. Kids are outspoken and honest, and I love that. It's too bad more adults don't act that way. Perhaps Brent didn't have good examples in his family? He might get better."

Olivia was pretty sure that Brent was only getting worse. She'd met him when he tended a bar at a restaurant in New Orleans where she'd worked. He'd moved on to several less dependable jobs from there until he landed in his construction career. She didn't think it was a career, but it covered his gambling habit and allowed him to keep ridiculous hours if he stayed out all night at a casino or illegal card house. The last few times she'd seen Brent, he looked like he wasn't sleeping and maybe had lost weight. She warned him that she wouldn't let him take Lucas if he didn't get his crap together.

"Maybe. But I doubt it," Olivia said and leaned into Alexavier's shoulder. He was a good guy, but she didn't share her real feelings or private details about her past. Her parents taught her at a young age to keep personal problems quiet. However, she did feel closer to Alexavier than anyone before him. They spent so many nights talking and getting to know each other that it was the only reason she could figure that she felt the way she did about him. But those feelings were foreign to her. Did you really know someone after six months? She grew up around people that she never understood.

She took a deep breath and tried to change the melancholy mood. "So, you ordered dinner?"

Alexavier smiled, "I went a little overboard, but I got your favorites and mine. Figured we could share?" He leaned over and picked up the first box he came to and a pair of chopsticks so he could feed her.

She laughed when he told her to open up, and then her stomach felt fluttery at the idea that the hot, powerful mayor would serve her a bite of food.

He told her funny stories about his day and then asked questions about her work. By the fourth bite of food, she picked up chopsticks for herself, and he grinned that she'd finally loosened up around him.

When they had plenty of food, they took the leftovers to the refrigerator and put them away. Alexavier poured more wine, and they returned to relax on the couch. He settled the old quilt she had lying on the chair over her lap and then pulled her into his side. "Did your mother or grandmother make this quilt?" he asked.

"No way, I bought that at a thrift store. My mother makes quilts, or at least she used to make them. She and a few other women from our church would put them together by hand. They were given as gifts from the church when someone got married or had a baby. Sometimes when someone was sick. Does your mom quilt?"

"Nah. My mother is a big cook."

"And that she does really well. Just ask Lucas. She's ruined Olive Garden for us."

Alexavier laughed. "Never been."

"Of course, you haven't. Your mom is the best cook ever."

"Your mom didn't cook?"

"Some, but we mostly ate at church. Everything there was like cafeteria food, you know. Like lots of casseroles or one-pot meals."

"And you never see them now?"

She shook her head but didn't answer. He'd noticed that she'd tried to change the subject already, and while he wanted her to open up to him, she wasn't ready.

"Well, that leads me to my next date proposal. Would it be okay if I took you to my Auntie's house for dinner? Lucas, too, of course. I can promise the food will be fantastic, but I can't promise that they won't ask a lot of questions."

Olivia took a deep breath. Was he serious? "You want us to meet your family?"

"Of course. I've already told them a lot about you, and they're going to bug me to death until they meet you and Lucas. It's okay if it's too soon for you, but frankly, I'm shocked they haven't driven over to the diner to have lunch and to say hello. They're nosy like that."

"Oh, my, God," Olivia said with her hands muffling her mouth. "Why? I mean, we've only been on one date."

"I think they can tell how I feel about you, Olivia. I've been trying to woo you for half a year. If you had let me take you out from the beginning, we would have been dating for months. You know me, and I know you. At least all the stuff that counts."

Olivia nodded. She'd purposely avoided talking about her family and ex, but he was right. He knew everything else about her and her thoughts and ideas about the world. They'd shared all the important stuff. At least the stuff that was important and relevant now.

"You still haven't slept with me," she said.

"Maybe I'm saving myself for marriage," he said straight-faced.

Olivia put her hand over her mouth to stifle her laugh. He'd been married before and dated tons of beautiful women, according to the social pages. "You're killing me, Alexavier Anthony Regalia."

He pulled her into his lap. "And you're using my full name?" he asked and then kissed her thoroughly. Again, they made out for an hour on the couch. He'd untucked his shirt, and her sleep shorts twisted around her. It was the hottest make-out session she'd had since the night before with him, and Olivia's body was on fire.

When they sat up, she could see how dilated his eyes were. He was just as affected as she was, and yet he stopped.

"Let me guess. You're going to go home?"

He kissed her again on the lips, "Yes, baby. I have an early morning, and so do you. But I'll be thinking about you all night and again all day tomorrow. Can I come over tomorrow night too?"

"Yes," Olivia whispered, wondering how long it would be before he stayed the night.

Chapter Twelve

Olivia got to the diner a few minutes late the following day. Miss Lynn had already dressed the tables and was sitting at the bar with Olivia's coffee waiting for her.

"Late night, honey?" she asked, smiling at Olivia when she came in.

"Not as late as I would have liked, but still late."

Miss Lynn laughed. "Well, he is one of the best-looking men I have ever seen up close."

"Tell me about it." Olivia closed her eyes and squealed in her hand. "He's got me so hot and bothered, and that's purely because he's sweet to Lucas. I haven't seen Lucas that happy in ages. I don't know what the hell, I mean heck, I'm going to do about him."

Miss Lynn reached her hand out and held Olivia's hand softly. "Maybe you shouldn't do anything except sit back and enjoy his attention?"

Olivia sat her coffee cup down. She wasn't the kind of woman that sat back and let things happen to her anymore. Her past taught her to stay focused and not get distracted by all the pretty things.

It was why she ended up in Maisonville and why she and

Lucas had an easy life. She worked to keep all the complicated nonsense away. Olivia wasn't a young, foolish girl that lived for the moment. Sure, she'd had some meaningless sex, but she didn't think it was funny when others said they were simply trying to make it to the end of the day. No way. She had to know she could handle tomorrow and the next day and the next. Lucas depended on her. She relied on herself too. But she did really want Alexavier, even if it would only last a little while.

Miss Lynn freshened up Olivia's cup of coffee. "Don't look so freaked out, honey. The man likes you. I can tell that Lucas likes him too. I think you could have a great time together and maybe it will become more, or maybe you will get a great friend out of the deal? Either way, you're better for having that man in your corner."

Olivia smiled and sat up straighter in her chair. "We are having a great time for now, but I'm not looking for more. And he's the lucky one to have my time."

"Absolutely," Miss Lynn agreed. She was used to Olivia's pride, and after seeing how nervous she was over Mayor Regalia, it was important to let her fake it for the moment. He was a strong man, though, and that might be exactly what Olivia needed to finally relax some of the control she'd been so tightly holding on to for the years that Lynn had known her.

The sweet girl didn't have a single family member or friend ever visit her or Lucas. She knew Olivia had an older sister, but she never came to visit. She'd even mentioned that her parents and some aunts and uncles were all still living, but none of them checked on her.

It didn't make sense.

It was much worse than if they'd all passed away. At least then, Lynn could believe someone cared about Olivia and Lucas but knowing they were out there and chose not to have any connections was unbelievable.

Miss Lynn scooted off her stool. "Look at the time. I better get that door open before they start knocking like yesterday." She laughed as she flipped the open sign around and unlocked the doors.

Olivia knew Miss Lynn had more questions, but she couldn't talk about Alexavier anymore. She'd already laid awake most of the night thinking about him. She also woke up to another waiting text from Alexavier, "Good morning. Hope you have a great day." She was starting to act like those silly women that made out in public, and she couldn't become that after making fun of them for so long.

Nope.

She needed to slow things down. Put the relationship or whatever it was on the right footing so she could focus on taking care of things for her son.

She slipped her cell phone into her back pocket. The cell phone that Alexavier bought for her. And she would give that back to him as soon as she had enough money.

After all, it was time that deadbeat Brent started paying up, and she was going to call him after the breakfast shift and give him the ultimatum that he deserved. Lucas needed a dad that helped take care of him. Financially and physically. Not a dude who showed up once every couple of months to bring him back home and watch television or something equally useless.

She would work every weekend until she had enough money for an attorney to file for child support if she had to. He couldn't keep promising to send money and then write her hot checks.

She was done.

⚓

THE DINER WAS slow during the morning and lunch shifts. Olivia waited on all the customers, and Miss Lynn interviewed another young woman for the open waitress job.

She appeared to be a gem and was ready to start at the diner on a trial basis as soon as she completed the new-hire paperwork. Suddenly, if Olivia needed or wanted a day off, it wouldn't be a burden on Miss Lynn or the kitchen guys who filled in on the floor when necessary. The kitchen helpers hated waiting tables, and when they had to leave their hiding place to work the floor, they would complain to the chef for days. They needed harmony at the diner, and if the dishwashers and line cooks wanted to only be in the kitchen, then it was time to hire another waitress.

The rest of the day was super slow, and Olivia left when Lucas' bus dropped him off. On days like that, Miss Lynn made him a snack to go and put it in a brown paper sack with his name on it. It always had a piece of fruit and random hot food like chicken strips, grilled cheese, macaroni and cheese, or something equally Lucas-friendly.

Once they got home, Lucas offered to help his mom take out the trash and unload the dishwasher. She knew he wasn't suddenly interested in household chores and sat him down to discuss the remote-control car rules.

He agreed not to go outside without asking again, and they worked on his homework together before heading out to ride bikes. Riding his bicycle was Lucas' favorite thing, and Olivia tried to make time for it several times a week.

She'd almost forgotten about the strange man from the park but suddenly felt like someone was watching them. She took a moment to look around. "Hey Lucas, let me check the chain on my bike before we go too far," she said, trying to distract him while she looked around at the cars parked on the street. She didn't see anyone or any strange vehicles, but she made a mental note to keep an eye out. It would also be a good idea to ask Alexavier if they got any information from the car license plate he'd called in.

They finished their bike ride, and then Olivia agreed to return Lucas' new toy car. She sat on the steps watching him try to get the car to spin in a circle. They laughed at the failed attempts, and then Lucas decided he would build a small ramp instead.

Olivia helped drag some old boards he'd found in the shed

behind their house while Lucas used a few bricks to prop the wood up, but they didn't have it quite right.

Frustrated at the situation, Lucas suddenly cheered when Alexavier drove up.

"Yes," he said, throwing his small fist into the air like he'd won a prize.

Olivia smiled at her son and Alexavier, who gave Lucas a high-five before walking over to plant a kiss on her lips. "Hey there," he said, and his voice was huskier than usual.

He had removed his suit jacket and handed her his tie before unbuttoning the first two buttons on his very clean white dress shirt. Holy smoke, she couldn't stop thinking about how sexy he looked that way.

"Hey," she said and was surprised at how desperate she sounded. She was crazy about the man and seeing him with her son did crazy things to her heart.

He reached for her hand and pulled her to his side so he could wrap an arm around her. "Lucas, want to help me carry some groceries into the house? We will make homemade pizzas after we build a proper ramp."

"Yahoo," Lucas said, whooping and running to the car at the same time.

He actually said, Yahoo?

Olivia reached for a bag, and Alexavier shook his head. "Let us men take the bags inside," he said, winking at Lucas.

Lucas grinned and looked proud as he walked past his mother carrying two full sacks.

Olivia rolled her eyes at Alexavier as he filled his arms with four more bags. "How much stuff did you bring?" she asked, walking into the house beside him.

"I can't take the credit. My mother and auntie showed up around four with an Italian salad already made and pizza dough plus all the toppings we needed to make at least four pizzas."

Olivia's eyes watered, and Alexavier hurried to set the bags on the kitchen counter. She swallowed back the emotion and turned away from Alexavier and Lucas so she could unpack one of the bags.

Alexavier walked over closer to her and helped take items from her hands. He didn't say anything, simply stood there next to her until she felt like talking.

"That was really sweet of them. Your family seems wonderful."

He realized it was the thoughtfulness that had gotten to her, and he didn't know what to say. Where the hell was her family?

"They are wonderful, but they are also bossy, pushy, nosy, a little bit crazy, and sometimes they drive me nuts. But I love them. It doesn't mean we don't have our issues. We just find a way to work them out. That's what family does," he said, pulling her and Lucas into a big hug. At the same time, he reached down and tickled Lucas under his arm, making him giggle and squeal.

It was the perfect way to diffuse the emotional moment.

"Now, let's go see if we can get that car to catch some air," he said, rolling up his sleeves as he and Lucas headed outside.

How could he always have so much energy for Lucas too?

Olivia watched the two of them talk and conspire over what they needed. Then they walked to the backyard and came back with more wood.

She didn't know what would happen between them long-term, but in the short-term, she knew that car was going to catch some air, they were going to enjoy some fantastic pizza, and that she and Lucas would meet Alexavier's family next weekend for dinner.

Chapter Thirteen

The rest of the week was perfect and predictable. Olivia and Lucas went to work and school, and at the end of each day, Alexavier came over to have dinner and hang out with them.

It was strangely comfortable, and Olivia tried not to think about how much she enjoyed his company.

Early Saturday morning, she rushed around so she could drop Lucas off with Sydney and Ryan for the day. She would work until four, and then she and Lucas would meet Alexavier in the city so they could eat dinner with the Regalia family.

She was nervous but refused to show it. Alexavier wanted them to come over, and she didn't want to disappoint him. He'd been so kind to her and Lucas, and it was the least she could do after all the effort he'd put into seeing them each day and bringing over or ordering dinner each night. He'd even bought a bicycle so he could go bike riding with them on Thursday after a full day at work.

Yup, she could have dinner and meet his family. At least, that was what Olivia told Sydney when she dropped Lucas off to spend the day with her.

"He sounds like a wonderful man, Olivia. He was charming and at home hanging out with all the boys and Ryan last weekend," Sydney said, sipping her hot coffee while curled up on the large leather sofa in the Gentry's incredible home.

Olivia nodded but didn't add anything to the conversation. She'd rushed around all morning, but she wasn't late and now had a few minutes to chat with her friend. Ryan had scooped Lucas up and had him in the kitchen with a giant bowl of cereal.

"Are your boys here or across the lake this weekend?"

"They're with Drake this weekend. I think Ryan plans to take Lucas fishing instead of working on the tree house."

Olivia hadn't made connections with anyone except Miss Lynn, Sydney, and Ryan since she was in high school. It was incredible to have a few close friends that cared about her son.

"He loves fishing with Ryan. I put extra clothes in his backpack. If it's not a lot of trouble, maybe you could hose him off before I get here?"

Sydney laughed. She was sure that both Lucas and Ryan would need hosing off before coming back into the house after fishing. "We'll have him showered and dressed when you get here. Why don't you text me when you're on your way? I'll make sure you don't have to wait. So, you haven't told me what you're wearing tonight?" Sydney wiggled her eyebrows suggestively.

Olivia laughed at her friend. She missed working with Sydney. "You're looking at it," Olivia said. She stood up and turned around in her black jeans and blue top. It was the best she had.

Sydney sat her coffee cup down. "You know, Olivia, I have a ton of dresses from my previous life that you can borrow or even have. I mean, there might be three that I would wear for Ryan. The rest, honestly, are not me anymore. They would look great on you."

"I'm taller than you, Sydney."

"Still, I bet they would look hot on you."

"I don't know," Olivia said and then casually looked at the clock on the wall. "I need to get to the diner, and look, I'll be rushing in and out tonight so that we won't be late."

"No worries. I'll put together a few things for you just in case you have time," Sydney hugged Olivia and walked her out. She knew her friend didn't have much money. Sydney was in a position to help, and she was going to do it. No matter how much Olivia resisted.

It was after two when Olivia and Miss Lynn could relax a bit. The new waitress, Daisy, came in and chatted with Miss Lynn. She then sat at the bar and drank iced tea. She smiled a lot but didn't talk much.

Olivia ran to the back to get supplies to restock condiments at the counter, and when she walked back into the main dining room, Sydney was sitting at the bar too. She had a garment bag with her and a big smile.

"You miss working here already?" Olivia asked.

"I do miss you guys. And Ryan and Lucas got in from fishing about thirty minutes ago and are napping. I couldn't stand the quiet and figured I'd bring these outfits here so you could try them on."

Olivia looked around the room, which was only half full now, but almost all the tables were hers.

Miss Lynn reached her hand over to pat Olivia's. "I've got you covered. Go try them on and let us see you in them."

Olivia nodded. She was hard-headed, but those two women were the same. Besides, it would be great if she could wear something from the stack of dresses. She wanted to look her best.

After thirty minutes of trying things on and having Miss Lynn and Sydney, along with a few of their regular customers, comment, they finally picked a blue wrap dress. It was the same color as Olivia's eyes and accentuated her curvy figure.

Olivia hugged the women and then went back to the storage room to hang up everything she'd tried on. When she returned, Sydney shook her head. "Those all fit you, and I will never wear them. Take them. It looks like you'll have occasions to dress up."

Olivia tried to refuse the clothes, but she didn't have anything that looked as pretty as those dresses. For the first time in a long time, she felt like a woman and not just a mother.

Sydney left, and the next couple of hours dragged along. She and Miss Lynn cleaned shelves and counters while waiting on the few afternoon customers. But for the most part, Olivia couldn't stop thinking about Alexavier and meeting his family. She was working herself up, and if she didn't settle down, she wouldn't be able to go through with it. She was practically shaking when Miss Lynn walked straight over and hugged her tightly.

"Those women are going to love you."

"How can you be sure?"

Miss Lynn leaned back so she could look into Olivia's eyes. "You are one of the loveliest women I have ever met, and that goes for your heart and not only your pretty face. You're genuine and honest and a wonderful little mom. Not to mention, that man really has a thing for you. Every mother wants exactly that for their son."

"Oh, Miss Lynn. He and I are simply getting to know each other."

"Honey, you've been talking to him since the cookout, which was months ago. That's a long time to get to know someone. Plus, he's taking it slow and easy, so he can make sure you get to know each other. It's special."

Olivia nodded. She got back to work cleaning out the coffee pot, but before she could finish, Miss Lynn rushed her out of the diner before her shift ended. She told Olivia that she didn't want to see her until Monday morning, which was an order.

Olivia knew Miss Lynn was sending her out of there so she would have more time to get ready and worried that she and Sydney were scheming together. Olivia had planned to play the whole dinner with his family cool. Now she worried that it meant even more than she'd wanted to acknowledge.

When she got to the Gentry's house, Lucas was dressed nicely in pressed khaki pants and a button-down blue shirt. "I grabbed those from some of John's old bins."

"You look nice, buddy," Olivia said. She'd expected Lucas to complain about dressing up, but he looked proud as he sat next to Ryan, watching old episodes of some western with John Wayne.

"Come with me," Sydney said and grabbed Olivia's hand to lead her into the main bedroom. "I put some shea butter soap in the shower for you and a silk robe hanging on the door. I thought you would like to shower quickly, and then I'll fix your hair and makeup."

"You and Miss Lynn are freaking me the hell out. I mean, heck," Olivia wiped her eyes. "This is only dinner."

"Oh, Olivia, I didn't mean to upset you. I know that you like this guy, and I wanted to help. Honestly, you look beautiful just the way you are now."

Olivia looked down at her clothes and knew she smelled like The Main Street Diner. It wasn't so bad if you liked the smell of fried chicken which was the special that day, but she didn't necessarily want to meet Alexavier's family smelling like fried food. "Thanks for everything, Sydney. I'll take a shower. And if doing my hair and makeup is still on the table, I'll take you up on it."

Sydney looked ecstatic. She was an only child and had no other girlfriends than Olivia and Miss Lynn. She had four boys, and the time with Olivia was as close as she would get to play with hair and makeup until Ryan gave her some little girls to dress up.

Forty minutes later, Olivia hardly recognized herself. Her hair was like silk and felt glamorous to the touch. Sydney put loose wavy curls in it, but whatever oil she used gave it the shine Olivia had always wanted. Sidney lined her top eyelids with black eyeliner, and after two coats of black mascara, Olivia's blue eyes looked like jewels.

Sydney had gone out to Olivia's car and gotten her blue dress, but it wasn't until she twirled around in front of the large mirror in Sydney's walk-in closet that Olivia realized she didn't have any shoes to wear with a dress.

She sat down on the padded stool in front of the makeup mirror. She was going to have to change back into her black jeans.

Sydney shook her head. "I know my shoes are too small, but I called Miss Lynn. She is on her way with a pair that she is certain will work."

Olivia shook her head. This was only a dinner. They were going overboard, and the next time Alexavier wanted to take her out, she wouldn't be able to replicate this look. He would be disappointed.

They heard Miss Lynn complimenting Lucas on how handsome he looked. Then she headed straight to the bedroom to join Olivia and Sydney. "Oh, my goodness. Olivia, you look breathtaking."

Olivia could feel her bottom lip trembling. She wasn't going to that dinner. It was all too overwhelming, so she secretly thought of an excuse for Alexavier and would swear Lucas to secrecy. She sent a quick text saying she worked late and was sorry, but they couldn't make it after all. Adding that she was too tired to drive all the way there and wouldn't be good company seemed reasonable. It was all she could do to keep a straight face as the ladies made over her.

Miss Lynn pulled out two pairs of shoes. She had one pair of three-inch heels with a pointed toe and a simple strap at the back. "I wore these when I was your age," Lynn said, smiling proudly. She then pulled out a pair of flat ballerina-looking slippers. They were silk but died a navy-blue color that complimented the dress. "I wore these at a wedding, and they were the most comfortable things." She laughed, "I never throw anything away."

Olivia tried them both on. They fit her perfectly. Sydney and Miss Lynn agreed that she should wear the heels but take the flats to change into after dinner or if the night ran late.

Olivia loved them for trying so hard to help her. Keeping a straight face, she never let on that she and Lucas were going home. When she walked into the living room to gather up Lucas, Ryan whistled, and everyone complimented her again.

It was just too damn much. Dang much.

Olivia got Lucas settled into the car, and once they drove down the road a bit, she told him the news. "I'm sorry to have made you wait so long, buddy. Would you be too upset if I bought us a hamburger and we went home and got out of these uncomfortable clothes?"

"What about Alex and his mom? Won't they be mad?"

"I don't think so," Olivia honestly didn't know what Alexavier's family would think after the late cancellation. She knew it was rude, but she would rather make him a little mad instead of a lot embarrassed. Olivia wasn't cut out for fancy dinners with the mayor and his family. She should have never agreed.

Lucas watched his mother's face in the rearview mirror above her head. She looked sad. He didn't like her to be sad. "I'm okay with hamburgers. But Mom, I like these clothes."

Olivia smiled back at her son. She felt like crying because he was the best thing in her life, and she wasn't sure she deserved him. Mother Trucker, stop with all these emotions, she thought. Olivia wasn't the kind of woman a man brought home to his mother.

She drove through McDonald's and let Lucas eat his fries in the car. They pulled into the small carport of her duplex, but before she could get the front door unlocked, Alexavier pulled into the driveway behind them.

Lucas held the McDonald's bag tightly in his hand and ran to greet Alexavier.

"Hey, little man. You look sharp," he said and then looked over to see Olivia. "Your mom looks pretty sharp too. A little fancy for McDonald's, huh?"

"Yeah. Miss Lynn and Aunt Sydney made her put on all that stuff," Lucas explained, trying to help his mother as he walked with Alexavier up the driveway.

Olivia could hear every word and simply unlocked the front door and went inside. Lucas sat his food down, and Alexavier asked if he would excuse them for a moment.

Walking straight to her bedroom, Olivia was sure that Alexavier would break things off with her. She could see the hurt in his eyes when he got out of his car, and it would be a long time before she forgot it.

He walked into her bedroom and closed the door. She sat on the end of the bed, waiting for his cruel words to come. That was how things went with Brent before she ran away from him. And he was the only relationship she'd ever had. If she'd known what could happen if she mixed antibiotics with birth control pills, she would've never seen Brent again.

Alexavier knelt in front of Olivia. He looked down at her high heels and ran a hand over her ankle. It was the first time he'd seen her in heels, and she had beautiful legs. He unbuckled the small straps and removed the shoes from her feet. He then scooted closer to her and settled his body between her legs. On his knees, he was almost at her eye level.

"Olivia, do you want to tell me what happened?"

Her stomach hurt like hell. Not heck. She shook her head.

Alexavier ran his hand over her cheek. "You look stunning tonight. But you know you don't have to do all of that for my family or me."

Olivia nodded but avoided his stare. "I didn't know what to expect tonight, and Miss Lynn and Sydney were trying to help. This isn't my dress or my shoes. I don't know how to make smoky eyes or whatever Sydney called this makeup."

"You look beautiful, but Olivia, I always think you look beautiful."

"Look, Alexavier, you're the mayor of New Orleans. I'm nobody. I got pregnant when I was twenty, and I wasn't married and didn't marry my son's dad. I'm a single waitress that can barely make the rent sometimes. What are you doing slumming with me?"

Chapter Fourteen

Alexavier's expression changed. For the first time, she saw him look angry. That was it. He was going to yell at her.

"First of all, I come from a working-class family. They aren't fancy, and they don't judge people based on their socio-economic standing." He gently turned her face to look at him, his voice was calm, but she could see his jaw tensing. "Have I ever said anything to make you feel not good enough? Have I given you the impression that I think I'm better than you?"

Olivia shook her head, no.

"I'm falling in love with you, Olivia Dufrene. I'm already crazy about you and Lucas. This week has been one of the most amazing weeks of my life. You kept saying that you couldn't believe I could work all day in my demanding job and then drive over here and still have energy for Lucas and you. I want you to know that I spend all day, every day, counting the minutes until I can be with you both. Coming here every night, coming here to play with Lucas and have dinner with you has been like coming home."

Olivia closed her eyes. She didn't want to cry and smear the black makeup that Sydney had put on her eyes.

Alexavier kissed her sweetly, but the kiss quickly heated.

Admitting his feelings for her made their attraction stronger. It took everything he had to reign it in, and when they stopped kissing, they remained a breath apart.

His voice was deep with emotion when he spoke. "Don't put yourself down like that again in front of me. You are an amazing woman and an amazing mother. I am lucky to be with you. I won't stand for anyone saying anything bad about you, not even you."

Olivia stared into his eyes. No one had ever stood up for her like that. No one. It hurt because his words echoed in her heart. She'd been lonelier than she would ever admit. Olivia had been entirely on her own for years before having Lucas, and suddenly in front of this remarkable man, she needed to pull herself together before giving too much away.

"Was your family mad when I canceled at the last minute?"

"They're used to me being late. Work. Besides, they eat late when the whole family gathers on the weekend."

Olivia looked confused.

Alexavier kissed her sweetly again. "I still want you to come with me, Liv, please?"

Olivia stood up and straightened out her dress. She walked over to the cheap mirror hanging over her closet door. Her hair was still silky, but it was a bit rumpled. She ran her hands through the long dark strands trying to smooth out the curls. She wiped the little bit of smeared makeup that was under her left eye and then felt Alexavier as he pressed his body into hers from behind. He wrapped his arms around her waist and pulled her back into his front.

"You look beautiful. Beautiful enough to eat," Alexavier whispered, but she heard the rasp in his voice.

"You mean to eat dinner with your family?" she asked with a half-grin.

"No, that's not what I meant, but it will do for now. You and Lucas should pack a bag so you can spend the night at my place.

That way, we don't have to rush back here to put him to bed. He's going to love my cousin's kids."

Olivia couldn't put into words what it meant to her that he always considered Lucas. She walked over to her purse and pulled out the flat silk slippers. "Do you think these would be okay to wear instead of the heels?"

Alexavier took the shoes, knelt before her, and slipped them onto her feet. He then reached over and picked up the delicate heels he'd taken off her. "Maybe you could bring these for later?" he asked, and her stomach tensed.

She'd thrown herself at him offering up sex at every turn. He'd declined enough that she'd stopped. Now his forward behavior made her nervous. What was wrong with her? She kissed him hard on the lips and then put the heels in her bag.

They talked Lucas into putting his hamburger into the refrigerator. Alexavier promised him dinner with his family, where there were at least five kids his age waiting to meet him.

Alexavier held Olivia's hand the entire time he drove across the twenty-four-mile bridge into the city. He talked to Lucas about the fishing he'd done that day and then about going deep sea fishing with him one day soon. He kept Olivia distracted with conversation. When he pulled onto his aunt and uncle's street, and she saw all the cars parked in lines on both sides, she got nervous again.

Alexavier told her to stay put until he came around and opened her door. He pulled her out of the car and into his arms, kissing her warmly. "They are going to love you," he reached over and ruffled Lucas' hair. "And this little man."

Lucas laughed. "And there's going to be other kids too, right?"

"Absolutely, buddy," he said, leading them up to the house. He knew his family was watching them, but he didn't let Olivia or Lucas know.

As soon as they walked into the house, though, his immediate family was standing there, ready to greet them.

Alexavier's mother and auntie each grabbed Olivia and gave her giant hugs. "Welcome. Come into the kitchen with us. Alexavier, go with the boys."

He hesitated, but when he saw Olivia laughing at the two pushy women, he hesitantly let her go.

Instead, Alexavier followed his uncle and father into the backyard. They had lit a fire in the large fire pit. It was a homemade job with cinder blocks and a giant hole dug into the ground, but it had a great bonfire effect, and all the family loved to gather around it on cool nights. Lucas met four boys and one girl that was close to his age, and before long, they were playing foursquare on the patio.

Olivia sat down on the barstool that the ladies pointed her to and then listened as they explained all the food they had prepared for the evening.

"You're such a beautiful girl. Alexavier said you were beautiful. Are you sure you are not Italian?" Auntie Francesca asked.

Olivia laughed. "I don't think so but thank you. You have a beautiful family. Lucas and I appreciate you having us."

"Oh, bellissima, we could not wait to meet the dear who has stolen Alexavier's heart," Alexavier's mom said, looking into Olivia's eyes.

Olivia gasped, and Maria Regalia grabbed her up into another warm hug. "You did not know?"

Olivia shrugged but didn't know what to say. She was in over her head with Alexavier and now his family. She couldn't muster up the confident woman she'd pretended to be since she was seventeen.

Maria kissed her on both cheeks. "My Alex has only brought one girl home before, and he married her."

His Auntie Francesca nodded. "God rest her soul, but it was not a warm marriage. She was a cold fish by nature, and once she got the cancer, it broke the little spirit she had inside. Still, he stayed by her. He's a good man."

"He is a good man," Olivia agreed. Alexavier had only talked about his wife and her battle with cancer briefly. She'd figured it was still too hard for him to discuss and so she didn't press him. She was surprised to hear from his family that they were not happy.

Alexavier's cousins Theresa, Gia, Mira, and Audrey joined the ladies in the kitchen. They helped pull some of the food out of the oven and then told Olivia about themselves.

Mira and Audrey were single, and Gia's husband was outside with the other men, but Theresa explained she was divorced. "Alex said your ex lives in the city?"

"Lucas' father and I dated, but we never married," Olivia admitted. She figured if they were going to judge her, then she needed to get it out in the open early.

Theresa sighed. "No wonder my cousin loves you. You are the smart one. I wish I hadn't married William."

Auntie Francesca nodded. "We all wish you hadn't married William." And all the other women in the kitchen agreed in unison.

Gia talked to Olivia about being a waitress. Gia had waited tables at a few restaurants owned by some other Italian cousins.

Auntie Francesca asked if Olivia helped cook at the restaurant.

"No. I'm afraid I'm not a very good cook. I mean, I can follow a recipe, but I haven't had much opportunity to try much. You all make better food than I've had in my entire life. Lucas and I ate everything you sent for that picnic and the pizza dinner."

"We can teach you, bellissima, anytime you want. You are welcome to come over, and we will show you how," Maria offered.

"Thank you. That is very sweet of you," Olivia said, and her voice cracked with emotion.

Auntie Francesca quickly changed the subject to keep her from feeling uncomfortable. "So, what questions do you have for us about Alexavier? We will tell you all the good stuff."

All the women in the kitchen laughed, making Olivia feel welcomed. They were all genuine and sincere.

"I'm afraid I can't think of anything," Olivia said. Truth be told, she and Alexavier had shared a lot about themselves, especially him, in the six months they texted and phoned each other. She felt like she knew him.

Audrey was the youngest of the adult cousins, and she asked, "Did he tell you about his crush on that lawyer? Do you know that bad guy Mathew Nunan who was in all the papers? He and Alexavier were friends, and he told Alex she liked him and wanted him to ask her out. He also told Alex that she liked aggressive men and that he should be more forceful with her if he wanted her to go out with him."

Olivia suddenly didn't want to know any of their gossip. They were referring to Ryan's sister Reagan. Olivia had heard that gossip. But Reagan didn't seem like his type.

Gia butted in, "It was all a lie. Alex hit on her a few times, and he said she acted like he was a bit crazy. Then, in the end, he realized that his friend was lying the whole time to keep him distracted from the illegal activity he was dealing in."

"How embarrassing," Theresa said. "Of course, he never explained if he was really into the kinky stuff."

"I wouldn't know," Olivia admitted. "He has been a perfect gentleman with me."

Maria walked over and hugged her. "Don't listen to them, bellissima. Alexavier never mentioned anyone to me before you."

Theresa giggled, "And that is all that counts to Auntie Maria."

Olivia smiled at the sweet Italian mama. Olivia didn't care about any other women Alexavier dated or wanted to date either. He wasn't a kid. She knew he'd had relationships before her. Obviously, she'd gone out with other men too. But what they had was fresh and new, and she hadn't had sex with anyone in almost a year, not even Alexavier. She was beginning to feel untouched and longed to have him in her bed.

She blushed at the naughty thoughts she was having of Alexavier in front of his mother, Aunt, and cousins. Being there made her want to be even closer to him. They were a strong, loving group, and seeing where he came from made her understand him more.

Alexavier had let the women have Olivia alone for over thirty minutes. He couldn't wait any longer. He walked into the kitchen, wrapped his arms around Olivia from behind, and kissed her on top of her head in front of everyone.

His mother smiled and went to stir her red gravy. "It's almost time to eat. Tell the boys," she said as she gave him a wink. He knew that meant she liked Olivia.

Olivia offered to help set the table or set up the food. "Bellissima, you do that every day. Alexavier tells me how hard you work to care for your son. Tonight, we take care of you. Now go on and help Alexavier get the kids and men inside. That is enough of a job for you." She winked at Olivia and then smiled as she went to pull out serving platters.

Alexavier held her hand as they left the kitchen, and then he gently pushed her up against the hallway wall and kissed her. "You doing okay?"

Olivia nodded. Her face was flushed, but she had goosebumps standing there in his arms. Had she ever wanted anyone as much as she wanted him? "Yes. I love your mother. Your aunt and cousins are great too. Thank you for inviting us."

Alexavier kissed her again and then led her outside to tell everyone it was time to eat.

Lucas ran over and told her about the new game he'd learned, and she went with him to wash up before dinner. It was going to be an event with sixteen people gathered around the table.

Chapter Fifteen

Olivia kept one eye on Lucas as they were all seated around a giant table by couples with the kids sitting together on one end. He was delighted to sit next to the other kids, and for the first time, she could see how grown up he acted for his age. He was charismatic and funny, and Olivia loved that he was confident. She didn't learn that until she was much older but knew how important it would be for him and how well it would serve him in life.

Alexavier intertwined his fingers with hers and gently squeezed her hand. "He's fine. They all think he's hilarious and were fighting over who would get to sit next to him."

"Really?"

"Yes," he whispered in her ear and then kissed her cheek. They heard his father clear his throat to get everyone's attention so he could say the blessing.

The Regalia family passed huge dinner platters around the table, and Olivia told Alexavier that she'd never seen that much food for a regular Saturday night dinner.

"You should see when it's someone's birthday," one of his male cousins said.

"We have to rent a place for the holidays because they all try to outdo each other, and no one's kitchen or dining room is big enough to hold it," another one of the men said.

Olivia's cheeks hurt from smiling so much. She couldn't remember everyone's name, and she kept trying to repeat them in her head. Gray, Tiny, Big Ted, and Mario were all she could remember, and then there was Gia, Theresa, Audrey, Mira, Auntie Francesca, and Mrs. Regalia, Maria.

It didn't take long for the group to circle back around to Alexavier and Olivia. His uncle was the first to start.

"So, was this date a setup?" he asked, and one of the other younger cousins laughed before he said the punchline. "Because I know someone that beautiful wouldn't go out with you on purpose."

All the kids laughed at the older man.

Then his cousin Mario grinned. "Olivia, did you know he's the mayor of New Orleans? What? And you still went out with him?"

"You guys can kid all you want, but it's obvious that you're jealous," Alexavier said, winking at Olivia.

For the rest of dinner, the cousins continued to pick on each other and told stories of how they got into trouble. It was fun, and Olivia didn't know what else to do but sit there and laugh.

She tried to help clear the table, but Auntie Francesca ordered Alexavier to take his girl out of the kitchen.

He swooped her up into his arms and carried her outside to sit by the fire while the kids played hide and seek in the large backyard.

They watched the kids scatter to hide, and then Alexavier wrapped his arm around Olivia to pull her closer to his side.

"You're warm," she said, snuggling in close.

"Are you cold?" he asked and then took off his jacket and put it around her.

"Now you're going to get cold."

He leaned in and whispered in her ear. "I've been hot all night watching you."

Olivia laughed until she realized he was serious. "Oh, Alex. Don't tease me."

"I'm not teasing. You and Lucas are going to spend the night with me, right? I have a spare bedroom on the other side of my house for him, and once he's asleep, I have a giant bed for us."

Olivia nodded. She'd wanted him for months. Lying her head on his shoulder, she watched the kids playing and tried not to over-think what was happening between them. Could things stay as good as they were right at that moment? Alexavier treated her and Lucas so well, and his family was perfectly lovely. It couldn't get better than it was right then. Could It?

The rest of Alexavier's family eventually joined them outside by the fire. His cousin Gia brought out coffee and some home-made cake.

Olivia drank half her coffee and ate a bite of Alexavier's dessert but told them she was too full to eat or drink anything else. Two minutes later, he stood up and told everyone that Olivia had been at work that morning by 7:30, and he needed to get her and Lucas home.

Everyone hugged her, Lucas, and Alexavier as they said their goodbyes. Olivia thanked Auntie Francesca and Mrs. Regalia again, and Lucas told them they were the best cookers he'd ever met.

Alexavier got them into his car and then smiled back at Lucas. "Good day, buddy?"

"Great day!" he said.

Alexavier agreed and winked at Olivia before he drove them to his place.

By the time they got to his house, Lucas was sound asleep. Just as Olivia picked him up, Alexavier took him from her arms. "I've got him."

She nodded and walked ahead of Alexavier into his sizeable, stately home. With wide eyes, she took in the impressive two-story entryway before stepping into a large living room with a stone fireplace. Suddenly she was ashamed of her tiny duplex. Alexavier had come over to her place so many times, and she'd never considered how awesome his house might have been. He seemed to like her house and never let on that his home was like something out of a magazine.

The beautifully decorated spare bedroom where they laid Lucas down was painted blue and had a generous-sized bed for the little boy. There was a fluffy bedspread with different cars embroidered all over it, and if Olivia didn't know better, she would have bet that Alexavier bought it specifically for Lucas.

Together, they tucked Lucas into bed, and after he settled, Alexavier held Olivia's hand as he led her back down the hallway into the living room.

"Would you like something to drink?" he asked.

She wondered if he was nervous too?

"Sure. I'll have whatever you're having."

Alexavier poured them each a glass of red wine. He then walked over to join her on the sofa.

"So, this is your place?"

"I bought it several years ago. Still trying to get used to it. The neighbors are friendly, but it's different from my old neighborhood."

Olivia nodded. "Your old neighborhood being where we were tonight?"

Alexavier smiled. She liked his family, and they liked her. "Yes. I bought a house in the old neighborhood close to City Park after graduating from law school. Then when I got married, we renovated a few things but didn't move."

Olivia twirled a strand of her hair as she listened to him. "You decided to move after your wife passed away?"

"It seemed like the right time," he said, watching her play with her hair.

"I'm sorry. That must have been hard for you."

Alexavier drank half his wine before setting his glass on the coffee table. She hadn't touched her drink. Instead, she listened to him carefully because it was the one thing he hadn't shared.

"Victoria was a unique woman. We met in college. She was getting her business degree, and I had started law school. We didn't date then because we were on different paths, or so she liked to say. A couple of years after I graduated, she'd sold some time management software to the firm where I worked, and we started dating."

Olivia finally picked up her wine glass and drank. She imagined Alexavier's wife was a fantastic woman to match the man, but it was hard to hear about her.

Alexavier hesitated as he measured her reaction to his words before explaining, "She wasn't from here and said she never liked New Orleans. Her parents were lovely people, though, and would come to visit when she had time for them."

He stopped talking and drank the rest of his wine. Olivia couldn't read his mood but figured it was hard to talk about his poor wife. Their entire interaction had been awkward from the start of this conversation. "We don't have to talk about this if you don't feel comfortable."

Avoiding her eyes, Alexavier ran a hand through his thick dark hair. It looked a bit tousled, and Olivia realized she'd never seen him that way. He was always flawlessly put together.

He reached a hand over toward her and squeezed her hand. "I don't want there to be any secrets between us."

Olivia worried her bottom lip with her teeth as she watched him. She didn't know what he would admit to her but was sure she would always have some secrets.

"Victoria has been gone almost as long as we were married. It's hard to believe. When we dated, she was a lot of fun and charismatic. Full of life. She threw a great party and was pretty good at the whole politician's wife thing. I was in awe of her."

"She sounds great," Olivia said, cooling her expression as she spoke. She had no right to be jealous of the woman and marriage he described.

"Yeah, great. Victoria found out she had cancer for the first time during a routine check-up while planning our wedding. She didn't tell me until six months after we were married. By then, it required serious surgery, plus the doctors wanted her on chemo. She refused to stop working or slow down on being the life of the party, so she had the surgery but not the follow-up medicine. We didn't need the money, and when I asked her why she wouldn't take care of herself, she insisted that she needed the independence."

"Maybe she was scared?"

Alexavier smiled. Olivia always acted so tough, but that was her outer shell. There was extraordinary tenderness inside her. "I was scared for her. But Victoria wasn't scared of the devil himself. She didn't want to lose her hair or look sick. When the follow-up exams came back clear, Victoria would argue that the doctors were wrong, and the chemo wasn't necessary. She continued to travel for work, and when I decided to run for mayor, she insisted on remodeling the house too. It was over the top, and she missed two checkups. Six months after I took office, it was too late. The cancer had spread, and while she finally agreed to the treatment, it didn't work," Alexavier saw Olivia's eyes water, and he stopped talking.

Olivia wiped her eyes and picked up her wine glass again. She moved closer to the arm of the couch away from Alexavier as she sipped her wine and then nodded for him to continue.

"Once the treatment started, she was angry all the time and kicked me out. I stayed with my parents to keep it out of the press. I did everything possible to get her to take me back, but she said she needed to focus on herself. For a while, she let someone from work move in with her. But eventually, she had to take a leave of absence from her job. The added rest didn't help. Finally, after trying every type of treatment out there, the doctors did what they could to make her comfortable. Once she was bedridden, she let me return. It was the hardest time of my life." Alexavier's face was dark.

Olivia abruptly jumped up. Lucas was standing in the doorway, half asleep, and she quickly ushered him to the restroom down the long hallway close to the room where he'd been sleeping.

Alexavier waited outside the bedroom as Olivia tucked Lucas back into bed. She'd practically run away from him and seemed to take an extra-long time with Lucas.

When she stepped into the hallway, her eyes were red. "I didn't mean to upset you, Olivia. It's just that I don't always get to control the information spread in the media, especially online, about me. And I wanted to be the one to tell you that I know I've made mistakes. The gossip about my marriage at times was brutal, and I hope it won't make you think less of me."

"It must have been impossible to watch the love of your life dying and not be able to do anything for her." Suddenly, hot tears rolled down Olivia's cheeks, and she couldn't stop the emotion that overcame her. She excused herself and went into the bathroom. Once she locked the door, she sat on the side of the tub and sobbed for Victoria, who died too young. She cried for Alexavier for becoming a widower in his early thirties. She also cried because she could never be the woman Victoria was to him and would never know that kind of love.

It took a little while before her tears finally dried up, and she held her head in her hands. It had been a long emotional day, and she was exhausted.

There was a light knock on the door, "Please, Olivia, let me in?"

She washed her face and tried to clean up the smeared makeup under her eyes. She unlocked the door, and Alexavier stepped inside. He crowded in close enough so she could feel his body heat, but he didn't touch her.

His eyes were still dark, and it made her knees feel weak. But his heart would always belong to another woman. It had to be the reason he wouldn't sleep with her.

When he reached over to move her hair away from her face, it felt too intimate. He saw her shiver and took a step back. "I know

I could've handled things with Victoria differently. We'd been friends once, and I should've refused to leave."

"You did what she wanted. She knew you loved her and probably wanted to spare you some pain." Olivia's bottom lip quivered as she spoke.

Alexavier stared at her lips, and his breath became irregular. "That would make the tragic story sound better, but that's not the truth. I thought I was clear."

"I think I get it," Olivia said, and her voice sounded stronger. "You can't get over her. It's okay. True love isn't something that happens to everyone."

Her voice didn't match her body language. While she made it sound like she understood, her eyes were red, and her nose was still pink from crying.

"Victoria didn't love me. She had loved the idea of having a glamorous wedding, but she didn't want to be married. She especially didn't want to be married to me. I wanted a relationship like my parents, but soon after the wedding started working more so I could be away from her. The cancer showed up, and she was on my insurance. She couldn't get her own policy. I thought she was trying to hide that she was afraid, and I promised that I would stay by her side. Once it went into remission, I was campaigning, and she loved politics. We were friends or at least friendly. But it wasn't love."

Alexavier looked toward the hallway when he admitted, "The friend from work that moved in with her was her lover. She told me in those last two months that she'd cheated on me from the beginning with loads of different men. Some were clients, and some were coworkers."

"What?" Olivia was devastated when she thought Victoria was his great love but hearing that he'd been in a loveless marriage upset her even more.

"When she allowed me back into our house, she was on strong medicine all the time to help her with the pain. She wasn't coherent or conscious most of the time. But she had a few decent days that led to some moments of clarity. She took that time to apologize to me about all the affairs. The truth killed me, but if I was honest, the signs of her cheating had been there from the beginning. I had to move past the anger. I made sure the last days of her life weren't more painful than they had to be. But I haven't forgotten how miserable that relationship was or what it was like to be around her. It wasn't until I met you that I forgave Victoria. I had to let go of all that resentment so I could love someone else. I'm ready for something more. Something better. I want that with you, Olivia."

Chapter Sixteen

It took a few minutes for Olivia to register what he'd said. He wanted something more with her. She took the half step it took to be in his arms and leaned up to kiss him. When he licked her bottom lip, she opened to him, and suddenly the kiss was so much more.

The emotionally fueled conversation had done a number on her. Part of her wanted to be home in her safe haven of Maisonville. She'd been through a lot growing up and being alone had been the only way she knew to heal herself. But she was torn because, for the first time in her life, she also wanted to be with someone. She wanted to be with him.

Alexavier held her tightly in his arms before leading her into his bedroom. "I'll give you some privacy." Was he leaving her? Olivia stood there for a half-second. She'd wanted Alexavier for months and had thought that tonight, he wanted to be with her too, but admitting his past vulnerabilities seemed to shut him down.

"I know I've given you a lot to think over, and I've slept on the couch as much as I've slept in here. If you don't mind, I'll grab some sweatpants and a t-shirt and then give you some space."

"I do mind," Olivia said, staring at him. "I don't sleep well in strange places."

Alexavier took a deep breath as he stepped closer to her. "I'm not sure I can keep my hands to myself if we sleep in the same bed."

Olivia gave him a sly grin. "Promise?" Then she lifted her arms, exposing the tie on the side of her dress. "Help me with this?"

Alexavier was comforted by the beautiful woman standing in front of him. Could he ever make her understand what she meant to him? He slowly untied her dress.

Olivia slipped out of the silky material to reveal a yellow lace bra and blue panties. She picked up the dress and laid it over the chair in the corner. Then she slipped under the covers of his bed.

Alexavier had never seen anything more beautiful than Olivia Dufrene in her mismatched bra and panties. He'd had women wearing the most expensive lingerie money could buy parade in front of him. But none of them were as stunning as Olivia. He couldn't get out of his clothes fast enough, and he wasn't the kind of man that rushed around for things. Sliding in next to her felt like home. He pulled her in close. She fit into his arms perfectly.

"You are so warm," she said and wiggled closer before she kissed his lips, chin, neck, and then chest. He let her explore for a moment, and then she heard what sounded like a primal growl before he wrapped his arms around her and then turned to flatten her on her back beneath him. When he pinned her wrists above her head and kissed her hard on the mouth, she was breathless.

"This okay, Olivia?"

She licked her lips and nodded. It was the hottest kiss ever, and she didn't trust her words to do it justice.

Alexavier traveled down her body, leaving a trail of kisses. It was hot until he reached her belly button, and she giggled uncontrollably. She was ticklish, which made him laugh too. Being with Olivia was fun and sexy, which is how he would describe her personality.

Before he could continue driving her crazy, she stopped him. "Please, Alex. I need you."

"Same," he whispered against her skin. "But baby, it's been a while. Let me savor you." And he spent the next two hours doing just that.

Afterward, Alexavier gave Olivia his t-shirt to wear and tucked her back into his front before he wrapped them both in crisp sheets and a goose down comforter.

Olivia couldn't remember ever being more comfortable, and when Alexavier's arm wrapped around her waist, she thought she might sleep for days.

"Rest, baby. I've got you," he whispered, and there was no way he could know how much that meant to her.

The next day, Olivia woke up alone in Alexavier's room. He'd tucked the blankets around her and closed his curtains to keep the morning sunshine out. When she looked at the clock on the bedside table, she jumped up. It was ten in the morning, and she hadn't slept that late since Lucas had been born.

She ran around the room looking for her clothes. She didn't want to go out into the other room wearing the dress she'd worn the night before, but she couldn't wear Alexavier's shirt.

She found her panties and bra folded on the chair where she'd left her dress, and right beside the chair was her overnight bag.

She smiled, thinking about Alexavier. He was a generous lover, but more than that, he was thoughtful. It wasn't anything like she'd experienced before him.

She pulled on her jeans and lilac sweatshirt, hurrying to find Lucas and make sure he wasn't worried about her. Stepping out of the bedroom, she sensed she was alone in the house. It took a moment for her to explore the spare bedroom, bathrooms, living room, and kitchen. Looking for her phone, she saw a note they'd left for her. She picked it up, and that's when Lucas and Alexavier walked through the front door.

"We got Beignets for breakfast," Lucas announced when he saw her. "From the real Cafe Du Monde."

"And coffee," Alex said as he walked over to her and planted a warm kiss on her lips. "Good morning," he said, smiling so much that his eyes were glowing.

Olivia had thought she'd never seen anyone as beautiful as Alexavier. Still, standing there in the morning light after letting her sleep in and taking her son to pick up coffee and French donuts, he took her breath away.

"My favorites," she said, accepting the cup he handed her and winking at Lucas. "I see someone has already had some."

Lucas looked down at the powdered sugar on his shirt and grinned. "Only one," he told her as he climbed onto the leather barstool at the long kitchen island so he could have more.

"It was a long way, and we needed the sugar, so we had the energy to walk back. Right, little man?"

"Right," Lucas said.

Olivia loved how happy Lucas was around Alexavier. He never seemed that happy around anyone else, especially not his father, Brent. Not that she'd brought anyone else over to their house, but he had met a few men interested in her at the diner. That never went well because Lucas usually ignored men that were fake trying to be his friend. It was a date killer. If Lucas didn't like someone, she figured his kid radar was more robust than hers, and the person probably wasn't worth her time.

She took the lid off her coffee and sipped it as she watched Alexavier put beignets on a plate for Lucas, and then they both flicked powdered sugar at one another and laughed.

Alexavier filled a small plate for her. They were fresh and hot, a lot like the man standing in front of her.

"Thanks," she said, and he leaned over casually and kissed her again.

"What would you like to do today?"

"What did you have in mind?" she asked, smiling at the innuendo her young son wouldn't pick up on.

Alexavier laughed when he peered over at Lucas, who acted unaware of them while he ate. He wrapped an arm around her waist and pulled her body close to his. Careful not to spill her coffee. His voice was low as he spoke into her ear. "I think you know exactly what I have in mind."

Before she could say anything, Lucas spoke up. "We talked about walking around the French place or going to the movies."

Alexavier laughed and then turned around and ruffled Lucas' hair. He knew from his cousins' kids that they might look preoccupied, but they always heard what was happening.

"It's called the French Quarter," he told Lucas.

Olivia smiled but shook her head. "I don't think that's a good idea."

Alexavier nodded. "I don't know what's playing at the movies, but I could get a private screening for us if you're interested?"

"Cool," Lucas said. "That superhero movie is out. Right, mom?"

"Yes, Lucas, but that's a lot of money."

Alexavier leaned in to kiss her again. "I got it," he said and stepped away, talking into his phone as he walked out onto his back porch.

When he came back in, he smiled at Lucas. "Alright, kid. We are ready to go in an hour."

"Yahoo," Lucas said and hopped off the barstool to high-five Alexavier.

Olivia shook her head. That was the second time she'd heard her son say yahoo. When did he learn that word? He also high-fived Alexavier a lot, and that was new too.

She looked at the two guys in her life and wondered how she'd gotten so lucky.

Chapter Seventeen

Alexavier dropped Olivia and Lucas at the back door of the AMC theater, where a man with a radio in his ear waited for them. He led them to a large screening room where one of the theater staff workers had set up popcorn and various kinds of movie candy onto a cart. There was also an ice bucket chilling bottles of soda and water.

A couple of minutes later, Alexavier walked in and smiled at them. "Little man, you can sit wherever you'd like. This whole place is for us."

"The whole place?"

"That's what a private screening means, buddy."

"Cool. Popcorn too?"

Alexavier nodded his head and handed him a bag of popcorn. "You can have whatever your mom says is okay."

Alexavier slid his fingers around hers as he sidled up next to her. "We're going to find our seats, kiddo. You can sit with us if you want or even stand up. Whatever."

"Mom?"

"Yes, buddy."

"Can I sit in the front row?"

Olivia laughed. Lucas always wanted her to sit on that awful first row, and she refused. "Sure. You heard Alexavier. You can sit wherever you want."

Alexavier grabbed a root beer, and he and Olivia sat in the middle row in the middle seats of the theater. Lucas started out in the front row, but once the movie began, he moved to a few rows in front of them, where he half stood, and half hung over the seats in front of him.

It was the perfect way to see a movie with a seven-year-old and your secret boyfriend, the mayor.

Olivia thought about how Alexavier felt like her boyfriend, although she wouldn't dare say that out loud. He'd made her very happy.

When the movie was over, she let Lucas pick out a box of candy, and he was able to eat the gummy worms when they got back to Alexavier's house. It was still early afternoon, and she'd figured Alexavier would be ready to take them home. But when she went to pack up their stuff, he asked for them to stay a while longer.

"I know you don't want anyone to see us together, and I can't offer you much to do at my house except for television, but I thought I could cook dinner before taking you home?"

"What's for dinner?" Lucas asked before Olivia agreed. She laughed at him and shrugged her shoulders.

Alexavier told Lucas that he was thinking of grilling out some steaks and corn on the cob. Lucas agreed that sounded good, and then after talking for twenty solid minutes about the movie they'd watched, he fell asleep in the chair in the living room.

Alexavier carried Lucas to the spare bedroom, tucked him into his bed from the night before, and then took Olivia straight to his bedroom to make love to her.

An hour later, Alexavier and Olivia moved to the large living room sofa, where he pulled a blanket over them. He turned on the television, but they both fell asleep shortly after turning it on.

It was two hours later when they woke up to Lucas sitting on the floor in front of them watching cartoons. He'd found the remote and quietly turned on what he wanted until they were awake.

"Hey, Lucas," a groggy Olivia said. "You okay?"

He nodded. "I'm hungry," he said and then turned back to his cartoon.

"Me, too," Alexavier said before he kissed Olivia and then jumped up. "We haven't had anything but junk food since breakfast."

Olivia shook her head. She rarely let Lucas eat the way they had that day. It had been a lot of fun, but she didn't have the heart to tell Alexavier that beignets weren't a nutritious breakfast either.

"I'll have the grill ready in a minute," Alexavier said. "Want to help me, Lucas?"

"Cook? Sure!" he exclaimed, jumping up to follow Alexavier.

Olivia offered to help, but Alexavier insisted she stay there and rest while the men took care of her. Lucas ran over and pulled the blanket back over his mom and handed her the remote. "We've got this, mom."

She almost teared up at her sweet boy trying to take care of her. She changed the channel to a buy-a-beach-house show and realized it was the first time in a long time that she had a moment to watch something she chose on television. At home, Olivia had a ton of chores looming over her every day, and the working-mom-guilt to read or exercise with Lucas constantly. She had never relaxed on the sofa watching television while someone else made something for her and Lucas to eat. She fell back asleep as she thought about how comfortable she felt with Alexavier and didn't wake up until the guys had dinner on the table.

They had a proper family-style meal with grilled steak, corn on the cob, and smashed potatoes. Lucas explained they decided to rename the dish because they beat them with a spatula on the cutting board and then moved them to the bowl. She laughed at the two guys tattling on each other and could only imagine the mess they must have made and had to clean up after the smashing event was over. They were proud of themselves as she told them she hadn't had a better meal since the night before with Alexavier's family.

It was a genuine compliment because no one cooked better than those Italian women except Miss Lynn.

They cleaned the kitchen together, and then Olivia apologized because they needed to get home so Lucas could take his bath and get to bed on time.

On the way there, they sang to the radio, and Lucas told them a few knock-knock jokes he'd learned. It was a quick trip, and when they pulled into her single-car driveway, it was bittersweet because none of them wanted the weekend to end.

Olivia invited Alexavier in, and to her surprise, he agreed to stay a while. He helped dry the floor when Lucas insisted on showering instead of bathing in the tub again. Alex also read stories to Lucas before he fell asleep.

Once Lucas was down, Olivia offered to make Alexavier a drink. He declined and said he would take a bottle of water. Then he walked her to her bedroom, and they showered together in her tiny shower. It was more funny than sexy since there was barely enough room for one person, much less two. When they finished, Olivia laughed that they had made a bigger mess than Lucas.

Alexavier cleaned up all the water and then joined her in the bedroom. He saw Olivia in bed and smiled as he asked, "What are you wearing?" He slid under the covers to discover she was completely naked. "Did you wear that for me?"

"Just for you," she said, and they made love for the third time that day.

Afterward, he pulled her body into his, and she laid her head on his chest. "Don't you have to get up early in the morning?"

"Yes."

"I understand if you have to leave."

"Do you want me to leave?"

"No. I like having you here," Olivia said. She wouldn't go as far as to ask him to stay the night with her, but she hoped he could tell that she wanted him there.

"Then I'll stay the night. I can leave early enough to get to the office on time."

"Really?" The look she gave him made him feel ten feet tall. He'd stopped short of beating his fists on his chest when she fell asleep in his arms.

The following day, Alexavier got up at five and kissed Olivia goodbye. She watched him get dressed and decided it was a great way to start her day. She couldn't go back to sleep after he left and so she showered and got dressed early. She then made breakfast for Lucas before she woke him up.

Lucas got up easily, and they had an easy morning, not having to rush around for him to catch the bus. When she got to the diner, the new girl, Daisy, was there getting instructions from Miss Lynn.

Olivia didn't say anything about Alexavier initially, but she was all smiles when Miss Lynn handed her a cup of coffee. It didn't take much prompting for Olivia to tell the sweet older woman all about her fantastic weekend.

"The mayor of New Orleans?" Daisy asked.

Olivia paused and looked at the new girl with brown eyes and sandy blonde hair. She was younger than Olivia, and no doubt had a story she was hiding, or she wouldn't have moved to Renaissance Lake alone in desperate need of a waitressing job. Usually, Olivia would have told her to mind her own business or stared so hard that the young woman would've wished she hadn't butted into their conversation. Instead, she smiled at Daisy and made the instant decision to be friendly to her. "Yes, Alexavier Regalia."

"He's really handsome. Congratulations."

Miss Lynn and Olivia laughed. Alexavier was handsome and Olivia, for the first time, felt comfortable enough to admit it to someone other than Miss Lynn.

Olivia didn't elaborate more about her weekend in front of Daisy, but she helped her set out all the condiments, and together, they prepared for the breakfast crowd. Daisy was a quick learner, and they had things ready in record time.

Miss Lynn jumped up and down on the inside over how happy Alexavier made Olivia. It was everything she'd ever wanted for her beautiful girl, but she couldn't tell Olivia that. Olivia would worry that it was too good to be true or too good to last. Miss Lynn had tried to set her up with other good men like Ryan Gentry, but Olivia would insist she was a one-person woman and Lucas was her only fellow. Lynn had watched Olivia struggle but also persevere on her own as she raised her son. She was proud, admitting that she'd learned to rely on herself at a young age. Olivia had also pushed away from others that were interested because she felt like they wanted something she couldn't give them.

No matter how close they were, Olivia never admitted what exactly that something was, but Miss Lynn understood the young woman had never experienced unconditional love. It was evident in the way she didn't talk about any past relationships, including with her family. It would take a formidable man to make Olivia happy.

Alexavier Regalia might just be the man to do it.

But, if Olivia needed to pretend things weren't getting serious with Alexavier and that she wasn't falling in love with him, then Miss Lynn would play along. They could smile and laugh together over the sweet things he did for her and Lucas until Olivia accepted the fact that he wanted more.

"MORE COFFEE, MISS LYNN?" Olivia asked as she breezed by the counter with another order. They had already gone through two more pots of coffee than usual. Daisy helped cover the floor while Miss Lynn kept the coffee brewing and the tea steeping for the larger-than-normal crowd. They'd expected things to slow down, considering the day would bring a lot of rain and severe storms later. The wind had already picked up, and dark clouds had moved in, but many of the construction workers and manual laborers had shown up to work, as usual, hoping the bad weather might hold off until the end of the work day. Countless men stopped off for breakfast and then hung out through lunch until they received the official word that work wouldn't resume until the storms passed. It kept the diner steadily busy.

Daisy had explained to Miss Lynn during the interview that she'd moved to the area from an island in Hawaii. She had an unmistakable sweet Texas accent but didn't admit to ever living there. The application was void of any references or previous employers, but Daisy admitted to waiting tables at a large restaurant loved by locals and tourists near the ocean. Olivia and Miss Lynn only had to give her a few instructions on how they did certain things, and she was off and running.

Still, the crowd kept all three of them busy, and it wasn't until eleven that Miss Lynn finally got a chance to drink her coffee and look at the paper. She was shocked when she saw the giant photo of Alexavier at Cafe Du Monde with Lucas. It was a fantastic picture of them, laughing and carrying two bags of beignets, and Alexavier holding a drink holder with two cups of coffee and a carton of what looked like chocolate milk.

The headline said: Is New Orleans' Most Eligible Bachelor Off the Market? The caption read: Mayor Alexavier Regalia with Coffee and Beignets for Three. Cute Kid!

While Miss Lynn loved that they were calling Olivia his girlfriend, she knew the pretty young woman would freak out. She hid the paper from Olivia and didn't say a word until one of their regular customers mentioned it at lunch. He asked Daisy if Olivia was dating the mayor, and when she shrugged, he said he was sure there was a picture of Olivia's son, Lucas, in the paper.

Olivia's face dropped when she heard the elderly customer talking about her and Alexavier. Hadn't she told Daisy it was a secret? Damn. No, darn. She walked over to the new waitress. "Don't tell anyone else."

Daisy nodded quickly and then practically ran away to refill water glasses instead of explaining that she hadn't said a word about her.

"What picture? What paper? Lucas hasn't been in the paper," Olivia said.

The retired man smiled slyly. "The new girl wouldn't tell me. So, are you, or are you not dating Mayor Regalia?"

Olivia faked a laugh. "Yeah, right. Do you think the Mayor of New Orleans would slum around with a waitress in the burbs when he could have his pick of women in the city?"

She then stormed off, looking for a copy of the darn paper.

Chapter Eighteen

Olivia couldn't find a single copy of the newspaper anywhere. She didn't understand it. Miss Lynn always got the paper and read it as soon as possible in the mornings. She would have grumbled if she hadn't gotten her copy to enjoy with her morning coffee.

Then she realized what had happened. "Miss Lynn, you have to let me see it."

"What, dear?" Lynn said wide-eyed.

"I'm not buying that innocent look. Give it up. I'm going to see it sooner or later. Please." She looked desperate, and Miss Lynn couldn't deny her.

"Now, don't get all in a twist. It's a great picture."

Olivia was sick thinking about the press having the scoop on them so soon. She took the paper Lynn sheepishly handed over.

When she turned the page and saw the giant picture of her son and Alexavier walking from Cafe du Monde, she gasped.

She put her hand over her mouth to stop the expletives that were about to come out. It was a great shot of both of her guys, but she'd expressed to Alexavier how important it was to her that things between them were kept quiet.

The handsome mayor of New Orleans wasn't just locally famous, he made the national news sometimes too. Olivia didn't want to be a part of any amount of publicity, locally or beyond. She didn't want her past brought back up, especially in front of her son. She was estranged from her family and didn't need them to think more terrible thoughts about her. Not to mention the fact that her ex was the jealous type, and although they weren't together, she didn't let him see her with anyone else. She didn't need to borrow trouble where he was concerned, and dating the mayor would get him riled up, which could cause problems for her and Lucas.

This paper was going to ruin everything.

Then she thought about Alexavier. They'd had the best weekend, but was he ready to announce to the world they were seeing each other? What if he was angry too?

She sat down on a barstool and put the paper down. "Dammit," she said and then put her hand over her mouth. One bad thing happened, and she immediately started swearing. She had to be stronger. Just because everything had gone to hell, she shook her head. Just because things had gone to the place of fire and brimstone, she couldn't lose her temper.

She took a deep breath. If she'd been honest with herself, she knew things had been going a little too well. She felt her stomach turn. She wouldn't curse in the diner, but she did want to give a piece of her mind to the reporter that must have spotted Alexavier and Lucas and snapped the picture without any regard for the mayor or her son's privacy. Her son was seven, and that reporter shouldn't have photographed Lucas without permission. Right?

Olivia folded the paper and handed it back to Miss Lynn without another word. She returned to working the diner floor and tried to keep her head up, although time dragged on, and the sky looked like it was about to break.

Finally, it was time for Lucas, and the weather hadn't gone sideways yet. Olivia felt lighter as she watched the bright yellow school bus come to a stop, and her son bounced down the steps, clearly happy from a great day at school.

But the universe wasn't done with her yet. Before she could

speak to Lucas, her phone rang, and when she looked at the screen, she could see it was her ex, Brent, calling. "Sh... Shitake mushrooms," she said before answering, "Hello?"

"What the hell are you doing, Olivia, and why is my fucking son in the newspaper walking with the mayor?"

Olivia smiled at Lucas and Miss Lynn. "I'll be right back," she said, holding her hand over her phone so Brent couldn't hear her."

She rushed out the back door of the diner for privacy. The air outside was electric, and Olivia's dark hair blew in the wind. She leaned against the building, trying to shield herself from the dust blowing up from the back parking lot. "What I'm doing is none of your mother trucking business. The mayor is a friend, of a friend of mine—" it was sort of true because she'd met him at Sydney and Ryan Gentry's house. "He is a nice man, and the reporter took that picture to make it look like something that it wasn't."

"Did you just say mother trucker? What the hell is up with you? And you know exactly what it looked like. It looked like my son was walking with him after picking up breakfast at Cafe du Monde!"

The not cussing was going to be an issue when she had to deal with idiot Brent. She had to stay on course. "Darn it. He isn't only your son. He's our son. And for that matter, he's mostly mine since you can't pull your head out of your rear-end long enough to send a dollar toward his care. You do know he needs to eat every day, right? He needs a roof over his head and a winter coat and shoes. There were school fees and supplies that he needed for school too. You haven't sent a dime in two months."

"Fuck all, have you stopped cussing, Olivia Dufrene? You don't sound like yourself at all, and don't change the subject. All you ever care about is money. I don't appreciate you bringing your lovers around our kid and then parading him around so the papers can post pictures of them."

"What I care about is Lucas having the things he needs, and

that takes money, you stupid piece of—" before she could finish her sentence, Olivia was knocked to the ground. She wasn't sure what hit her, but she screamed from the force. Looking down at her skin, she could feel the charge of electricity, making her tremble. Before she could get up, Alexavier came running outside.

He'd heard the crack of lightning, which sounded like the sky had opened up, right before Olivia screamed, and his heart sunk until he could get to her. Alexavier dropped to his knees and wrapped his arms around her. "Are you alright?"

"Y-Yes," she said, but her voice was low, and when she looked at her phone, it was dead. "The lightning was super close."

"We need to get inside," he said as he helped her stand up and guided her back into the building. They were in the back room of the diner when he helped her sit on top of a table. He gently ran a hand over her cheek. "You're sure you are okay? I thought I heard you yelling at someone."

"I was on my phone and—," she held up her cell phone, and smoke was coming from it. Alexavier quickly grabbed it from her hands and looked at her.

"How close was that lightning strike?" he asked and then reached for her hands to check out her fingers and then made her show him the bottom of her shoes. The canvas tennis shoes she was wearing were a little worn, but the rubber on the bottom of her left shoe had been completely melted and was black.

Suddenly, he held her face with both hands and stared into her eyes. "You're sure you're okay, Olivia? I think that lightning struck you. The charge certainly took out your phone."

"What?" she asked, forgetting all about Brent and the newspaper for the moment. Alexavier had just bought her that phone, and she would pay him back. She'd have to pay him back for a phone that didn't work, and she'd still be without one. She shook her head. Everything had been going too well, which was what happened to her when she started to get comfortable. She knew better. Life didn't work out like that for her.

She put her head in her hands. She had to pull herself

together. She'd taken care of herself for a long time and Lucas too. She couldn't afford to fall apart because a decent man paid her a little attention.

"I need to get back to work. Miss Lynn is going to wonder what happened to me. And Lucas is going to have homework to get done," she rambled on, avoiding his stare. Olivia couldn't look at him. She was disappointed in herself for letting things go too far, and now she would have to slow it all down. Way down.

Alexavier lifted her chin so she would look at him. His eyes were warm as he stared at her. "There are only a couple of customers in there, and with the weather, there probably won't be much more."

He kissed her forehead. "Do you want to tell me what's really wrong? Is it the picture in the paper?"

Olivia nodded. It was silly, but sometimes when she was around him, she didn't feel like she had to be strong.

He pulled her into his arms again. He knew she would be upset, so he'd had his assistant clear his late afternoon schedule and headed straight across the lake to Olivia. The paper had been out for a few hours before he saw it, or he would have been there sooner.

"I know you didn't want to be in the public eye, and I promise to protect your anonymity as much as possible. My office has already contacted the paper and lodged a complaint about the picture of me walking with a minor boy. We told them he's a family friend, and it was irresponsible for them to post the picture without permission."

"But it's out there, Alex. Brent saw it and went ballistic."

"That's who you were talking to before I walked outside?"

She nodded in response.

"Well, we will deal with him together. I'll let him know that it won't happen again."

"He's bad news. You don't need to talk with him or be associated with him whatsoever. For that matter, you probably don't need to slum around with me anymore. I'm not good for you. I'm not good for your reputation. How is it going to look when everyone finds out that you're dating someone like me?"

Alexavier paused as he stared at her. She couldn't read his expression and wasn't sure if he agreed. Perhaps he was looking for a way out?

He leaned in and said, "I don't want to discuss this here. Let's go back to your place?"

"Miss Lynn needs me."

"Miss Lynn is fine. She has that new girl and almost no customers. We need to go home and talk, Olivia," Alexavier said. He held her hand as he led her back into the main room of the diner to find Miss Lynn and grab Lucas so they could go home.

Chapter Nineteen

The weather raged outside as they pulled into the small one-car carport at Olivia's duplex. Miss Lynn insisted on sending three to-go boxes home with them for dinner. She was sure she wouldn't have many customers that evening, and the special would go to waste. Red beans and rice were a staple on Mondays and one of Lucas' favorites.

Alexavier offered to drive Olivia and Lucas home in his SUV. The excessive rain had flooded several roads in the small lake town, and he worried about them in her small car.

Olivia wouldn't admit it, but the lightning had rattled her earlier. Now the rain was blowing sideways, and the storm was getting worse. She was a strong independent woman but felt relieved to have Alexavier with them.

As usual, the covered carport didn't provide much shelter, and all three got wet as they ran from the car into the house. Lucas thought it was great fun getting soaking wet from the rain until his mother insisted he change into his pajamas. As soon as he left them alone, Alexavier crowded Olivia against the refrigerator in the small kitchen. "You're pretty wet yourself. Need some help changing your clothes?"

Olivia smiled but shook her head. "I'm fine. Thanks," she

said, and he could see she was still shaken from what had happened earlier. But she wasn't going to talk about it.

Alexavier led Olivia by the hand back through her bedroom and into her bathroom. He pulled a towel out of the linen cabinet and proceeded to dry her dripping wet hair, neck, and then face. She watched him as he wrapped the towel around her shoulders before slowly unbuttoning her blouse.

"Take this off," he said in that low deep voice that could make her do almost anything.

She did as he asked, and then he blotted her damp skin. She was lost in the moment until she heard Lucas close his bathroom door. "I'm sorry. Lucas is going to come looking for us."

"You don't have to be sorry. I love that kid. I would love to take care of you right now too, but I'll see what he's up to while you dry off and change into warmer clothes. We'll continue this later tonight when he goes to bed." It wasn't a question, and she wasn't sure why she liked that so much, but she did.

After he left her alone in the bathroom and shut the door, she took a deep breath and sat on the side of her bathtub. Why did Alexavier have to be the freaking mayor of New Orleans? Why couldn't he be an electrician or a delivery driver or someone less visible? She couldn't deny how attracted she was to him, and it was only getting more intense the more time they spent together. He was incredibly thoughtful and super attentive. She didn't even know she liked that much attention or affection.

She heard a tree limb blowing wildly against the outside wall of her bathroom and stood up. The storm was going to scare the daylights out of her. She shimmied out of her jeans and then dried off her legs before finding a pair of black leggings and an off-white thermal shirt to put on. As soon as she slid socks onto her feet, the lights went out.

She could hear Lucas making scary noises in the dark and then giggling. There was still a little light outside, but inside the living room where he and Alexavier were, was probably dark as pitch.

She heard Alexavier calling her name and then saw the light

from his mobile phone shining her way down the hallway. "Need some help?" he asked with Lucas right behind him.

"Don't be scared, Mom. We'll save you from the ghosts. Oooooo," Lucas said, continuing to make noises he figured a ghost would make.

"I'm fine," she said, emerging from the depths of her messy closet.

Alexavier held out his hand, and she grabbed onto him as he pulled her close. "I'm not sure it will come back on too soon. We heard the transformer from down the block go out. It lit the sky up in an electric blue color," he said as they made their way back toward the living room.

"Good thing Miss Lynn gave us red beans and rice," Lucas said, plopping down on the beanbag chair in the middle of the living room floor.

"Are you hungry, buddy?" Olivia asked.

"Yes, ma'am," Lucas answered as he leaned back in the flimsy seat so his head would touch the floor.

"Okay, let me light some candles, and then we'll sit around the coffee table to eat," she told him, and he jumped up to help her.

While Lucas helped find all the candles Olivia had stashed in the pantry, and under the sink, he told Alexavier how they never got to eat in the living room.

"I guess it's a special occasion then," Alexavier said, smiling at Olivia.

"We could tell campfire stories around the candles, too," Lucas said in another scary voice.

"What is up with all these scary stories, son?" Olivia asked. He'd never really been into the macabre, and she felt she was missing something.

"Halloween is coming up, Mom," Lucas said as he shook his head at her.

She had forgotten about Halloween. Suddenly, his behavior made a lot more sense. Olivia felt relieved that she hadn't missed something big going on with him while distracted with finances and the new relationship that she wasn't sure could go on much longer.

Alexavier moved in close to her. It was like he knew what she was thinking. "All boys and girls love Halloween. What's not to love, costumes, candy, and parties?"

Olivia shook her head at Alexavier and Lucas when they bumped their fists together and then made an explosion sound and sign with their hands.

She'd learned more about Halloween when she first moved to New Orleans. It was a big deal there, but where she'd grown up, no one was allowed to celebrate. In fact, her parents told her it was a pagan holiday. She'd never once gone trick-or-treating as a child or teenager. Once she got away from her parents and hometown, she could see that it was more of a retail holiday, and she allowed Lucas to go last year.

"There is a big parade in the city. Maybe you two would like to come with me?"

"Oh, I don't know," Olivia said, thinking again about the photograph of Alexavier and Lucas.

"Oh, mom! Please! Think about it?" Lucas pleaded.

"We'll talk about it later, honey," she said, not looking up at him or Alexavier.

Alexavier instantly knew he should have waited to ask Olivia when they were alone. He felt terrible putting her on the spot.

She lit five candles in jars, and they placed one in the kitchen, one in the guest bathroom, and the rest on the small coffee table.

Lucas and Alexavier carried the food to the living room, and then the guys poured everyone a drink. They sat on the floor around the small wooden table and talked about their day, and then Lucas told one of his scary stories. It was funny to see him act it out. He'd become more animated telling stories just like Alexavier, who acted them out for him.

Olivia, Lucas, and Alexavier laughed and had fun eating and talking in the dark together. It felt like real family time, and

Olivia's heart hurt a little because it was what she'd always wanted for Lucas.

By 7:30, it was time for Lucas to take his shower, but the power was still out, and he agreed to take a five-minute bath instead. Alexavier showed him how to make shadow shapes on the bathtub wall with his hands while in the bathtub. He was thrilled to learn a new trick.

Olivia cleaned up the food boxes from the living room and put the pillows back onto the couch while Alexavier read to Lucas. She knew Alexavier acted out at least two of the stories every night and did a fantastic job with the different character voices. It still surprised her each time Lucas chose Alexavier to do it.

The house was quiet without any power, and she could hear the wind howling through the trees and the rain beating down onto the metal flashing of the fireplace chimney. It was a good thing Lucas was going to bed because the night sounds were spookier without the hum of electricity. As she relaxed on the sofa, she could barely make out Alexavier's voice coming down the hallway as he read Lucas his last story. The heavy rain and Alexavier's tone almost lulled her to sleep, but unexpectedly, there was a light knock on the front door.

Pausing to make sure she heard correctly, someone knocked again, a little louder. Olivia crept to the door to open it. "Yes," she said as she pulled the door back, and that was when Brent stepped inside, invading her space.

"Money doesn't seem to be a problem for you now, does it? Since when do you drive a fucking G-wagon, Olivia?"

She'd never seen Brent look so threatening, and she tried to take a step back, but he kept pace with her. When Olivia's back hit the wall behind her, she gasped, and that was when Alexavier stepped into the room from the darkened hallway.

"Is there a problem?" Alexavier asked using a menacing voice she'd never heard him use before, but she was thankful for him.

"Yeah, there's a problem. Who the fuck are you?"

Alexavier stepped in front of Olivia and into Brent's face. "I'm your problem if you don't back the fuck up," Alexavier said without blinking an eye.

Brent paused to stare at Alexavier. Brent was scrappy but Alexavier was fit and much bigger. The expensive suits were a distraction, but his body was a work of fine muscle art, and he could hold his own in a fight. At least Brent must have believed it because when Alexavier didn't budge, Brent backed up.

"You're the mayor of New Orleans, aren't you?"

"And who are you?"

"I'm the father," Brent said, trying to sound important, but Alexavier knew that Brent hadn't been around to see Lucas in months, and he certainly didn't take care of him.

"What do you need, Brent?" Alexavier asked as he shielded Olivia.

"That's none of your damn business," Brent said, making one last attempt to seem intimidating.

It didn't work.

"She's my business. For that matter, so is Lucas. I'll give you one more chance to explain why the hell you're here at this late hour. Otherwise, I will show you the door."

Brent looked terrible. While Alexavier distracted him, Olivia looked closely at her ex-boyfriend. He hadn't shaved, and his clothes looked disheveled. It was a look she remembered well and one that scared her. It was his I'm-in-desperate-trouble look that Olivia had seen before when he gambled excessively.

"Lucas is my son, and there is nothing you can do to change that, Mr. Mayor," Brent said as he backed up closer to the door. "Olivia, I don't appreciate you hanging up on me this afternoon or blocking my phone calls. I don't want my son in the paper or on the news with this guy, or I'm getting a lawyer. You know I will, and I will get custody."

Olivia stepped out from behind Alexavier. "Lightning struck my phone, and it doesn't work now. I know you heard the sound before it went dead. And don't you dare threaten me with a lawyer. You haven't sent a dime in months for Lucas. No judge would give you the time of day."

"Are you sure about that, Olivia? You've been running from something since I met you. I bet you're still running. Those kinds of secrets make everyone suspicious. Including judges and even your new friend here, the mayor."

Olivia closed her eyes. Brent must be in a bind, or he wouldn't have threatened her. He only questioned her past when he was backed into a perceived corner. But Brent never thought about their son. Olivia didn't intend to drag things out in court, and she certainly didn't want to discuss her past with anyone, especially not in front of Lucas.

Alexavier saw the worry on her face. "Alright. Your time is up tonight. If you would like to make arrangements to see Lucas or talk to Olivia then you will have to do it at a reasonable hour," Alexavier said and backed Brent out the door.

Outside on the small porch, the two men stared at each other. "I'm not intimidated by you or your money," Brent said with his teeth clenched.

"You should rethink that, Brent," Alexavier said. "I will keep this civil as long as you do. But the minute you try to hurt her or Lucas, then you'll find out just how formidable I can be."

Brent turned and ran back to his truck in the rain. He couldn't believe Olivia was dating Alexavier Regalia. He didn't like it one bit, and he wasn't going to stand by and let that jerk push him out of the picture.

Chapter Twenty

Olivia was embarrassed when Alexavier walked back into the house. She'd silently hoped he would never meet Brent, but she knew that was foolish. Brent may not have been around for a couple of months, however, it was bound to happen eventually. He would step out of their lives or be unreliable for a while. She guessed gambling had a lot to do with that behavior. However, at some point, he would pull himself together and finally bring her child support money and Lucas a toy.

Time had taught her that Brent was irresponsible, and she refused to fight with him. It didn't seem to do any good and always upset her or Lucas more than it ever did Brent. He was undependable and inconsistent but mostly unaware. His behavior made life difficult for Olivia and Lucas, and they had learned to live with it or in spite of it.

Olivia had suspected that Brent was borrowing money from some bad people again. He'd done that when she was pregnant with Lucas.

Alexavier was on the phone when he walked back into her house and locked the door. Talking quietly but firmly, she heard him discussing security.

Olivia poured them some wine and brought it into the living

room. There would be no avoiding the conversation when he finally finished his phone call and calmed down. She set her wine glass on the coffee table as she pulled at the frayed edges of the quilt lying over the back of the sofa. When Alexavier finished his phone call, he walked directly over to Olivia, pulled her close, and kissed her.

When he eased her back onto the couch, he was watching her closely. "Are you okay?"

Olivia nodded as she avoided his face and picked up her wine glass. Was she going to try and avoid the conversation about Brent again?

Barely taking a drink from her glass, she set it down again. "Alexavier, ask me what you really want to know."

He didn't hesitate. "Has Brent come here like that before trying to bully you? Is there something else I should know about him?"

Olivia swallowed hard as she tried to gather her thoughts. Alexavier was the most successful man she'd ever met. Being in the public eye wasn't foreign to him. The tragedy of his wife getting cancer, the heartache of her betrayal, and then her death had all happened while he was in office. Then, six months ago, he'd almost been killed by someone he thought was his friend. Olivia couldn't be the source of more pain for him.

He was beautiful on the inside as well as the outside. No wonder she had let her guard down and gotten closer to him. But the media would eventually discover everything, and she couldn't embarrass Alexavier. He'd been through so much already.

Telling him about Brent would be enough to set him in motion. She could avoid her transgressions because he would be gone in the morning, fleeing like everyone in her past. Things had gone too far anyway.

She wiped her face with her hands and sat up straighter. "Brent never comes over here unannounced like he did tonight. I've never seen him angry like that. Ever. He has a gambling problem, and that's why I took Lucas and left him. We weren't in love, but I got pregnant and stayed with him after I had Lucas because I didn't know what else to do."

"And you think his problem could affect me? Do you owe money? How are you involved, Olivia?"

She shook her head. Maybe she should be offended, but she'd been accused of worse by people she trusted her whole life. "No. I'm not involved with betting. I can play a mean hand of Uno, but I don't know how to gamble."

She stood up and walked into the kitchen to put her full wine glass into the sink. She didn't feel like drinking and honestly didn't understand why Alexavier was still there. Wouldn't meeting Brent and hearing of his gambling problem be enough to scare anyone off?

Alexavier followed her into the dark room and wrapped his arms around her. "Dealing with Brent isn't going to be a problem for me."

Olivia leaned back into his warm, hard body for a moment. It was everything she wanted and couldn't have. "You don't know the whole story."

He urged her to go back into the living room and sit with him on the sofa. She curled back into her little corner again, and her blue eyes were like steel. "I'm not like the other women you've gone out with, Alex."

"Thank God for that," he said, not missing a beat.

Olivia rolled her eyes. He wasn't going to make it easy on her, so she had to tell him all the gory details. "I moved to New Orleans when I was nineteen. I worked in bars and restaurants downtown and the quarter to pay for rent and necessities. Eventually, I got promoted to shift team leader, and things were pretty good. Brent was the bar manager there, and we became friends and eventually more.

"He was a nice guy, and it wasn't serious until, well, you know, I got pregnant. It was three months before I told him, and it took him about a month to stop freaking out. Then when I was seven months along, I came down with gestational diabetes, and the doctor made me stop working. Brent let me move in with him and helped me out since I didn't have much money."

Alexavier looked like he wanted to say something, but he sat there and listened without saying a word.

"We lived in a rundown apartment that was above a bar in the quarter. Three flights up with no elevator, and the stairs were difficult to manage as I got closer to my due date. Brent worked nights, and I was so tired that I slept most afternoons. It was rough, and we hardly talked to one another. I slept in the bedroom, and he took the couch, or if he slept in the bedroom, then I would sleep on the couch. He was gone more and more, and then one particular day, he didn't come back. He was gone for three days, and I was scared, not knowing what to do, when two big men showed up at the apartment.

"They had a key and let themselves inside. I thought they would rob me, but they said they were there because Brent had borrowed a lot of money from their boss and hadn't paid it back. I told them he wasn't home, and they told me they knew that and had waited to make sure I was alone. They were going to make him pay for his mistakes by hurting me."

Alexavier closed his eyes and swore. "They hurt you?"

"They scared me. I was wearing a baggy t-shirt and leggings, and they didn't know I was pregnant. I screamed like a banshee when they chased me around the room. One of them picked me up and dragged me into the bedroom, but when he threw me onto the bed, my shirt flew up. He stared at me for a long time, and when the other one came into the room, they both said they couldn't hurt a pregnant woman. They told me to tell Brent they had been there. They left after that, and I cried for an hour.

"Brent worked off the money he owed and then said he'd stopped gambling."

Alexavier reached over to hold one of her hands. "He didn't?"

"He did, for a little while. Then he bragged that he was winning so much that he shouldn't stop. He said he didn't have a problem and that I misunderstood what he'd told me. His version was that he said he wouldn't borrow money from the bad men again. Not that he wouldn't gamble. I went back to work six weeks after Lucas was born and tried to save a little money every paycheck. I knew it was only a matter of time before Brent owed someone else again. I'd hoped to be gone before they returned to punish him by hurting us."

"They came back?"

Olivia nodded. "Nine months later, Brent borrowed money from the same loan sharks as before, and when they came calling, they'd found me alone with baby Lucas. Since I wasn't pregnant anymore, they were going to use me to teach Brent a lesson. Lucas cried uncontrollably when he heard me scream, and I managed to talk them into letting me put him in his nursery.

"It was a miracle. We escaped that day out the bedroom window. I was able to balance him and a backpack full of baby stuff plus the cash I'd hidden under his crib mattress. Everything fell into place at that moment, and I'm not sure why but it worked out perfectly. I'd wedged a chair under the doorknob, which gave me enough time to get us out of there. The men were huge, but for some reason, the chair held the door closed. Lucas, who'd been screaming his head off, suddenly stopped. I hustled us out the window and onto the metal fire escape, and he didn't move a muscle or make a sound. The metal staircase was rusted in the closed position when I'd moved in with Brent. He'd even tried to make the stairs move once to show me how safe it was to live on the third story, but they didn't budge. Suddenly at the exact moment, I needed that fire escape, it was in perfect working order and touched the ground below, so I didn't have to jump a single foot from the third floor as I'd feared. I got to my car with Lucas, but instead of finding my way to the highway, I ended up on the long causeway bridge that led to Maisonville. I needed to stop to get some water to make Lucas a bottle and ended up at Miss Lynn's diner. She made the bottle for me and didn't ask any questions when I came in without wearing shoes. Miss Lynn simply found me a pair of sandals. She even found a place for us to stay, hired me, and let me bring the baby to work until I could afford a sitter. It was like my life started over when I showed up in Maisonville."

"They didn't follow you?"

Olivia shook her head. "Brent said he paid them back again, and after some time passed, he started sending me child support money for Lucas. Eventually, I let him see Lucas, and when he got a little older, I let him go for a weekend here and there. I didn't want Lucas to grow up without a father. But honestly, he hasn't been much of one. Lucas doesn't want to go with him anymore because all he does is play video games or sleep all day instead of spending time with Lucas. He's behind on several child support checks, so I haven't had to deal with telling Brent how Lucas feels."

Olivia stopped talking before admitting that she had never felt for Brent what she did for Alexavier. And apparently, Lucas felt the same way. She and her son had never been happier, and why would Brent want to ruin that for them? It didn't make sense. Olivia hadn't been with Brent in over six years. He never seemed to care about Lucas either.

"You must have a guardian angel, sweetheart."

"Must have."

Alexavier was reeling over Olivia's getaway story. How could Brent have put her and Lucas in danger? He watched her face and could see what telling the story had cost her. Blowing out the candles she'd lit around the house, he used the flashlight on his phone to lead them back to her bedroom. They didn't talk anymore, but he held her close until she finally fell asleep. The events of that evening had disrupted his plans, but he needed to be next to her. What young mother would know to keep a bugout bag for her baby in case they needed to run? She'd learned that from somewhere, and Alexavier laid awake wondering what else she had escaped.

Chapter Twenty-One

Tuesday morning, it was cold, but the rain had stopped, and everything outside seemed clean and fresh.

"It's freezing," Lucas said when he got up.

"That's why we're going to have some oatmeal for breakfast, little man," Alexavier said.

"Oatmeal?" he asked. He wasn't sure he'd ever eaten oatmeal before, but Alexavier seemed excited about it.

"It's delicious. I put brown sugar and cinnamon in mine. Add a little butter and then cream, and if we're acting fancy, then we get some crushed pecans too."

Lucas laughed because Alexavier made faces when he said they were fancy for adding pecans.

"Did you sleep well last night?" Alexavier asked when he put the oatmeal down for the three of them.

Olivia was still in the bathroom getting ready, but the two guys began eating.

"Yes, sir. And this is good," Lucas said and then picked up his milk to take a drink. He didn't remember ever having the oatmeal stuff before, but he loved it.

"When I was a kid, my mother would make oatmeal for me on

cold mornings. It was one of my favorite breakfasts. It makes you strong." He flexed his arm muscle and then had Lucas do it too.

Olivia came into the kitchen and saw the guys flexing as they finished up their breakfasts. "I'm pretty sure I didn't have any of that stuff in the pantry."

"Nope. I made a grocery run this morning. I've been up since four and needed to get my workout in."

"Four in the A M?" Olivia said, shaking her head, and then she walked over to sit with them at the table. Alexavier leaned over and kissed her sweetly on the lips.

He knew she was thinking about their previous conversation and how close they held each other once they went to bed. The honesty of what she'd been through and what he might face with Brent was freeing. It felt like a big moment for their relationship.

"The bus is going to be here any minute Lucas," she said, and he began rushing through his breakfast.

"I thought we could drop him at school this morning instead of him riding the bus. I have to take you to the diner, and isn't it on the way?"

"Are you sure we aren't a heap of trouble? I could call Miss Lynn for a ride, and Lucas takes the school bus every day."

"You are two of my favorite people, and I feel privileged to help in any way possible."

Lucas didn't say anything, but he smiled really big when he heard Alexavier's comment. He liked him. He really liked him.

ALEXAVIER HELD Olivia's hand while they drove Lucas to school and then on the way to the diner where she'd left her car. He kissed her goodbye for ten minutes until she told him to let her get to work. When she got out of the car, she felt a bit dizzy.

She had fallen hard for Alexavier, which happened super-fast for her. Sure, they'd talked for months, but the actual dating had just begun. She put her hands up to her lips, which looked bee-stung from all the hot kissing. She was acting like a lovesick fool, and she didn't even feel bad about it. All these years, she'd made fun of couples for their excessive PDA, but she couldn't stop herself from wanting to make out with Alexavier constantly.

Public displays of affection should be outlawed, she would say, and all of a sudden, she couldn't get enough.

Nothing could wipe the smile off her face or take away the bounce in her step. She was in love. Truly in love for the first time in her life.

She swung open the diner door with a big fat good morning on her lips when she saw Miss Lynn's serious expression. Following the older woman's eyes, she saw Brent sitting in a booth alone, and the diner wasn't open yet.

Olivia swallowed hard as she walked over to where he was sitting. He ran his hands over his face and hair, and there was no mistaking the anguish in his expression.

"Brent? What are you doing?"

Miss Lynn was still in her line of sight, and she watched as the sweet woman shook her head in warning to Olivia. She'd never seen Miss Lynn look so worried. Walking over and handing Olivia a cup of coffee, Miss Lynn put her arm around her. Lynn hoped it would give Olivia strength for whatever was coming next.

Brent put his hands down on the table, and that's when Olivia saw the knife he was holding.

"What the hell is going on, Brent?"

"Don't look at me like that. It's not what you think," he said in a weak voice. He looked exhausted, and she knew he hadn't been home or slept since he'd barged into her place. Black circles framed his eyes, and he wore the same clothes he had the night before.

"He barged in the door this morning behind me. He's been sitting here for an hour," Miss Lynn said.

"You're gambling again, right? Let me guess, and you're in big trouble with those guys from before?"

Brent nodded. "It's worse than before."

That little bit of news made Olivia's pulse race. Reliving it while she told the details to Alexavier had thrust her back to that last day in the apartment. She remembered every word, every threat they'd made against her in an attempt to teach Brent a lesson. She could still feel their hands all over her before Lucas started screaming and crying. It was why she was willing to jump out a third-story window onto a fire escape that she thought wouldn't work. She had to save her son even if she got hurt or killed in the process that day, and fortunately, things worked out. What were the chances that would happen again?

Miss Lynn didn't know the details behind Olivia walking into her diner that night many years ago with baby Lucas on her hip. But she'd always figured it had to do with Brent. Brent had a gambling problem?

Olivia wasn't ready for her closest confidant to hear the sordid details of her life before Maisonville. Brent coming around once in a while was already awkward. She hugged Miss Lynn, and the older woman nodded, leaving Olivia and Brent alone.

"How much worse? Tell me what you've done," Olivia demanded quietly. Why was he there? They weren't together anymore and hadn't been in over six years. What did she have to do with his life anymore?

Olivia sat down across from Brent. She stared at him and wondered what she ever could have thought was appealing about him. He was handsome by most standards, but his behavior made him incredibly unattractive.

"I couldn't stop myself this time. I borrowed a crazy amount, and I can't pay it back. I'll never be able to pay back that much money."

"I-I don't have any money, Brent. I barely make enough to take care of our son on my own. Why don't you leave town? Start over somewhere else?"

He lowered his eyes at her. He was angry. And he had that knife. Olivia tried to put the thought of him hurting her or himself out of her mind as she tempered her expression.

He continued flipping the knife between his fingers and then, without warning, stabbed it into the table before glaring at her. "You don't understand, Olivia. They have eyes everywhere. If I so much as look at a bus ticket or fill my car up with gas, they would grab me. When they realized I couldn't pay them back, they wanted me to work for them. They had me out with some of their goons and wanted me to break some guy's fingers. When I wouldn't do it, they beat the shit out of me. I tried to keep you out of it, but they remembered you."

"What are you talking about?" Olivia threaded her fingers together to stop her hands from shaking.

Brent could see she was scared. "I couldn't work for them anymore. I owe them big, and to pay back that kind of money, they wanted me to hurt someone. I couldn't do it. I couldn't. I told them to kill me instead, but they said that wouldn't do them any good. I owed them cash, and they couldn't get money from a dead guy."

Olivia's eyes were locked onto Brent. He'd left the knife jutting out of the table as he glowered at her. He was desperate. She could understand him being scared. Those men were scary. But why was he mad at her?

She kept her voice low. "So, they think I have money?"

"No, you see, the guy they wanted me to cut the fingers off wasn't the guy that owed them money. It was his lover. They go after a man's family if he owes them money, so he'll do anything to pay them back and save them."

"I'm not your lover, and I've never been your family," she said. "Do you know what those men were going to do to me, Brent? How could you?" She suddenly thought about the man watching them at the park. She was sure he'd been a reporter or someone following Alexavier. Was he there watching her? Or worse, would he have hurt Lucas?

"I'm sure they're following me, but I thought you should know they've been watching you too. They like their chances of getting money from your new boyfriend, the mayor. I mean, he's got tons of money, right? He'd pay to keep them away from you?"

"What?" Olivia couldn't believe what he was saying.

"Fuck Olivia. What were you thinking by going out with someone like that? It's like you're taunting me."

Suddenly she wasn't sure who was watching her relationship with the mayor. Brent or the mob? "It has nothing to do with you." She couldn't help the tears in her eyes. She looked out the window to avoid Brent's stare.

When she looked back at him and saw him smiling at her, she was done. He'd ruined everything that could have been great for her, and she would not forgive him.

"Get out, Brent! Get the heck, no, get the hell out of here now!" she said as she stood up from the booth.

"I'm sorry, Olivia. I didn't mean for this to happen. I wouldn't have put you or Lucas in danger on purpose."

She stopped and stared at him in horror. "W-Would they hurt a child?"

"They're the ones who showed me his picture in the paper."

Olivia was sick with worry. Lucas was at school, but she suddenly needed to see her son and make sure he was okay. She didn't know what to do first.

Miss Lynn had watched Olivia and her ex from the bar and then hurried over to open the front glass door. "You should go, Brent. Don't come back here," Miss Lynn said.

Brent stared at the floor as he walked to the door and then stopped and turned toward Olivia. He'd thought she would live her stupid little life in Maisonville and then realize she wanted him back. She talked tough, but he could tell she'd been sheltered growing up. There was no hiding how surprised she'd been over life in New Orleans. He'd taken her to restaurants, clubs, and festivals. She'd never done anything or been anywhere. She needed him. "No matter what you think, I do care about what happens to you and Lucas," he said and then turned and left. He would make her understand.

Olivia watched him walk out, and Miss Lynn locked the door behind him. Olivia was shaken and had to pull herself together. She'd already considered her options if things with Brent went badly again. Of course, that had been years ago, and Olivia had gotten comfortable. She needed a minute to regroup and figure out where she and Lucas could go next.

Chapter Twenty-Two

Olivia couldn't stop the chill that ran through her. She was cold down to her bones, and Miss Lynn wrapped an oversized sweater around Olivia's shoulders and hugged her tightly.

"Things are going to be alright, Olivia. You hear me?" The sweet older woman kissed her cheek and then looked into her eyes. "Together, we will stop Brent."

Olivia nodded. She knew Miss Lynn would do anything to help her, but after seeing Brent with the knife, she wasn't sure if she even knew what he was capable of anymore. He had an addiction. Gambling didn't get the press that salacious addictions like drugs, alcohol and even sex addictions received, but it was as life-altering. Brent was incapable of stopping himself, and his behavior would hurt everyone around him.

She had to protect Lucas but also Miss Lynn.

Using the diner phone, Olivia called the school and told them she was on her way to check Lucas out early. She then grabbed her keys and rushed out of the diner, promising to return soon. There was no way Olivia could concentrate until Lucas was in her sights. Once she picked him up, she could decide what to do next.

While Olivia was gone to pick up Lucas, Miss Lynn called the

Maisonville Sheriff and offered him a complimentary breakfast. When Olivia returned, she would nudge her to talk to the sheriff and get his help. While it had been difficult to hear the entire conversation between Olivia and Brent, she did hear about his gambling habits. Then there was the passive-aggressive way he played with that knife. He was threatening Olivia. Perhaps if Brent knew she would involve the authorities, he would stay away from there?

Olivia pulled into the school driveway, and that was when she knew she was being followed. The gray sedan was shiny, and the polished chrome glowed, but the man inside looked like he'd had a few miles on him.

What kind of mobster followed a mother to her child's school? She lost her mind a bit as she stormed up to the sedan's driver-side window.

She beat on the window and yelled, "Mother trucker do we have a problem?"

The forty-year-old man with a scar down the right side of his face smiled at her. "Mother trucker?" He laughed.

Olivia didn't see the humor in it. Apparently, the stop cursing plan had worked, and when she needed to yell something at him, it was what came out first. He'd tailed her since the diner. Was he really going to hurt her in broad daylight over her ex-boyfriend's gambling debts?

"Why are you following me?"

"Well, ma'am, I'm being paid to do it."

"What?" So, he blatantly admitted he was there to harm them because of Brent?

"What kind of man threatens a woman and her child?"

"I think you need to talk to Alexavier Regalia."

"He isn't in this. I won't ask him for money to bail Brent out, so you may as well do whatever you're going to do to me. But please, leave my son out of this."

She'd been fired-up when she saw the man behind her. The momma bear in her came out swinging with no regard for her own safety. Realizing the mobsters were ruthless, she would sacrifice herself if they would leave her precious son alone.

"Please, I'll go with you if you, just let me get him safely to the diner."

"No, ma'am, you don't understand. I'm here to watch over you. Regalia hired me to keep watch."

Olivia's mouth went dry. What the heck was going on? "Alex hired you to watch over us?"

She saw him nod, but when he began to speak again, she turned around and walked toward the school office. She'd woken up next to Alexavier, which felt like the best way to start the day, and without warning, it had become the worst day ever.

Her heart pounded out of her chest as she thought she was approaching someone that worked for the New Orleans mob. Learning that Alexavier had hired a security guard for her made her heart hurt differently. She didn't want to be this person. She wished she could simply be with Alexavier, but that wasn't how her world worked. She would never have a happy ending.

It was time to get her child and then try to create another peaceful life somewhere else, so her son could be safe and happy.

🐚

BACK AT THE DINER, Olivia was relieved to see that Daisy and Miss Lynn had everything covered. It was perfect timing for Miss Lynn to find someone so proficient, but it made Olivia a little sad to imagine not seeing the place anymore. If Olivia could be honest with herself, and currently she couldn't, she would admit that she loved the older woman like a mother and didn't want to leave her.

She watched as Miss Lynn brought Lucas a large chocolate milk and a bacon biscuit along with a new crossword puzzle book for kids. She was sweet with him and always had treats and prizes waiting for Lucas. He got busy with the new book, and Olivia considered what options she had for their future.

It couldn't have been a worse time for things to go badly.

Brent not paying her child support when the school year had just begun was the worst. She'd spent the few extra dollars she'd had on Lucas' school fees, school supplies, and uniforms. Olivia had always run a little low on funds when school started but immediately started saving again. There simply wasn't enough money to get them into a new place somewhere else, and she dreaded the only option out there. Before she got emotional over it, Miss Lynn nudged her to go and sit down with the sheriff.

Olivia appreciated Miss Lynn but, in her heart, understood there were no real options for her there. Still, she asked him how safe anyone was if the mob came after them.

Sheriff Gallegos had worked in a big city precinct for most of his career but then moved to Maisonville. He had dealt with restraining orders and organized crime, which were difficult to stop. He told her he wanted to be honest with her. "I can put the diner and your house on rotation and drive-by more often, but unless someone makes a threat against you or Lucas, there isn't much we can do."

"So basically, we have to get hurt before anyone believes we're in danger?" She looked away from him. Gangsters like that would only need one time to do irreparable damage to her or her son. She stood up and, without another word, walked back over to the counter to sit with Lucas.

The sheriff followed her. "Look, Miss Olivia, maybe if you could give me more details about what is going on, I could do more?"

Olivia ran her hands through Lucas' hair and then looked up at the sheriff and shook her head, no. She knew the truth. No one could help her.

Miss Lynn stepped up and thanked Sheriff Gallegos for stopping in and then offered him some free pie and coffee to take with him before she ushered him away from Lucas and Olivia.

"What's wrong, mom?" Lucas asked, watching her.

"Nothing for you to worry about, kiddo," she said, trying to keep the worry off her face.

She knew the police couldn't do anything. That was why she'd run away from New Orleans and Brent the first time.

The only thing that would keep them safe would be to get out of town. It was simply the awful truth of Olivia's life that she didn't have any family that could protect them. Her parents hadn't spoken to her in years, and there was no way she could go to Florida and ask for their help.

She wasn't sure where exactly her sister even lived. Then there was the family home in St. Marksville. She had abandoned it when she moved to New Orleans, and no one else had moved back in. Someone was paying the minimal electric and water bills because she still got the statements, probably her folks but she was certain they had never gone back. She could swallow her pride and move back there. She wiped her eyes. She wouldn't go back there for anything except to save her son.

Lucas reached over and patted his mother's hand. "Maybe you should call Alex?"

Olivia's eyes watered. Lucas had said what she'd felt, but she couldn't burden Alexavier. He couldn't get involved. The mob was dangerous. She had to protect Lucas and Alexavier from Brent and his criminal lifestyle. No one could know what she was planning.

Unexpectedly, the security guard, who she'd confronted an hour earlier, walked into the diner, and handed her a phone. "Mr. Regalia needs to talk to you."

Olivia shook her head. What else could go wrong?

Chapter Twenty-Three

Olivia's chest hurt as she accepted the phone from the man with a scar down his right cheek. Without saying a word, he stepped back, and she took a few steps away so she could talk in private.

Alexavier had told her he'd be in meetings all day and possibly unable to come over that night. She hadn't expected to hear from him.

"Olivia, what's wrong?"

How could he know something was wrong after she simply said hello?

"Nothing? Why would you think something was wrong?"

"Rex told me that Brent was in the diner this morning. Rex had gotten there shortly after I left and didn't know Brent was in there until he came out. He said you looked unhappy, and then you checked Lucas out of school. And did you also talk to the Sheriff?"

Alexavier hadn't missed a thing. Of course, that was all thanks to Rex, the bodyguard she didn't know was watching her. She had to pull herself together.

"Um, about that, I don't need a bodyguard. He scared me half to death when he followed me into the school parking lot."

"I apologize for not telling you, Olivia. I meant to tell you last night, but then I got distracted." A lot happened last night but she instantly thought about how he held her in bed as she fell asleep. She would miss the hell out of him.

He cleared his throat several times before he spoke again. "I should have told you, Liv, but he's nonnegotiable," Alexavier said. "You need someone when I'm not there."

Olivia wished it was as simple as having a bodyguard outside, but she knew the men coming for her and Lucas wouldn't stop. They'd gotten to her each time before, without being seen coming or going. She couldn't chance Lucas' safety.

"Sweetheart? Are you still there?"

She loved when he called her sweetheart. She would miss him terribly. "I'm here."

"Can you tell me what happened this morning?"

They'd gotten close over the past six months, and most of that time had been them talking over the phone. Alexavier picked up on little nuances in Olivia's voice more than anyone else ever had. Still, she couldn't tell him everything. "Brent wanted to talk about the child support he owed me. That's all. Lucas wasn't feeling well, and the Sheriff comes over for breakfast all the time. No biggie."

There was a long pause, and she worried Alexavier would press her for the rest of the details. She didn't want to lie to him, but she couldn't have him trying to save the day. He would try and swoop in and take care of everything, but in the process, he might get hurt. She couldn't let that happen because of her. She needed to gather up her son and go before his position as mayor was compromised in some way. He'd already been in a terrible situation months ago, and it had been in all the papers.

She wouldn't drag him into another. No doubt that Brent's mob contacts would be news fodder, and then they would dig into her background, and all of her past would be eaten up by the local gossip hounds. It was a slippery slope, and she didn't want Alexavier caught up in the slide. Get it together, Olivia.

"So, Brent is going to pay the child support he owes?"

"Yes."

Alexavier paused awkwardly again. Darn, did she answer him too quickly? She tried to explain. "It will take him a little while, but he said he would do what he could. And I'm fine. I looked unhappy because I never enjoy talking with Brent."

"Huh, okay, and Lucas must not be too sick if he's at the diner?"

"I think he was overly tired from the weekend. We'll leave early today so he can get some extra rest."

She answered him carefully while at the same time trying to come up with a way to get rid of the bodyguard. He would no doubt follow her home too. And she couldn't have him paying such close attention to her. So far, his watch had been quite eventful especially when she confronted him and yelled like a crazy person for everyone at the school to see.

She needed to find a way to distract him so she and Lucas could slip away.

Alexavier's voice startled her. "Are you still there, Olivia?"

"Yes. Sorry. So how is your day going?" She finally had the sense to ask him about his day like she would in a normal conversation.

"It's been hectic."

"I know you're busy. We can talk about all of this later."

"I'm never too busy for you, beautiful. No matter what happens with you or Lucas, I want you to know you can call me."

Olivia tried not to get upset hearing his sweet words. He always said the right things to her, and she wished her life could be different. If only she had followed a different path and could date a powerful man like Alexavier. Instead, he'd be ashamed, and she couldn't stand to see the look in his eyes as she saw in her parents. Then there was the whole relationship with idiot Brent. She didn't belong with someone in the spotlight like Alexavier.

He'd done an incredible job as Mayor and cracked down on crime more than anyone who'd held office in recent years. But even his city reform initiative hadn't completely gotten rid of the mob. Sure, they had gone underground, and most people didn't know they were still around. However, according to Brent, they'd simply gotten clever about their business and stayed off the radar. Extorting money from gambling addicts' families was only one of the ways they kept afloat.

"Thanks, Alex. No need to worry about us. We'll be safe tonight." She was relieved to actually say something true. She would keep Lucas safe. She would take him somewhere no one would think to look for them.

She just needed to get off the phone with Alexavier. Because when he used that deep warm voice on her, it made her want to tell him everything, like how much she truly loved him. It felt strange to admit even to herself that she was in love with Alexavier Regalia. It had to be real, or her heart wouldn't hurt so badly. While her head told her she was doing the right thing, her heart hated the idea of her walking away from him and her life in Maisonville when everything was finally getting good.

Her excuses seemed to work as Alexavier sounded relaxed. "I didn't realize you would be home early and sent your replacement phone to the diner. The courier service should be there in an hour or so."

"You shouldn't have bought me another phone, Alex. I was going to replace it when Brent paid me."

She would never be able to repay him for two new phones. She closed her eyes and tried to remain calm. He explained to her how happy he was to do it and how necessary it was for her to have a phone when she was alone with Lucas. While he spoke sweetly again to her, she realized he'd given her the perfect excuse to get rid of Rex for a while. Everything was falling into place, and even if she didn't want to leave secretively, she couldn't deny that everything was lining up so she could get away with it. And that was the way her life had worked out ever since she'd escaped to New Orleans and then to Maisonville.

"Thanks, Alex, for everything you've done for Lucas and for me. We appreciate you more than you will ever know." She promised to call him that evening when she got her new phone set up. Then she was consumed with remorse when they said their goodbyes. She made sure to tell him again how much their time together had meant the world to her. She couldn't bear to think of how hurt he would feel when he realized she'd taken Lucas and left town.

If she only had another choice. But she'd witnessed firsthand how Brent was spiraling. If he was freaking out, then she should have already left town. The last two times the men came after her, Brent hadn't even known about it until after it had happened. They were terrifying, and it took her years to stop keeping a duffel bag packed with getaway clothes and provisions. She didn't think she could handle them showing up in Maisonville.

Olivia calmed her expression before she returned to the main dining area. It wouldn't do any good to fool Alexavier and Rex, if Miss Lynn figured out her plan. That woman would insist on protecting them and shout it from the rooftops.

If those men found out how much Miss Lynn meant to her and Lucas, they would surely use her against Olivia. She wouldn't let that happen.

She walked over to Rex, thanked him, and handed him back his phone. Then she told Miss Lynn that Alex would probably head over soon, and she and Lucas would go home and rest for a while.

Miss Lynn hugged her fiercely and then whispered in her ear. "Alexavier is a strong man. Keep him close." She hugged Lucas before handing him a to-go bag full of treats.

Usually, Olivia would scold her for spoiling him and then tell Lucas he couldn't eat any candy before eating dinner. But that didn't seem very important anymore. She let him dig out whatever he wanted to eat and told him he could have some of the candy in the car on the way home.

She hugged Miss Lynn again and then gathered Lucas' things so they could get out of there. She also made Lucas hug Miss Lynn again, and then she blew her a kiss from the doorway as she held Lucas' hand, before they walked through the parking lot to her car.

Rex followed behind her, and she tried not to tear up when she looked around the neighborhood she wouldn't be returning to again.

As soon as they got home, Olivia packed up all their necessities. It only took twenty minutes to gather what they needed. Next, she filled in the gaps of the pantry and the bathrooms where she'd removed items so it wouldn't be obvious that they'd left town for good.

It was only stuff, and she would explain to Lucas that those things weren't important. Besides where they were going, it would be best not to call any extra attention to themselves. Of course, her driving into town would probably cause enough of a stir. She didn't need a bunch of bags and boxes loaded in the car to get the neighbors to come out to see what she was doing. They couldn't seem to help themselves when it came to her. Olivia Dufrene was one of their favorite topics of discussion, and everyone seemed to watch her for most of her young life. Of course, there were no secrets in St. Marksville because everyone was famous in a small town.

Setting the bags by the front door, Olivia tried to forget about her past. Getting Lucas to a safe place was all that mattered. She could do this. Adding a single bag with a few food items next to the large duffel bag, she assessed everything before deciding she was done. Then she watched Rex sitting in his car for another twenty minutes before walking outside to speak to him.

He rolled down his window when he saw her coming his way. "Hey, Rex. Sorry to bother you. Alexavier said he sent my new phone to the diner. I would get it, but Lucas is taking a nap, and well, I don't want to wake him up. Would you mind?"

Rex looked at her and then turned around to look around her neighborhood and house. She could tell he was weighing his decision.

"The school traffic will start soon, but if you go now, you should be back here in no more than ten minutes."

Rex texted Alexavier who approved the errand if Olivia agreed to stay inside the house with her doors locked until Rex returned. She held up her right hand, promising she would lock up to make him and Alexavier happy.

She headed into her duplex and watched out her side window as Rex drove away. Then she ran to her car, throwing all the bags she'd packed into the trunk as she hollered for Lucas to grab his coat and pillow.

Everything was loaded when she turned to see Lucas returning to the house. A minute later, he came out with his electric car and as many books as he could carry.

Her heart sank as she watched Lucas clinging to his favorite possessions. They probably would never see Maisonville or the rest of their things again, so she didn't stop him. If he wanted those few items, then she would make room for them. She helped Lucas buckle up and then checked her watch to double check their time. Just in case Rex made it to the diner and back faster than Olivia predicted, she drove out the back way of her neighborhood and then headed toward the highway.

It would take two and half hours to get to St. Marksville, and Olivia hadn't told Lucas anything. She began explaining.

"Hey buddy, are you ready to go on an adventure?"

Chapter Twenty-Four

It was half-past five when Olivia pulled into the small town of St. Marksville. The moment she drove across the parish line, her stomach hurt. No doubt, residents of the quiet town would know the minute she showed up. After all, she still had the same car and looked pretty much the same as when she'd left over ten years ago.

However, it was dinnertime for "respectable" folks, as she'd been told so many times, and most people would be home. So, there was hope that no one would be around to see her and Lucas as they arrived.

Lucas sat up straighter as they neared civilization. He'd remarked along the way how there was nothing but fields everywhere.

She told him it was sugarcane and that she would get him some to try soon. Once they entered the town limits, she pointed out the small medical center where she'd been born and then the small school where everyone went from kindergarten to high school.

Trying to smile when she felt like throwing up was tough, but Lucas didn't notice. She slowly pulled into the driveway of the house she'd grown up in and immediately saw the grass was cut but several boards on the house needed to be scraped and painted.

Her father had kept all of that up when she was a kid. "Cleanliness was a sign of Godliness," he would say.

When she moved away, she figured it would all fall into disrepair but perhaps her parents were paying to have the yard kept up. It didn't matter. Olivia couldn't pay anyone to do the work, and she would do all the maintenance herself. She pulled up as close as the one-car garage would allow and then shut off the car.

"Here we are, Lucas." She kept her smile as she helped him out of the car and grabbed an arm full of things.

"You grew up here?" he asked. His face showed how much he disapproved of the old house. Their duplex in Maisonville wasn't much, but it was clean and neat. The landlord worked tirelessly to keep up the maintenance, and her old family home showed years of neglect.

"It was nicer back then. We can paint and make it look as good as new, buddy. Pick out which room you want, and we'll paint it too. Sound like fun?"

"But what about my school?" he asked, staring at her.

Her heart ached for him, but she didn't let it show. "No worries. You are going to go to my old school. And make a bunch of new friends."

Lucas nodded, but he wasn't so sure about going to a new school or making new friends. He did love painting, and the idea of being set free to pick stuff out for his new room made him happier. He headed off down the hallway to locate which room would be his.

Olivia finished unloading the car, thankful that none of the neighbors peeking out of their windows came outside to speak to her. After pulling her car into the small garage, she went inside to begin the exhausting work of cleaning every surface in the house.

At some point, since she'd left town, someone had covered all the furniture with large white sheets, so at least it wasn't thick with filth. Olivia carefully rolled the sheets up in order to capture the dust and took them out back to shake out. Then she had Lucas help her roll up the large area rugs so she could throw them over the clothesline and beat them with a broom. Lucas thought that was particularly funny and helped her by using an old mop handle.

Two hours into the house cleaning, when Olivia finished mopping the floors and found that the central air and heating units still worked, Lucas told her he was starving.

"Sorry, kiddo. I lost track of time. How about a peanut butter and jelly sandwich tonight?"

Lucas nodded and followed her into the kitchen. They each ate a sandwich, and then she pulled his sheets out of the dryer and put them back on the double bed in the room he'd claimed.

He fell asleep after one story, and Olivia dragged herself to the shower. Being in the house flooded her with memories, none of them good. It wasn't fair growing up naïve and happy for sixteen years, to have it erased by terrible people with even worse behavior.

Swearing she would never go back there, Olivia felt like it was a cruel joke that when she needed a refuge, it was her only option.

Damn Brent and damn his gambling. Coming back to the place where she'd taught herself how to cuss like a sailor brought it all back to her. She shook her head. She couldn't start talking like that again. But when she thought about Brent, it brought out all the wrong words.

What kind of man would put his son in danger? The same kind of man and woman that would abandon their daughter, she thought.

She would never understand Brent or her parents because being Lucas' mother was the most important thing to Olivia. As she pulled a blanket out of one of her bags and headed for the old couch in the living room, she figured going back to St. Marksville proved it.

A little beam of moonlight came through a slit in the living room blinds, and she stared up at the ceiling. Olivia didn't want to sleep in any of the bedrooms as long as her mind replayed the past.

How could she enroll Lucas into the awful little school she'd attended? Honestly, when she had been his age, she was happy and clueless. The elementary teachers had been lovely, and he'd probably fit in fine for a while. But it would matter that he was her son. It would also matter that his father wasn't there with them. Everything mattered in that little town.

She would have to try and channel some of the good stories from her childhood to tell Lucas especially since there was no way around their situation. Perhaps it would be good for him since he was a boy? Boys seemed to receive preferential treatment when she was in school, and things couldn't have changed that much since she'd left.

Olivia pulled the covers up higher. She didn't have to enroll him immediately. She could take a few days before she had to take Lucas to the school and face all the mean old ladies who worked there and hated her.

In the meantime, she would make an adventure out of fixing up the house and getting settled. Lucas was already enjoying cleaning her childhood bedroom and making it his own.

Olivia had moved into her parent's bedroom after they'd left during her high school senior year. She'd turned eighteen in December of that year, but by Thanksgiving, they'd packed up. They told her they were retiring to Florida. She'd thought they'd come back once in a while and surely would be there for her high school graduation. Two weeks after they left, her father called her. He let her know that she'd embarrassed the family, and they couldn't forgive her for ruining their relationships with other church members. They decided she could stay in the house because they had paid it off years earlier, but she had to pay for everything else. She didn't even know what bills she had to pay until the city shut off her water. She found a way to manage the meager money she made working as a waitress at a dive bar on the outskirts of town. But what hurt the most was that her mother wouldn't speak to her at all.

It took some time before people found out her parents had

left. She didn't want anyone to know, so she hid it for as long as possible. Maybe it was denial, or that she liked having a secret that no one else knew for a change. No matter what the reason, it was a devastating time for her.

She'd never gone a day in her life without seeing them, and she was scared to be alone in the house at night. Every night she would lie on the couch and think about how terrible she must be for her parents to leave her. Of course, they'd never stuck up for her once she became a teenager. Not once. But still, her mother cooked dinner at night, and they all sat at the large oblong table together as a family.

The cussing and brash behavior she'd adopted was a defense mechanism to keep the bullies away, but she knew it upset her mother. She didn't know that it could make her mother not love her anymore.

She thought about Alexavier and his family. His big Italian family with all of their large personalities. They loved each other. His mother adored him, and although his politics didn't always follow her ideals, nothing would change how they felt about each other.

Olivia dried her eyes with her t-shirt and rolled over on her side. She had that kind of love for Lucas. There was nothing he could do that would make her not love him. He could rob a bank, and she'd still visit him every day in prison. She'd probably bake a file inside a cake for him. Smirking at the idea of baking a weaponized cake, Olivia accepted she was just too much for the people in that ridiculous little town.

ALEXAVIER WAS in a meeting when the security guard he'd hired to watch over Olivia and Lucas called him and left a message. He was heading into his next appointment as he listened to his voicemail and then immediately apologized that he would have to cancel due to a personal matter.

It only took him a few minutes before he was in his car driving to Maisonville when he called Rex back. "What in the living hell, Rex?"

"I know. I know." Rex had worked for Alexavier for years and had managed his security for most of that time. He'd personally taken down the man that had threatened Alexavier during his first term as mayor. And Rex and his team had thwarted a few more radicals looking for their few minutes of fame by hurting a famous elected official. He'd tried to warn Alexavier that he was too accessible and needed to keep a security team all the time. Recently the mayor had gotten lax on having them around and only used Rex and his team for large events.

Of course, the last occasion he'd coordinated for the mayor was on a yacht for his birthday party which was a disaster. Two of the mayor's guests went overboard that night, and one of them drowned. His team hadn't identified the two men responsible and later they abducted Alexavier. Rex tried to resign afterward but he nor his team were guarding Alexavier at that time. Still, Rex felt responsible since the two incidents were related.

Alexavier hadn't blamed him or his team. But Rex understood how important Olivia and Lucas were to the mayor and that guarding the man's family surpassed guarding him any day. It didn't matter that Alexavier had agreed for Rex to leave them alone while he picked up Olivia's new phone. Rex blamed himself and deserved to be fired.

"None of us could have predicted she would leave," Alexavier said. He'd never known Rex to be careless, and he didn't blame him, but was angry about the situation.

"I regret to tell you that she was damned convincing, boss." Rex was in Olivia's duplex and looking around for any sign of her planned exit.

Alexavier had to agree with Rex. Olivia wielded power over men that even she didn't completely realize. He'd suspected something was wrong. She wasn't herself when they spoke on the phone, but he had no idea that she was working on a plan to run away.

"You've checked the house?"

"Still in it. Nothing is missing except Miss Dufrene's purse and car."

"They're missing, Rex. My girl and Lucas are gone." Alexavier ran his hand over his dark whiskers. He shaved every single morning, and by early evening, he needed to shave again. Olivia liked his razor stubble. She'd said it was sexy. Why hadn't she told him the truth when he'd talked to her? He would have moved heaven and Earth to help Olivia, yet she pretended everything was fine. He'd figured once he saw her face to face, she'd admit whatever was concerning her.

Alexavier was wrong.

He sped across the bridge to her place because he needed to see for himself that she was gone. Then he was going straight to the diner because if anyone knew what was going on, it was Miss Lynn, who clearly was the one and only person Olivia trusted.

Chapter Twenty-Five

Alexavier walked through the small duplex making sure to check every room. He saw Olivia's toiletries missing as well as Lucas' things. If he hadn't spent time with them there, he wouldn't have noticed the little things. Like the fact that Olivia had extra shampoo and Lucas had more than one toothbrush. However, she favored the coconut-scented variety for her hair that was gone, and Lucas liked his racecar toothbrush, which was also missing. He noticed that Olivia had taken her favorite blanket, a small pillow, and a few clothes but left everything else. Lucas took a small stack of his favorite books and left the rest. He also didn't bring any toys, but the remote-controlled car Alexavier had bought him was gone.

Alexavier couldn't explain it, but he knew they weren't coming back. One more time, he had Rex go through minute by minute what had happened that morning with Olivia. Then he headed to the Main Street Grocery, better known as Miss Lynn's Diner.

The new waitress, Daisy, greeted him when he walked through the door, but Alexavier didn't speak. He walked directly up to the lunch counter, and when Miss Lynn turned around and saw him, she put her hand over her chest. "What's happened? Is Olivia hurt? Lucas?"

There was no mistaking her concern, and it told him that she didn't know Olivia had left town. Alexavier shrugged and then sat down at the bar. Miss Lynn was his plan A and B.

She reached across the counter and patted his hand. "Mayor, what's happened?" He explained that Olivia took Lucas and left town while she sent Rex on the errand to pick up her phone.

"I think she'd planned it all day. I clearly gave her the excuse she needed to get rid of Rex so she could slip out undetected. I just don't know why." Alexavier stared at Miss Lynn, and she felt so sorry for him and Olivia that she wanted to cry.

True love was a gift. Miss Lynn knew that personally. She also knew that Olivia had never experienced love. She might not have even recognized it when Alexavier showered her in it.

Lynn had to help them.

"I should've known," Lynn said, being hard on herself for not recognizing the pain Olivia was in all day. She thought about the extra hug Olivia had given her and then how she had Lucas give her another big hug before they left.

"They were saying goodbye to me."

"What?" Alexavier watched the older woman swipe a few tears away with her apron.

"This afternoon. Before Olivia left, she hugged me again and thanked me for something, then she had Lucas hug me one more time. She even blew kisses at me from the doorway before they walked to her car. How did I not see what she was doing?"

Alexavier reached out and held Miss Lynn's hand. "She didn't want you to know."

Miss Lynn stood up and walked around the counter to sit next to Alexavier while Daisy took care of the diner customers. "She's scared. While Brent was here, I thought she was mad at him, but it wasn't anger. She's afraid of something happening to Lucas."

Alexavier appreciated the love Miss Lynn had for Olivia and

Lucas. Olivia wasn't close to anyone except her friends from Maisonville, which made the fact that she'd left town even more confusing.

Miss Lynn watched Alexavier war with his feelings. "That Brent is no good, I tell you. I knew it the first time I laid eyes on him, and not a thing has changed in that man since."

Alexavier smiled at her. She seemed to love everyone. He could tell she liked him from the start. But Miss Lynn was sharp and called it as she saw it with people.

"Olivia told me he'd stopped by to discuss the child support he owed her."

"That's highly unlikely. Brent had a knife and bullied his way through the front door when I unlocked it. He caught me off guard, but it won't happen again."

He watched as Miss Lynn pulled a very small silver handgun out of the double lining of her apron.

"I've gotten comfortable here over the years and keep it under the counter. Brent reminded me that it doesn't do much good to keep it down there when someone rushes up behind me in the early morning hours."

Alexavier could see the gleam in her eyes. Lynn reminded him a bit of his mother and he loved her spirit.

"So, what about the knife, Miss Lynn."

"Oh, well, he waved it around a little while talking to me, but when Olivia came in, he hid it under the table. I warned her he was off, so she kept calm as she sat with him. Then the damn fool stabbed it into the table. He told her things were bad. Worse than before. Apparently, he's a gambler and owes some money."

"Have you seen him like that before? Was Olivia upset? What does that have to do with her and Lucas? I mean, sure, he can't pay her child support but hell, I could take care of them." Alexavier tried to stay focused. He had so many unanswered questions. Like where could she have gone? She didn't have much money or any credit cards. How would he ever find her?

Miss Lynn was as upset as he was. She blamed herself for not kicking Brent out of the diner before Olivia got there. "You don't think he did something to her?" she asked nervously.

"No, ma'am. I think she left before that could happen." He stood and buttoned up his jacket.

"Don't give up on her, Alexavier."

He saw the desperation in Miss Lynn's eyes.

"Don't worry, Miss Lynn. I'm going to find our girl."

He kissed Lynn on the cheek and then stormed out the front door of the diner, with Rex following behind him.

Outside in the parking lot, Alexavier stopped next to his SUV, facing Rex. "I need you to track down Olivia's ex so we can have a chat. He's in some trouble, and it sounds like he's indebted to the local mob. Bring Cage and Reaper with you. Give me a call when you have him. I don't know where she is, but we need to know what she's running from in order to figure that out."

Rex understood. The mob wouldn't easily let him pick up one of their stooges. They couldn't take a chance on Brent squealing and would snatch him off the street before Rex or his team could find him.

"And Rex, I don't have to tell you how important this is, right?"

That was the zinger. Rex blamed himself no matter what Alexavier had said. Hearing his boss and friend, Alexavier, remind him how important the case was, took something out of him. Rex nodded at Alexavier and then headed back to the city. It would be a busy night if Brent was running around with or from the mob. They'd gone underground since the mayor hired his great new police chief, who attacked crime in the city like a villain. But they were watching and forever waiting in the wings in case they could jump back in the spotlight and run things again.

Alexavier had been patient, but if organized crime was trying to make a comeback in New Orleans, it was time to shut them down. He knew the best way to stop organized crime was to interfere with their ability to extort money. That and arrest every last one of the bastards on any charges they could press against them.

They'd threatened his city and his woman for the last time. But first, he needed Rex to grab Brent.

❧

ALEXAVIER HEADED to his parent's house. He'd had a long day of duty as the mayor, but his adrenaline had been pumping like a freight train since he got the news about Olivia and Lucas. He needed to recharge.

When he walked through the door, his mother was waiting for him. She yelled for his father, who came running. "What's wrong, Alex?" she asked, putting her hands on his face, and staring into his eyes as if she could read his mind.

He leaned down and kissed his mother on both cheeks. They walked into the large kitchen where she'd been cooking when his father stepped into the room.

"Son?"

Alexavier walked directly over to his father and hugged him.

Looking at both of them, he finally answered. "I'm fine. It's Olivia and Lucas. They're in trouble, and I don't know how to help them."

His father had a seat near the counter, and his mother twisted her hands in her apron repeatedly. "Where are they?" she asked, wondering why he didn't bring them to her. She'd already accepted them, and once she'd done that, she had expectations.

He smiled at his mother. Before he could answer, his Auntie Francesca, uncle, and two cousins showed up. Clearly, his mother called reinforcements as soon as she heard he was upset and coming over.

They all had seats as his mother served pasta and bread around the large kitchen island.

"I don't know where Olivia and Lucas have gone. Her ex showed up, and I think he's in some trouble. She sounded upset over the phone, but when I asked her about it, she said she was fine. She made some excuses and said she'd explain later. If she's in some kind of trouble, why wouldn't she tell me? Let me help her?"

Alexavier needed his family. He'd been young and foolish when he'd met his first wife, Victoria. She didn't like how they butted into the couple's business and had told them on more than one occasion to stay out of their marriage.

His family hadn't liked Victoria from the beginning, but he hadn't listened. It was a miserable marriage, and he couldn't take back his arrogance from long ago. But he wouldn't make that same mistake again.

Alexavier's mother reached across the table to hold his hand. Her eyes were filled with love. "Alex, she's a strong woman. She's not had anyone strong enough to rely on before you. It will take some time for her to accept it."

His cousin Theresa nodded. "And her son is everything to her. She might have come to you if it had only involved her, but not when little Lucas was also in trouble. She's fierce and will forget her own health and happiness for him."

Alexavier looked at Theresa. She was a hot mess on her best days but could make more sense than anyone when it was necessary.

"Where would she go? She doesn't have anyone. She doesn't have a lot of money."

His father put his fork down. He was a man of few words. It was always the family joke that he wasn't quiet, he frankly couldn't get a word in with all the women. Everyone looked at him as he coughed and wiped his mouth with his napkin.

Alexavier's mother swatted his dad with her cloth napkin so he would hurry up. "Son. You know her better than anyone. Where is her family? Where's she from?"

Alexavier shook his head. Olivia didn't talk about her childhood, family, or hometown. She only told him the basics. She was from a small town and estranged from her parents since she was a teenager. Most of the information he had on her came from Rex.

In an attempt to protect Alexavier, Rex ran a background

check on Olivia. There wasn't much information, but he'd found out she was from St. Marksville. She'd been born there and graduated high school from there too. Her parents still owned the house Olivia grew up in but had bought another house in Florida before she graduated high school. She also had an older sister, Beth, but she lived in Tennessee. Olivia didn't mention friends from her hometown. It was as if she hadn't lived before moving to New Orleans.

"She doesn't have anyone. No family. She grew up in a tiny town called St. Marksville. The only thing she ever said about it was that it was a one-stoplight town, and a team of wild horses couldn't drag her back."

"Did she have any other choices?" his auntie asked.

Cousin Theresa shook her head. "It wouldn't take wild horses if she tried to protect Lucas."

Had Brent not given her any other options?

The entire Regalia family started talking at the same time and eating like it was their last meal when Alexavier's phone rang.

It was late, but Rex and his men had located Brent's apartment and had some news. He sent an address to Alexavier so he could meet them in the French Quarter but didn't explain further. Alexavier knew that wasn't a good sign. When Rex and his men were quiet, things usually were at their worst. Had Brent been hurt, or was the mob hot on their heels? Alexavier wasn't sure, but knew he needed to get to them as fast as possible.

Chapter Twenty-Six

Olivia woke up with the sun. She'd removed the filthy curtains the night before, and when the moon beamed through the broken slats of the blinds, it didn't seem like a big deal. However, sunrise was a different story. She peaked at the glaring light with one eye and tried to pull the covers over her head. The old quilt was threadbare, and it didn't help.

Dragging herself down the hallway, she peeked in on Lucas. He was sound asleep, which gave her some peace. In the early morning hour, she felt raw and vulnerable over the decisions she'd made that led her back to St. Marksville. After swearing she'd never come back, she had to swallow her pride and would probably have to beg her way into the judgmental community. It was for Lucas. He depended on her, and she would protect him with her life. Somehow, she'd find her strength for him.

However, early in the morning hours, she missed Alexavier, Miss Lynn, Sydney, and Ryan. She wanted her routine of having breakfast with Lucas, seeing him off to school, and then heading to the diner. She longed for the happy little town of Maisonville and how it seemed to give her hope. But no matter how much she missed everyone and everything she'd left behind, it didn't change the circumstances that led her back to her hometown.

She'd known Brent was a bad decision when she went out with him. He showed off how important he was by taking her to places he frequented and proving that everyone knew his name. He had no idea that she'd grown up where everyone knew everything about her. It wasn't that cool. Still, she went out with Brent for a few weeks because he had a good sense of humor. He'd seemed exciting at first, but it quickly ended when she realized he drank excessively and gambled even more.

Reckless behavior had no place in her life. Olivia understood at an early age that to keep safe, she needed control. Unfortunately, she had a weak moment and spent one night with Brent. Who gets pregnant after one time?

She'd been on the pill for two years and hadn't realized what was going on with her body until she missed her period. You could set your watch by her cycle which always came every 29 days. Overwhelmed at the thought of having a baby, Olivia couldn't stop the intense love she instantly felt. She loved that kid more and more every day, and while she wished she'd never met Brent, she wouldn't trade Lucas for anything.

She took a deep breath and headed to find the old French coffee press in one of the kitchen cabinets that her parents had left behind years ago. Olivia had never used it before, but back then, she hadn't needed coffee. At five o'clock in the morning, it was the only thing that got her moving.

Caffeine would motivate her to get the house thoroughly cleaned. Plus, it might give her the nerve to venture out and pick up the extra supplies she needed once Lucas was up.

She carried her coffee outside onto the patio and jumped when she saw Miss Goings next door staring at her through the window. The older woman hadn't changed a bit since Olivia had moved away. She strangely looked the same age and still loved to watch everything Olivia did in and outside of her house.

Olivia covered the old lawn chair with a towel and wiped off the table with a wet wipe as the older woman kept watching. Did she ever sleep?

Finally, when Olivia finished cleaning her space and had a seat, she turned and waved at the older woman, and she twisted her face so tight that Olivia couldn't stop the laughter that bubbled up inside of her.

Things hadn't changed in the stuck-up little town, but she sure had, and it wasn't going to break her down anymore.

In the early morning, she wondered what Alexavier was doing and then felt the sting in her heart. He woke up at five every day during the week, so he could get his workout in before he showered and headed into the office.

Was he thinking about her like she was thinking about him?

❦

ALEXAVIER HADN'T BEEN to bed. It was five in the morning, and he couldn't get Olivia and Lucas off his mind.

Truthfully, he hadn't stopped worrying about them since he got Rex's phone call the day before telling him that Olivia and Lucas were gone. After he'd walked through their small duplex and then spoken with his own family, it had gotten worse.

Rex's next phone call sent Alexavier to meet with him and his team, Cage and Reaper. They'd gone to Brent's apartment and found the place ransacked. Not like someone was looking for something but more like they were there to destroy the area, so it was uninhabitable. It didn't look like he'd slept there in a while, but they had some clues to report back to the mayor.

The solid iron gate was open, and Alexavier headed down the dark walkway into a bricked courtyard off Royale Street. He quickly found the green-painted door and knocked three times.

Reaper opened up with a big smile. "Hey, Boss."

Alexavier shook his head. He'd told Rex, Cage, and Reaper to call him by his first name. They mostly called him Boss or Chief. The three men had watched his back more times than he could count, and he finally agreed that they could call him anything they wanted. He was glad the nickname wasn't as bad as Reaper's.

He shook Reaper's hand before walking inside. The unassuming house on the outside hid what a gem it was on the inside. He'd noticed the fountain and intricate brickwork in the courtyard, even in the dark. But Alexavier was surprised to find the house's interior was just as impressive. There was an exposed brick wall on one side of the open living room and kitchen area. Dark painted cabinets and cement countertops that looked designer-made instead of remodeled by an ex-commando. Reaper's home was a work of art waiting on a home improvement magazine to find it.

Rex and Cage were both sitting on a large leather sofa but stood to shake his hand when he walked into the room. Cage offered to get him a beer, but he declined. They hadn't found Brent, and Alexavier figured the news wasn't good. He needed to be clear-headed and focused to come up with his next course of action after they explained what they had found.

"We split up so we could track him down faster. Brent made his rounds in the city, and we had a lot of ground to cover in a short amount of time," Rex told him. "The construction jobs weren't in progress like he told Olivia. I went to each location, and they were destroyed. Remember the arson fires from a few weeks ago? Those were his construction sites," Rex said.

Cage leaned forward. "He'd been frequenting a strip club in the quarter and fooling around with one of the girls. She said he had changed in the past month and no longer could afford her. When she wouldn't dance for him for free, he lost his temper. The bouncer threw him out on his ass. He fought with the bouncer and then waited for the club manager one night and beat the hell out of him. That was nine days ago."

"I found the underground card-house where he'd been gambling. He'd won a good bit of money, and they said he went to Harrah's casino downtown to buy into some of the high roller games. He'd bragged that he was moving to the big leagues. He lost it all there within two weeks. That was when he started borrowing more money than he could pay back." Reaper opened his bottle of beer and took a long drink before he continued. "Joey Giordano owns the place. It seems they let Brent get indebted, so he would have to work for them. Word on the street was that Brent had worked for them before."

"So, you think Brent refused to work for them again?" Alexavier hadn't expected to hear Brent had joined the underground mob. Joey Giordano was small-time. His father had been head of the most prominent crime family in the city, but he'd died of a massive heart attack six years ago while attending a concert in the park. He'd been dancing with his wife one minute, and the next, he'd dropped dead. Joey had only been out of college a few years and didn't seem to have his father's business sense. The crime family had aged out of business mostly and only enjoyed the romance associated with their bygone glory days. Joey owned businesses, but they appeared legit, and he didn't seem to have any local leaders or politicians helping him. Of course, the district attorney was famous for prosecuting crooked business owners and politicians with vigor. Coupled with the Police Chief and the fact that Alexavier had given them the money they needed to get the work done, crime was locked down in the city.

Rex shook his head. "I don't think it would have insulted Brent's delicate moral sensibilities if that's what you're asking. I mean, he certainly didn't have any other career opportunities, and he'd run with Joey and his cousin for several years back when Joey's old man was still controlling things."

Alexavier scrubbed his face with his hands and then looked at Rex. "Then explain to me why they would go after Olivia and Lucas? It seems to me that since she left him six years ago, they wouldn't hurt her as a way to get back at Brent. Wouldn't they go directly after Brent?"

Reaper nodded. "Exactly what we thought, boss. I wouldn't be surprised if Brent was wearing a pair of cement shoes and dropped in the river at this point."

"Dead?" Alexavier didn't want Brent to hurt Olivia and Lucas anymore, but he didn't want the man to be dead. It would upset Olivia and certainly hurt Lucas.

Cage shook his head. "He may not be dead. He could have gone underground. But he's a ghost one way or the other, right now."

Alexavier shook his head. It was the worst news he could have gotten. They'd spent the entire night looking for Olivia's ex and following up with his supposed mob ties. None of it had led them to Brent, and they weren't any closer to finding Olivia and Lucas either.

Rex made a list of all the businesses Joey Giordano owned and who he ran with. Alexavier called the police chief, and in an hour, law enforcement would start raiding every one of those establishments.

Rounding up bad guys was something Alexavier was proud of, but it would be different than when he first took office as mayor. He'd felt like it was personal back then because he'd grown up in the city and loved everything about it. He'd hired law enforcement that loved New Orleans, too, and together, they did whatever it took to clean things up. But this time, stopping gangster activity and running down Brent would be the key to helping Olivia and Lucas. They felt like his family and making them safe was his responsibility, and it didn't get more personal.

Chapter Twenty-Seven

Olivia drank three cups of coffee before Lucas woke up. She'd wiped down everything in the living room, removed the old blinds with a screwdriver, and rehung the curtains she'd washed.

Lucas wrapped his arms around her waist when he walked into the room.

"Morning, buddy. Did you sleep well?"

He nodded his head. "I didn't know where I was when I woke up. At first, I thought we were at Alexavier's place." He wiped his face and looked sad.

Olivia wished they were at Alexavier's house too, but she couldn't admit that to Lucas. This was their new life, and she needed him to be happy.

"Nope, this is our new adventure, Lucas. Do you want to go pick out some paint for your room today? I thought we could drag some of this old furniture and stuff to the curb and maybe head to the hardware store?"

Lucas shrugged. "I'm hungry."

"Let's get you some cereal, and after you eat, we can head out to pick up that paint. You're going to help me paint, right?"

That got Lucas to smile a little as he nodded, and it lightened

Olivia's mood too. It would take a while for them to settle in, and paint was the cheapest way to make the place their own.

It took Olivia and Lucas a little longer than she'd expected to carry all the trash to the curb. She ignored two men who came outside to roll trashcans to the curb, too, then stood in the street talking about her while they pointed her way. She didn't remember their names, but they'd lived there forever like her folks.

"Do you know them, mama?" Lucas asked. The neighbors were still outside and watched Olivia and her son when they pulled out of the driveway to head to the hardware store in her old car.

She waved to the men as she passed them and loved the shocked looks on their faces. "I don't remember their names, but since we just moved in, let's be polite, baby."

Lucas didn't wave to the men, and she heard him grumble under his breath, "They're not polite, staring."

She couldn't help the smirking because he was definitely her son. Learning to stop cursing was one thing but teaching him to stop smirking would be another level she wasn't sure she could master. It was part of her genetic makeup, and she was convinced it was part of Lucas' too. She could only hope that the hardware store would be easier to handle.

It didn't take Lucas but a few minutes to pick out the color he liked. "This is the color at Alexavier's house, right?"

Olivia nodded. It was a white linen color and not what she'd expected from him. "Yes. You sure you want to use that color, kiddo?"

"Of course. If Alexavier likes it, then I like it."

Olivia nodded her head and tried not to tear up. Lucas missed Alexavier as much as she did, and it was hard not to think about the man every second.

As they neared the counter, Lucas added, "Besides, I want to make sure he likes our new house when he comes to visit, so maybe he will stay with us."

Olivia bit her bottom lip so she could control her emotions.

She would have to tell Lucas that she and Alexavier weren't together anymore.

Trying to concentrate on something else, Olivia looked around the small home improvement store as they walked toward the checkout counter. She saw Mr. Robichaux standing there and suddenly all thoughts of her life in New Orleans and Maisonville fled her mind.

"Well, well, well. I never thought I'd see you back in this town again." He was a deacon at the church she used to attend. He'd watched her grow up and then treated her like trash. Clearly, he was about to say something more, but Lucas stepped out from behind her and put two paint brushes on the counter.

Lucas looked exactly like her but with brown eyes. Mr. Robichaux froze. "This your boy?"

Olivia's mouth went dry. She wished she hadn't brought Lucas to this horrible place. If anyone said one awful thing to her son, she was going to mama bear her way through them, and in St. Marksville, that meant she would certainly go to jail. Even the local sheriff was on the town's side regarding Olivia Dufrene.

Lucas hadn't read the situation and stepped closer to the counter and held out his hand to shake Mr. Robichaux's hand. "Hi. I'm Lucas."

Olivia stood frozen as Mr. Robichaux reached behind the counter and pulled out a lollipop so he could hand it to Lucas. The man smiled as he used to at her when she was a young girl. "Please to meet you, Lucas. Doing some painting, I see."

Lucas told him all about painting his new room and cleaning up his mom's childhood home. Mr. Robichaux was soaking it all in, and Olivia could imagine how he would tell all the others everything he'd learned. But he was genuine and kind to Lucas. He smiled the whole time he spoke and even told Lucas he had a firm biblical name. "You know Lucas or Luke in the bible was a beloved physician. He was a scholar and wrote beautifully. I bet you're smart too."

"I make all A's in school," Lucas said, then he thanked Mr. Robichaux for the lollipop.

Olivia was shocked over the kind exchange, and, with a half-smile, stepped up to pay for the items they'd picked out. Mr. Robichaux didn't speak to her except to tell her the total price.

Olivia handed him cash as he looked up at her. He counted out her change and then offered to carry her paint to the car. She was flustered, and before she could decline, he had the bags in his hands and walked out beside Lucas.

"Where's your dad, Lucas?" he asked. Olivia had wondered how long it would take for him or someone else in town to pry into their business.

Lucas thoughtfully answered Mr. Robichaux. "Oh, he's still in New Orleans. He works there, you know. But we are getting the house all fixed up to surprise him."

Olivia bit her bottom lip to keep the emotion out of her voice. "Lucas. We don't need to bother Mr. Robichaux with all our family business."

Mr. Robichaux put the bags into the trunk of Olivia's car while she opened Lucas' door so he could climb inside. When she turned around, the older man was still looking at her.

She met his eyes but didn't speak. He nodded his head and then whispered. "Nice boy you have there, Olivia."

She nodded at him and leaned against her car as he walked back into his small store. Mr. Robichaux's son, Mark, had been in her grade throughout school. They'd been friends as small children, but her parents and his had been strict. Once they became teenagers, they weren't allowed to hang out. She'd thought that Mark would ask her out in high school, but once she'd started getting into trouble, he'd avoided her.

She'd been labeled a hellion by everyone in town, and everyone shunned her. So why was Mr. Robichaux being nice to her and her son?

As she buckled her seatbelt, she could see Lucas watching her in the rearview mirror when she looked up.

"Hey, Lucas. Why did you say that to Mr. Robichaux?"

He shrugged his shoulders, and she thought for a minute that he wouldn't answer her. "Well, we are fixing up the house."

"Yes, baby, but your father won't live with us."

"I know. I like to pretend sometimes."

Olivia took a deep breath. She'd had the same conversation with Lucas before when kids from his school had a mom, a dad, plus grandparents come to watch their class sing Christmas songs or put on a play. "You and I are a great team, buddy. And your father and I are friends. You know that, right? I mean, families come in all shapes and sizes."

"I know, mom. I wasn't pretending about Brent."

She watched him smile at her. He'd been calling his dad, Brent, for the past few months, and she hadn't corrected him. It was kind of funny and made Lucas sound like a little adult. He giggled and then whispered loudly because that was the only way Lucas knew how to whisper, "I was pretending about Alexavier."

Closing her eyes, Olivia took a deep breath before starting the car. She shouldn't have moved back to St. Marksville, and she shouldn't have let Lucas start calling his father by his first name. And for the life of her, she shouldn't have allowed Lucas to meet Alexavier.

She was making so many mistakes and had to try and be better. Be stronger. It was rare for her to go on a date with anyone. Forget about letting them meet her kid. Just her luck, Alexavier up and turned out to be a great man. Not only was her heart breaking, but soon, so would her son's.

§

ALEXAVIER WANTED to buy his police chief a superhero cape and demand it be worn at all press conferences.

Patrick Morales was in his late 30s but had been a marine for eight years and then a police officer for nine before being promoted to chief. He was organized, tough but fair, and above all else, a leader.

Alexavier called him at eight that morning, and by nine a.m., he had a task force on the move and raiding Joey Giordano's businesses. They'd found stolen property at one of his garages and, before noon, obtained a search warrant for Joey's home. The raid on his house resulted in them arresting him for suspicion of organized crime and possibly the disappearance of Brent.

The local police called in the FBI, and what had been suspicious behavior was now elevated to a federal investigation that crossed state lines.

It hadn't taken the local news long to catch on to the story, and when Alexavier tried to visit the police chief, they accosted him with questions.

"Mayor Regalia is it true that Joey Giordano is in custody?" a short brown-haired reporter asked from the front of the crowd.

"Did you meet with Chief Morales this morning and prompt the raids to all of the Giordano family businesses?" A man with a giant microphone yelled at him before he could answer the first question.

"Can you tell us how long the FBI has been investigating Joey Giordano?" The brown-haired man asked next.

Mayor Regalia held up his hands and smiled his charming politician smile. "I'm afraid you all will have to wait for an official statement from Chief Morales' department. I'm only here to see the chief and have a cup of coffee."

Several people in the crowd laughed. Alexavier had become famous for an Instagram page called Regalia and his coffee. Someone had set it up early during his first campaign for mayor. He didn't even know who was doing it or if it was only one person. But pictures of him drinking coffee started popping up on the app, and before he knew about it, there were hundreds of different pictures of him drinking coffee in various places around New Orleans.

At last count, there were over three thousand pictures of Alexavier, and the page was followed by thousands of people. Sometimes the pictures made the evening news. A "Where's Mayor Regalia" tagline was added at some point and had become locally famous as a New Orleansesque Where's Waldo.

He gave the press a relaxed smile and then waved to the crowd before he turned and went in search of Chief Morales.

"Alexavier," Patrick Morales said as he waved to him. "We're over here."

Chapter Twenty-Eight

Chief Morales explained to the mayor that the FBI assisted his task force with the morning raids. The Giordano family owned more establishments than they'd previously known about and were spread outside of his jurisdiction. "It was a collaborative effort like I've never seen," he said.

Alexavier listened as he read off the list of places. "There was a garage on Chef Menteur, two strip clubs; one in the Quarter and one in the East, a card club in the Warehouse District, a restaurant in the Bywater, a pizzeria in Fat City and another in Kenner, and several rental properties in Mid-City and Metairie." He grinned, "And a tile store on the Westbank."

Alexavier had known about the card house and the strip clubs, but he had no idea Joey Giordano had been that busy. He'd known they couldn't eradicate the Giordano Mob Family completely, but everything they had on the family said they were no longer a real problem.

When Mayor Regalia was first elected, his most extensive plan was to clean up crime and corruption starting with the mob. The Giordano's were wealthy and had plenty of influential people in the city doing their bidding or at the very least looking the other way whenever they conducted business.

It was the reason Mayor Regalia fought so hard for Patrick Morales. He was confident Chief Morales would be up for the task, but before they could take the crime boss down, Oscar Giordano had a heart attack and died.

Oscar would have been a formidable adversary because he was well-liked in the community. He'd grown up in New Orleans in the fifties and kept tight control over every facet of his business.

It was because of Oscar Giordano's tight reign that no one was able to pick up where he left off. When he dropped dead, The Giordano Mob Family business did too.

Chief Morales said it wasn't dead, only dormant, and that was why they kept an eye on Oscar's only son, Joey Giordano.

Until Olivia and Lucas had been threatened, and Brent had gone missing, there hadn't been a single reason to look any harder at Joey Giordano. Other than the card house, all the other businesses were legitimate, and he'd kept out of trouble.

Had Joey been more cunning than they thought?

Alexavier ran his hand over the thick stubble on his face. He hadn't shaved since the day before when he was with Olivia. He couldn't believe she'd been gone for only a day and a half. He looked up at Chief Morales. "Any word about Brent?"

The chief shook his head. "The feds are in there with Joey now. He's admitted some impropriety with the card house. Said it had been his father's business and that he had inherited it. Some of the old fellas from his father's day still go there, so he let it alone. He's swearing that he had nothing to do with any stolen car or goods. Says the rest of the businesses are legit and that he's been straight for years."

"What did they find?"

Morales shook his head. "They're working him pretty hard in there, but honestly, I don't think they have enough to charge him. They are bluffing and trying to get him to turn on whoever is running the family business his father built because he's certainly not doing it."

No one was genuinely concerned about Joey taking over his

father's business. He'd been a man-child who came home from college with a lot of playfulness still driving him. Joey loved fast cars, playing dice, and women. Still, he was his father's only son and had grown up around the family business from childhood. His father had been the biggest mob boss in New Orleans' history.

Alexavier stared at Chief Morales, not believing what he was saying about Joey Giordano. They'd raided all those businesses and found nothing?

"Let me rephrase that, Mayor. We didn't find anything that we could arrest him for, and Giordano knows it. The stolen stuff at the garage belonged to one of the mechanics who bought them hot off someone else. There was some drug paraphernalia at the garages and the strip clubs, but it looked like it had been in the employee locker room areas. Nothing big enough to hold him and no evidence of anything bigger."

Alexavier listened to every word. "What about Brent's apartment?"

"He denies ever being there. He does own the building but offered up the surveillance tapes for us to take a look at and verify he and his men haven't been there."

"Do you think he's innocent?"

Chief Morales turned and motioned Alexavier to follow him into his private office. Morales shut the door behind them and had a seat at his desk. When Mayor Regalia sat down, Patrick leaned forward. "Joey's definitely been trying to run the family business. But he's not the asshole his father was behind closed doors. The man probably doesn't have to be either because his father was smart enough to use his relationships with local authorities to wash his money so he could invest it legally. Freaking Joey is a trust fund kid. He doesn't have to do anything illegal. Once his father died, Joey could have left here and reinvented himself. He just loved his father and couldn't do that. He's playing at being a mobster but not doing anything serious that could put him behind bars."

"You don't think he did something to Brent?"

The chief shrugged his shoulders. "He says he's friends with Brent. He went to school with him."

Alexavier stood up and paced the floor. Olivia fled because she was scared for her son and herself. That was real. Brent was gambling again and told her it was worse than before. He'd frightened her, again. If Brent was Joey Giordano's friend, then why would Joey threaten to hurt Brent's ex-girlfriend and kid?

Alexavier's head was swimming with all the information and then all the questions he had when Chief Morales stood up. "Let's go talk to the feds. They're done."

Thirty minutes later, the federal agents and their department chief explained they didn't have enough to charge or even hold Joey Giordano. "He's smart. He's covered all his bases. We can't hold him or charge him with anything, yet..." was all Alexavier heard.

The men shook hands, and once the feds left, Alexavier asked Chief Morales if he could talk to Joey. "He's free to go. So, I guess it's up to him," Chief Morales said before leading Alexavier to the room where they'd all questioned the suspect.

Alexavier grabbed a bottle of water before walking into the room with Joey Giordano handing him the unopened drink.

"Thanks for seeing me," Alexavier said. Chief Morales had told him he was free to go and gave Joey a choice of whether or not to stay and talk to the mayor.

Strangely he agreed to stay.

"Well, since I was in the neighborhood, figured it was the neighborly thing to do," Joey said with a laugh. "Nice to see you, Mayor Regalia."

Joey Giordano opened his water bottle and took a drink before twisting the cap back on tightly. He'd been questioned for several hours but didn't look worn out or rumpled. He had a smile on his face that made his golden-brown eyes glow. He was Italian like the mayor but had lighter hair and eyes.

They didn't know each other personally. Joey was a good ten

years younger than Alexavier, but Alexavier had cousins that knew Joey well. The Giordano's threw money around, and it didn't always sit well with the other alpha men in his pack. Nevertheless, Joey was a happy guy with a smug demeanor.

"I'll get right to it," Alexavier said, not wanting to waste any more time. "Do you know Olivia Dufrene and her son Lucas?"

"Can't say that I do."

Alexavier observed Joey's face looking for any sign of recognition. Either Joey was cold and more calculating than he'd given him credit, or he honestly didn't know them.

Keeping his calm, Alexavier pulled out a picture of Olivia and Lucas at the park when he'd taken them on their first date. Joey Giordano stared at the picture but still nothing.

Next, Alexavier showed him the picture that had been in the newspaper of him and Lucas walking back from Cafe du Monde. It didn't take but a second before Joey smiled and nodded.

"Cute kid. Friend of yours?"

Alexavier remained calm. "You know him." It wasn't a question.

"Yeah."

"Tell me about Brent."

Joey moved his chair back a little when he heard Brent's name. "What do you want to know?"

Alexavier locked eyes with Joey but didn't answer. When negotiating a business deal, he'd learned to stop talking so the other person he was dealing with would fill the silence.

He watched the young Giordano swallow visibly and then ran a hand through his light brown hair. Then he began to talk. "We went to high school together. Been pretty good friends since then. He doesn't know when to reign-in the good time, if you know what I mean."

Alexavier shook his head. "I'm afraid I don't know what you mean."

Joey smirked. "Brent likes to party and sometimes doesn't

know when to stop. I've gotten him out of more than a few scrapes."

"Drinking? Drugs? Gambling? Something worse?" Alexavier asked but never took his eyes off Joey.

"Sure. Brent's not much into drugs, but he can drink like a fish. And he loves to play cards. He also likes the strip club more than most, has a sidepiece there and can't seem to stop showering her with gifts he can't afford."

Alexavier showed Joey the picture of Olivia and Lucas again. "So, you know who they are now?"

Joey nodded. "Don't know how Brent ever got her to go out with him."

"Do you know where she and Lucas are now? How about Brent? When was the last time you saw him?"

Joey leveled his eyes at Alexavier. "Look, man, I know you must have a thing for her. She's a looker, and I don't blame you. But Brent is still an idiot over that girl. He goes to the strip club and fools around, but she's all he talks about. He has some plan to win her back, and he isn't going to take no for an answer."

"You didn't say when you last saw him."

"I don't know. A couple of days or so ago. Brent was being an asshole, and one of my guys had to throw him out of the club."

Alexavier took a deep breath, trying to keep himself together. It felt like he was running in circles, and he was the type of person that could typically get things done. What was he missing? He wasn't any closer to finding Olivia and Lucas. His plan to find Brent hadn't panned out, and now questioning Joey Giordano only made him more frustrated.

"Brent told Olivia that he'd gotten into trouble again with gambling. He said he borrowed more money than he could pay back. Said the men he borrowed from were going to send someone after her and their kid. Like before. He was referring to you. He scared her to death, and she took Lucas and ran."

Joey shook his head. "No way Brent said I would do something to her and her kid. Besides, he's borrowed money from me before, and we settled it between us."

"You may be a better friend to him than he is to you, Joey. Six years ago, two men broke into the apartment when Lucas was a baby and were going to hurt her to teach Brent a lesson for not paying what he owed. He said that was your men and that it would happen again. It terrified her." Alexavier felt his jaw tense as he told Joey how frightened Olivia was about the men coming after her. It killed him to know she was out there running away from danger when he would have protected her.

Joey stood up and pushed the chair back abruptly. He, too, was losing a bit of his self-control. "I don't know what the hell Brent is doing. But I don't hurt women, and I sure as hell don't hurt kids. If Brent did something wrong and I was pissed at him, then why wouldn't I go after him and kick his ass?"

Alexavier shrugged. "I'm simply telling you what he told her. Thought you might be able to shed some light on what was happening."

Joey headed for the door. Apparently, their conversation was over. Before he walked out, he turned to Alexavier. "I've got no beef with that girl or her kid. But I don't like what's been implied about my character. I'm a businessman. Plain and Simple. You better find Brent and question him before I do." Joey Giordano didn't raise his voice or change his easy expression as he spoke. Then, he nodded at Alexavier before turning and walking right out of the New Orleans Police Station.

He may not have known where Olivia, or even Brent were, but one thing for sure, he was not a plain and simple businessman. And Alexavier wasn't any closer to finding Olivia and Lucas.

Chapter Twenty-Nine

Alexavier and Chief Morales discussed the details of the conversation he'd had with Joey Giordano. Things didn't add up, and the only answer was that someone was lying.

Chief Morales didn't want to be the messenger of bad news but had a flaw of being brutally honest. "You're sure about this woman? I mean, Joey Giordano wishes he could follow in his father's footsteps, but he's mostly kept his nose clean. Brent is gambling. While he appears to be addicted to it, the only person he's hurting is himself. Ms. Dufrene wouldn't be the first woman to fake danger for attention?"

"You don't know her, Patrick." Mayor Regalia didn't call the chief by his first name at work. They were friends, but he kept it strictly professional in front of others. It was the tell-tale sign that Alexavier was too personally involved to make a clear decision regarding her.

Chief Morales lowered his voice. "You're right. I don't know her. But I have known some beautiful women in my life who were attracted to power. They would do anything for attention from a powerful man."

Keeping his calm in stressful situations was one of Alexavier's best features. He could hold a placid expression, and underneath that facade, rage with anger. This wasn't one of those times.

Patrick Morales watched as his friend and mentor, Alexavier Regalia clenched his fists, and his neck turned red. Had he ever seen the man angry? "I was simply looking at this from all angles, mayor."

"She's not the angle."

They stood in the middle of the police station staring at one another. Finally, Chief Morales conceded. "Maybe you're right —" before he could finish his sentence, Alexavier stepped closer so only Morales could hear.

"Damn right, I'm right. Olivia Dufrene is one of the sweetest women I've ever met. She's sassy and independent on the outside. It's probably been a defense mechanism from a young age because on the inside, she's soft and a bit fragile. Keep an eye out for Brent and the other eye on Joey Giordano. One of them or hell, both of them are behind this." Mayor Regalia stepped back and straightened his tie and buttoned his jacket before he turned and strode away.

Patrick hadn't seen Alexavier act that way over a woman. Ever. His friend had it bad for the missing Olivia Dufrene, and he hoped for Alexavier's sake that she was the person he thought she was and not involved in the scheme.

OLIVIA AND LUCAS spent most of their day painting his room and then started on the living room. They used old linens she'd planned to throw away as drop cloths and happily removed the dated-looking pictures her parents had hung all over the house.

By the end of the afternoon, they had gotten more done than she'd have ever thought. The light paint that Lucas chose had brightened the place up along with the music and dancing they did while they worked. The house had a lively vibe for the first time.

Olivia cleaned the last paint brush while Lucas showered and tried to scrub as much paint off his hands as possible. They needed some dinner, and she'd promised to check out the bicycles in the garage to see if they could ride them.

She'd hated to leave Lucas' bicycle. However, there were several in decent condition inside the old garage, but she didn't know about the tires.

They ate a quick dinner and then worked together to pump up the tires on two bicycles. Olivia told Lucas they could spray paint his electric red if he wanted, and he laughed.

Riding bicycles seemed like a good idea, but as they rode around the second block, Olivia was ready to drop. She wasn't sure where Lucas got his energy from but decided it was unfair that kids had more than their moms. "Slow down, buddy! I can't pump my legs any faster tonight."

Lucas slowed down for her but laughed at the faces she made at him and the exaggerated pedaling she did on the bicycle.

They rode for half an hour more, then Olivia told him they needed to get home before it got too dark. On the way back, she noticed a dark blue pickup truck that had been parked on their street earlier was now following behind them.

She told Lucas to be the leader, so he wouldn't see her staring at the truck. No matter how hard she tried, she couldn't see the driver through the tinted windows before the truck turned at the next street.

The mob guys didn't know where she grew up, and there was no way they would travel that far only to teach Brent a lesson.

Would they?

Still, she made sure to lock the house up tight and closed all the blinds once they were in for the night. Then she and Lucas both cleaned up and got ready for bed.

Lucas pulled out his books and performed the first one for her as Alexavier did for him. It was entertaining and made Olivia laugh. Next, she read to him, making sure to use different voices for the farm animals which impressed Lucas.

When they finished all the books, Lucas hugged her tightly before turning over toward the wall. "You're getting better at the voices, mom."

"Thanks, kiddo." She smiled at the compliment.

"No one is as good as Alex, but when he gets here, he can read them with me."

There would never be a good time for her to tell Lucas, and she had to Mom-up to admit the truth. "Kiddo, I've been meaning to talk to you about Alexavier."

He turned back over to look at her.

"You and I needed to move here, but Alexavier is the Mayor of New Orleans, and he won't be able to come."

Lucas shook his head. "No, mom. I know he's busy. We talked about it. But he likes us. Really likes us. He is coming." His confident little face made her want to cry. Lucas snuggled under his covers and closed his eyes again.

Stunned over his words, Olivia lay there. Lucas was so sure of himself, and she didn't have the heart to disagree with him. She, too, wanted it to be true, and was there any real harm in pretending for a little while longer?

Alexavier got into his car before he checked his phone. He was furious but not at Chief Morales. The chief's comments were his way of looking out for Alexavier. His friend hadn't met Olivia, or he would have known better.

The situation wouldn't feel so dire if they had located Brent. The more time passed, the worse it looked for Brent's wellbeing. Whoever was after Olivia and Lucas might have settled the score with Brent instead. The worst part of it all, Alexavier wasn't any closer to finding answers or locating Olivia and Lucas.

It was getting late, and the mayor needed to check in with his assistant to clear his schedule further. He was running on zero sleep and needed to go home and recharge.

It was midnight when he heard his phone ringing. He'd slept like the dead.

"You're not checking your messages anymore?" Rex asked.

"Yes. Been busy, Rex." Alexavier explained everything they had done, from raiding Joey Giordano's businesses and home to sitting down with him to ask the hard questions.

Rex was amazed that Mayor Regalia could get that much done in a day, especially without any sleep. But the man always surprised him. "You don't think Joey Giordano is involved, do you?"

"I wouldn't say he's completely innocent. There's something he's not telling, but I don't think he knows anything about Olivia and Lucas. He also doesn't seem to know where Brent is, and if Brent is smart, he'll keep it that way."

Alexavier had slept on his couch and felt much better after a few hours of rest. He listened to Rex's point of view on the Giordano information and then remembered that he'd said he'd called him earlier.

"What else have you got, Rex?"

After chasing down every lead they could on Brent, Rex and his team decided to dig further into Olivia's past. In the process, they came across something that he'd wanted to tell Alexavier but now dreaded.

"I'm afraid it's bad news, boss."

Chapter Thirty

Sunrays woke Olivia up again at five in the morning. She'd rehung the curtains in the living room and thought that would prevent the sun from beaming through, but they were thin and no match for the bright early morning light.

She threw off her blanket and slugged her way into the kitchen to make coffee. While the grounds were steeping in the French press, she went to peek in on Lucas. It was so easy to love that kid. He slept like an angel and seemed to roll with whatever life threw at them. Honestly, the move should have shaken him up more than it did, and she was thankful to see him sleep comfortably.

Olivia returned to make her cup of coffee and thought about all the upheavals they'd had in Lucas' seven years. He didn't remember the move from New Orleans or the separation from Brent. But Brent was always unreliable, and whenever he didn't show up for his visitation weekends or canceled a trip to the zoo, aquarium, fishing, or whatever he fake promised their boy, Lucas acted relieved not to have to go. It was probably the reason why Lucas had latched on to Alexavier so quickly. Right?

She thought about how comfortable Alexavier was with Lucas and incredibly sweet. For a man without children of his own, he sure had a comfortability that she hadn't expected. Of course, Alexavier seemed to do everything better than most people. He kissed her better and loved her body better.

Olivia shook her head and tried to stop thinking about Alex. Lucas was so sure he was coming to them that it had made her hope for it, too. It was silly. She was silly. She'd been on her own since she was seventeen and didn't have time to fantasize about things that couldn't be.

She looked around the house and saw how much progress she and Lucas had made. Her kid had a strong work ethic like her, and they could move mountains as a team. However, she didn't want him to have to work so hard because giving him a happy childhood was important. Making things routine would help him settle down in their new home and help it feel normal. That was why they would go ahead and register him into the school that morning. He would be at school all day, and she could finish the house and hopefully find a job too.

It was time for her to make it feel like home for Lucas and to accept things as they were. She couldn't think about how much she wished it was different. It was how it had to be, and she warred with her feelings for most of the early morning until Lucas woke up.

A couple of hours later, Lucas found her in the laundry room. She was finishing up the rest of the linens and would make the bed in the main bedroom after she painted there.

"Hey, buddy. Ready for some breakfast?"

Lucas nodded his head while he hugged her tightly. He'd been a little snugglier than usual, and she figured it was the move and maybe some of the uncertainty he'd seen in her. She had to get control.

She put on a smile and excitedly told him about the local school. "I think we should go check it out this morning. Get you registered, and you can start tomorrow. That way, you can meet everyone and have the weekend for them to miss you."

Lucas agreed, and after cereal, he went to get dressed.

By 8:30, they were sitting in the parking lot and staring at the brick buildings. Olivia pointed out the ones that belonged to the lower school and the large playground that went with it.

Lucas smiled, and she knew he was trying to look excited for her, but he missed his friends and school in Maisonville.

It took Olivia a second to get herself together. She missed Maisonville too. Miss Lynn was her best friend and had been the mother she'd never really had. Plus, she didn't look forward to seeing anyone she'd grown up around, and enrolling Lucas in school would ensure she saw half the town.

She plastered a smile on her face and held Lucas' hand as they slowly walked to the lower school office.

The heavy red metal door closed behind them, when Olivia immediately noticed the old Formica floors and the familiar smell of crayons and pink erasers. There was also the faint smell of spilled milk and bleach that would get stronger after lunchtime.

Pictures colored by the elementary classes filled the hallways celebrating the fall harvest and the upcoming harvest carnival. They didn't celebrate Halloween at school or in St. Marksville.

She'd forgotten about the harvest festival they had instead of costumes and spooky themes. The entire town came out for the event. She would have to explain to Lucas how different things were in the small town. She had avoided the conversation, but he needed to know since he was about to start school.

They stepped into the small office and waited for the secretary, Mrs. Kline, to finish her phone conversation. Mrs. Kline had worked as the lower school secretary for over thirty-five years. She'd gotten a little rounder and softer with age, but she had the same sparkly brown eyes and a cheery smile that made her popular with the little kids. She would give them hugs along with band-aids when needed and was a favorite amongst the parents.

Olivia had liked her when she was young too. Of course, at that time, she'd been sheltered and only seen the good in people and things. But she would never forget how unforgiving Mrs. Kline was when she discovered the trouble that Olivia had gotten into in high school. In fact, she'd led the charge against Olivia and said she'd always known she was a troublemaker and had never really liked her.

It had crushed Olivia at the time. Like all her childhood memories were a lie. And no one was loving and kind.

Setting her hurt feelings aside, Olivia acknowledged that St. Marksville was their only option, and she would do anything for her son. Clearly, that was true as she bit her lip and smiled at the round, two-faced woman who hung up her phone and stared expectantly at Olivia.

"Well, who do we have here? Olivia Dufrene, don't tell me this is your son?"

Mrs. Kline walked around her desk and handed Lucas a pumpkin patch sticker.

"Yes, ma'am. This is Lucas. We just moved back to town, and he needs to register for school."

Olivia handed over Lucas' last report card, shot records, and birth certificate.

"I'll request the rest of his records from his school in Maisonville," Mrs. Kline said, smiling at Lucas again. "You know, Lucas, you are tall for your age. I would have never guessed you were seven. You might be the tallest in the second-grade class."

Olivia didn't like Mrs. Kline, but she appreciated the effort the woman was making so Lucas would feel comfortable.

"Would you like to meet your teacher? I can walk you down there right now. I think Mrs. Dow is starting their reading lesson."

Lucas looked at his mother.

"He's not staying today. We have a few more things to do before we're settled from the move."

"I understand. I hope we'll meet your husband at the harvest carnival. You know it's only a week or so away."

Olivia smiled back the same fake smile Mrs. Kline was giving her. "He's a busy man. We'll have to see if he's available."

"Oh, yes," Mrs. Kline was bubbly now. She obviously missed the mocking tone of Olivia's voice. "I hope you and he will join the parents' association. We always need young couples to help keep the group's energy up. You know, for the sake of the kids and the school community."

"Most definitely, Mrs. Kline." Olivia lied and then held Lucas' hand so they could leave.

Mrs. Kline leaned in to whisper to Olivia, "I was sorry to hear about your parents. They'd moved to Florida?"

Olivia nodded and turned so she and Lucas could get out of there. She'd thought she was strong enough to handle the residents of St. Marksville, but she might need a little more time.

She and Lucas were quiet as they got into the car, and Olivia started the engine. Why did Mrs. Kline bring up her parents moving to Florida? They had been there for over ten years. Was that her way of telling Olivia that she knew they'd moved to Florida without her? She seemed sad for Olivia and Lucas.

Screw that.

She didn't need that woman's pity. Besides, it was years too late.

Olivia sat there with the car running in the parking lot for a few minutes because she couldn't make herself put the car into drive. Explaining things to Lucas was difficult when she was ashamed of her past. But making nice with everyone in town would be the only way to keep the peace. It might be the only way to keep them from making Lucas' life a living hell. She knew that firsthand, and she couldn't let them get to him too. However, she'd told him that it was wrong to lie, and she'd told a whopper of one to the lower school secretary.

"Hey, Lucas."

He locked eyes with her as she looked at him through the rearview mirror. Olivia took a deep breath before turning around to face him as she spoke.

"I shouldn't have told a story about my husband being busy."

Lucas smiled and tried not to giggle. "It's okay, mom. It's fun to pretend sometimes. Besides, Alex may like pretending when he comes to visit too."

Olivia shook her head. How would she teach her son that lying was wrong if she couldn't stop doing it herself? She had to sit him down and explain once and for all that Alexavier would not be joining them.

She looked back at his perfect smile and smiled back at him. She would wait until after dinner or bedtime, and they would have a serious discussion about Alexavier again.

In the meantime, she needed more paint. She and Lucas had used all that they'd bought, and she still needed to do the main bedroom and the hallway.

They stopped at the local hardware store again, and Mr. Robichaux smiled at Lucas. "Hey, there, kiddo. Run out of paint?"

Lucas smiled. "How did you know?"

Mr. Robichaux grinned. "You looked like a painter the first time I met you, Lucas. There was no way y'all could stop with only one room. And it takes more than a couple of gallons to paint a whole house."

Lucas nodded.

Olivia agreed and told him they did need more paint. While Mr. Robichaux put his base can in the machine and punched the code that would allow the device to add the tint they needed, his grown son Mark walked behind the counter.

"Olivia Dufrene as I live and breathe," Mark Robichaux said.

"Hi." Olivia smiled back at him and then held Lucas' hand to keep him from pulling down any more paint color cards. "This is Lucas."

"Well, how do you do, Lucas."

Lucas smiled at him. "Do what?" Lucas asked, and Olivia laughed.

"No, baby. He's asking how you are doing."

Lucas grinned. "I'm doing great."

Mark patted Lucas on the head as he walked out from behind the counter with their paint. "I can help y'all carry this to your car.

Olivia paid Mr. Robichaux and then walked Lucas to his door while Mark put the paint into her trunk.

"You look well, Olivia."

She stared at Mark with a blank expression.

"I mean, motherhood suits you. You look happy."

He'd been her friend years ago and even stood up for her with the pervy coach, but when things got really bad, he'd backed down. She tried to forgive Mark because the pressure had been intense for everyone to condemn her. He'd been a kid when it happened but so was she, and he'd let her down.

Olivia opened her door and then turned toward Mark. "Thanks. Lucas is a great kid. And I am happy."

She didn't sound very convincing about being happy, but Mark seemed to buy it. After all, when she'd seen him last, she was being dragged down the aisle at church and out the front door. Anything would be happier than that day.

She closed her car door and saw that Mark was still standing there. She reversed her car and then paused to roll down the window.

Mark wiped his face with his big doughy hand and stood there silent until she looked like she would drive away. "It's good to see you again, Olivia. It's nice to see you doing well after learning about your folks in Florida."

Olivia nodded and then slammed her foot onto the gas pedal so she could get out of there. She didn't even say goodbye as thoughts of her parents raced through her head.

What the hell happened to her parents, and since when did everyone in her hometown give a shitake mushroom about them or her?

Chapter Thirty-One

Olivia could feel Lucas' eyes on her. "Hey, Lucas. What do you say we go to the park before we start painting?"

He shrugged.

"I could really use some fun, and I happen to know a place that has the largest slide you've ever seen."

That got his attention.

"Really?" he asked with a little more enthusiasm.

She was thankful that her seven-year-old son could be distracted. "Yup. You're going to love it." She explained how she used to play at the same park as a kid and how her sister would chase her up the ladder and down the slide or even swing for an hour with her.

It was overcast, and no one else was at the park when they arrived. Olivia was thankful for that one gift. She wanted some fun with her kid and didn't want to have to talk with anyone else.

Lucas was amazed at the large curving slide, and Olivia smiled when he ran to the very top and quickly slid down toward her yelling, "Yahoo."

She followed him up to the top again and slid down behind him. They laughed and talked for thirty minutes about all the cool things at the park. Since Olivia had been a kid, they'd added an old train car and a sand pit with excavating toys.

It was precisely what Lucas needed, and it helped her feel better too. They played at the park for forty-five minutes, and when a minivan full of kids and a couple of moms pulled up, they decided to leave.

Lucas talked the entire way home, and it lifted Olivia's spirits. He was a funny storyteller and had a great imagination. He was growing up so fast, and she loved watching how his mind and personality worked.

Olivia grabbed the paint as Lucas headed to the side door in the carport and walked inside. He'd ran ahead of her so he could change into his painting clothes, and she laughed at how excited he was to paint the house. What kid enjoyed working that hard she mused as she brought in all their new supplies. She set everything down on the floor, and when she looked up, she saw the blinds in the kitchen and living room were open. Her coffee cup from earlier was also sitting on the counter. She was sure she'd washed her cup and sat it upside down in the sink to dry along with Lucas' cereal bowl.

Then it dawned on her that she hadn't unlocked the door for Lucas. Her entire body began to tremble as she quickly ran to find her son.

Lucas didn't have on shoes when she grabbed his hand, and they ran out of the house together. Olivia didn't stop until they were on old Miss Goings' porch.

She rang the doorbell several times and then explained to Lucas that everything would be alright. Miss Goings opened her front door but didn't speak. She stared at Olivia the same way she always did, with a pinched expression.

It didn't matter if her face was a permanent scowl or not to Olivia. She needed to use a phone and wouldn't allow the meanest neighbor on the street to dissuade her.

"I'm sorry to bother you. I think someone has been in our house. Did you see anyone?"

Miss Goings shook her head. "I was napping."

"Please, can I use your phone?"

Miss Goings opened her door wider to allow them inside.

Olivia whispered to Lucas not to touch anything and then quickly dialed the sheriff's office. While she explained that she needed an officer, Miss Goings opened her pantry and offered Lucas a treat.

When Olivia got off the phone, she was shocked to find her son and Miss Goings chatting about the park as they ate oatmeal cream pie cookies together.

"The sheriff will be here in a minute. I-I need to meet him. You ready, Lucas?"

"He's fine. We're enjoying our snack. Take your time." Miss Goings smiled, and Olivia couldn't remember ever seeing her do that. She didn't have words to express how thankful she was at that moment. Having Lucas tucked away safely was a relief.

She thanked the older woman and then stood outside on Miss Goings' porch until she saw the police car turn onto the street. When the car stopped in front of her house, she was surprised to see it wasn't the older Sheriff Bowman but instead his son Zachary.

"Olivia Dufrene," he said as he rushed up the driveway to meet her.

"Zachary Bowman."

His eyes roamed her entire body as soon as he closed the door to his car. But when he stood in front of her, he was respectful and kept his eyes on her face.

"What's going on?" he asked, and she appreciated that a police officer in St. Marksville was taking her seriously.

He asked her to wait while he went through the house and spent a good twenty minutes looking in every room. Then he asked her to come back into the place and show him what had her concerned.

She pointed out the window coverings she kept closed, the

coffee cup she'd washed and left in the sink, and then turned to point toward the side door that was unlocked when they returned. She couldn't be sure if anything else was disturbed because she'd grabbed her son and then ran out of the house.

He offered to walk her through the rest of the rooms so she could point out anything that was out of place. Kindness from residents in St. Marksville seemed to be her undoing, and she had to force the tears in her eyes away. He didn't say a word as she avoided his stare. It took several awkward moments of her looking up at the ceiling without blinking until her tears dried up, before they looked through the house together.

There wasn't anything missing, but someone had moved things around in her bathroom. They had also put her shampoo and soap on the top shelf in the shower where she could barely reach. There was also a wet towel that she and Lucas hadn't used.

"Why would he take a shower in your bathroom?" Zachary asked, and Olivia shivered at the idea someone had been naked in her house.

"Is there anyone you can think would do this?" he asked.

"I didn't leave town under the best circumstances, you know. Maybe someone doesn't want me back here?"

Officer Zachary reached his hand out and patted her forearm. It was meant to be comforting and he wasn't flirting as he did in high school. "You're in for a big surprise around here, Olivia. Things have changed a lot since you left."

Olivia looked past him at the windows in Miss Goings' house that had the same lace drapes they'd had for as long as she could remember. "Things sure look the same as they did when I left."

"You, of all people, should know you can't judge a book by its cover, Olivia."

"What is that supposed to mean?"

Zachary held up both hands in surrender. "Sorry. I'm not great with words. But I want to be clear about this with you."

Olivia felt her heart pounding in her chest. Could he hear it too? She'd learned to be strong and stand up for herself. It was important to her that in this town, in her old house, that she showed him and everyone that she'd made it in spite of them. But instead, she stood there wide-eyed and waited for his judgmental comments.

He surprised her instead. "You were a good person, Olivia. A really good person, and well, maybe you didn't get a fair shake because you were young and people blindly followed someone else."

Olivia stood frozen as she tried to comprehend what he was saying to her. He thought she was a good person?

Zachary swallowed hard and then leaned in closer. "I don't mean maybe."

Was he apologizing for what had happened to her? All she'd ever wanted from her hometown was for just one person to believe her. She'd left thinking there wasn't a soul on her side.

What had changed?

Zachary was a year younger than her in school. She'd had several classes with him and had cheered him on in football. He'd always been a big kid and was an even bigger man. Yet, he was quieter than most and avoided getting into trouble. He never missed school or church, probably because his dad was the sheriff or maybe because his mother was the church pianist. Zachary's entire family had been there that day when she'd been thrown out of the sanctuary. She could still see his horrified expression when she was dragged down the aisle.

"Thanks, Zach," she said. It was all she could manage because she was still trying to pull her emotions back.

Officer Bowman smiled at her, and it gave his face the same boyish charm he'd had in school. "Try not to worry, Olivia. We still don't have much crime here, and I'll be on duty all night. I promise to drive by your house once an hour to keep an eye out."

"Okay." Olivia paused and then asked, "Zach? You do believe that someone was in my house, right?"

"I believe you, Olivia."

"Thank you." She watched him walk back to his car and then open the trunk. He pulled out a metal rod and something else she couldn't see.

"I think this will fit into the track of your sliding glass doors. When you're not using them, it's a good idea to keep this in there. And this is a can of pepper spray." He walked back into her house and showed her where to place the rod. Then he showed her how no one could open the door even if it were unlocked with the track blocked. He then showed her how to use the pepper spray. It may not stop a bad guy entirely, but it will slow him down long enough for you to run or hit him with an iron skillet or something."

Olivia laughed. Zachary Bowman had made her feel better than she'd thought possible. She quietly followed him back outside, and he turned around before getting into his police cruiser. "It was probably some teenagers fooling around in your house especially since they didn't take anything. When I catch them, I'm going to scare the hell out of them," he dipped his head at her and added. "Good to see you, Olivia."

She stood in the driveway until he was gone and then looked around. In many ways, it was the same place she'd left, but in others, it was better.

St. Marksville had been the place that taught her how cruel the world was, and now maybe it could show her something more. She considered how Mr. Robichaux, his son Mark, Mrs. Kline, Miss Goings, and now Zachary Bowman had all been nice to her. In a million years, she would have never believed any of that could happen.

She took a deep breath and headed back next door to collect Lucas and thank Miss Goings. They had painting to do, and she planned to get the main bedroom in order. It was closer to Lucas' room, and she wanted to be near him.

They spent the rest of the day working on the house. Lucas laughed and sang along to some music as they worked. He was a trip, and she felt lighter just being around him. They finished painting except for a little touch-up work and then began moving furniture around before she made the bed and hung clean curtains. The house felt brand new.

It was seven when they hauled out the rest of the trash, and Lucas held his stomach and complained about starving to death.

"You go shower, and I'll make dinner," Olivia offered and quickly popped a frozen pizza into the oven and mixed up a bag of ready-made salad.

She and Lucas sat on the floor in the living room, using the coffee table for their food, and ate almost everything. "It wasn't as good as Alex's mom makes, but I still liked it."

"I guess so since you ate four pieces."

Lucas giggled and then flexed his muscles to show her how strong he was getting.

"You're growing up too fast, buddy."

She always told him that, and it made him smile. He liked getting bigger. After cleaning up and reading several books, Lucas began to doze off on the couch. Olivia helped him to bed and then finally got to shower. It was only half-past eight when she finished up, but she decided to check all the doors and windows and then headed to bed early. She and Lucas had to be up at seven in the morning for school, and she wanted his first day to be easy.

She tossed and turned in bed as she thought about Alexavier, Brent, and the mob guys. She would love to see Alexavier but couldn't let Brent know where she and Lucas went. He probably wouldn't figure out they were gone for at least a month or longer. Brent was in over his head, and he needed to forget them and take his trouble somewhere else. She didn't want to keep Lucas from his father, but Brent didn't care if he put them in danger. It was her worst nightmare, not being able to protect her son. It was terrifying.

After an hour, Olivia got out of bed. There was no way with her mind racing that she would fall asleep. Remembering the chamomile tea she had in the cabinet, Olivia headed to the kitchen to make herself a cup. She was only halfway down the small hallway when she thought she heard footsteps outside.

She scrambled to find the mace Officer Bowman had given her and then peeked out several windows. She couldn't see anyone. But whoever was out there was going to get a face full of pepper spray if she could stop her hand from shaking.

Chapter Thirty-Two

Olivia heard footsteps in the carport. Were they circling the house and looking for a way inside? She wanted to be brave and confront the intruder, but she was trembling. What if she couldn't spray the mace accurately enough? What if it was more than one person?

Rustling sounds got louder, and she ran to find a chair to brace under the carport door handle. If they decided to rush the locked door, it would hopefully deter them.

Next, she heard the wooden gate opening into the backyard. Whoever it was must know about the sliding glass doors. It was the only entrance into the house from the back except for the window in her bedroom that was painted shut when she lived there ten years ago.

She slipped into the living room and stood against the wall beside the glass doors. She had to get herself together. If it were one man, then she would spray him in the face with pepper spray. There might be enough to get two of them.

She heard the door rattle. Whoever it was had managed to pick the lock, but it wouldn't slide with the metal rod holding it into place. Would they try and break the glass?

Suddenly she saw blue lights flashing through her front

windows. Zachary had said he would drive by her house. Whoever had tried the glass doors suddenly stopped. Had they seen the blue lights flashing from back there?

She wanted to run out the front door and flag down Zach, but she was afraid the would-be intruder might get to her before she could get away.

The blue lights continued to flash through her windows, and then she realized the police car had pulled into her driveway. There was a loud knock on her carport door, and she hesitantly moved the chair to look out the peephole.

It was Officer Bowman.

She quickly unlocked the door, and when he saw how scared she was, he stepped into the house. "I saw a truck parked at the end of your street that wasn't there earlier. And your back gate is open."

Olivia nodded. "I heard him walking around my carport."

Zach saw the chair beside the door.

"I put it under the doorknob to keep him out. But then I heard him going into the backyard. He unlocked the door, but that rod you put in it kept him out."

Zachary pulled his gun as he ran out of her house and through her back gate into the backyard. She closed the door, locked it, and then ran to the back door and turned on the light. The yard was small, and there was no place for anyone to hide. Whoever had been outside was gone.

The officer flashed his light into the neighbors' yards, but there wasn't anyone there. He nodded Olivia's way and then walked the perimeter of her yard again to look for clues. After a few minutes, he met her at her side carport door again. "There were some muddy footprints in the back. He jumped the fence, probably when he saw my lights."

Olivia took a visible breath and couldn't believe how lucky she was for the officer to show up when he did and scare the intruder away.

"I'm going to drive around the neighborhood and see if I can find this guy. Lock up again and put the chair back under the doorknob."

Olivia nodded, and he saw the worry in her eyes.

"Olivia, he probably won't come back tonight. But after I look around for him, I will be back to check on you. Okay?"

"Okay."

Officer Bowman hurried to his car and was quickly headed down the street with an enormous spotlight so he could light up every yard in sight.

Olivia peeked in on Lucas before she checked all the locks again, verified the chair was stable against the side door, and the rod was still tightly placed on the glass door track. She then made some coffee and sat in the kitchen until Zachary returned.

It was forty-five minutes before she saw him again and the fine tremble in her body betrayed her when she opened the door for him.

He patted her shoulder and gave her a reassuring smile.

"Y-You didn't find anyone?"

He shook his head. "No, but that probably means some teenagers that live around here did it. They could have easily run home to hide."

Olivia wasn't so sure. "You think kids could pick a sliding glass door lock that easily?"

"YouTube has these kids skilled in everything petty criminals took years to master. But I'm pretty great at my job too." He winked at her and headed to the back glass doors.

She watched as he removed the metal rod and pulled the door open. He then took out some black powder and dusted the door for prints. He was meticulous as he focused on his work. When he finished, she smiled at him, "YouTube?" she asked.

He laughed. "Not exactly. I interned at a forensics lab when I was in college. I wasn't sure if I would come back here or if I wanted to move to a larger city. I even considered the State Police for a while."

Olivia followed him into the kitchen and moved things out of his way so he could set his bag down on the counter.

"Would you like a cup of coffee?" she asked, already heading to the cabinet to get him a cup.

Zachary stayed for an hour, drinking coffee, and talking about his life over the last ten years. He went to college out of state, which surprised her. His mother passed away from cancer while Zach was in school. He came home more often after that to help his father, and that was when he met a girl. After he graduated, he moved home for good. They were engaged for a year, but things didn't work out. He was married to his job now.

Olivia listened to Zachary and refilled his coffee cup. He was a sweet man and a conscientious police officer. Zachary Bowman cared about the community, and she admired his honesty. He didn't try to pretend to be something he wasn't, and the power of his position didn't make him feel powerful. Instead, he was humble and saw himself as a servant to his hometown, like his father.

It was rare to meet someone so selfless, and Olivia surprised herself when she hugged him. He blushed, and she stepped back and laughed.

"I'm not trying to hit on you, Zach. I appreciate you looking out for my son, Lucas, and me."

"I would do anything to help you, Olivia. I think I owe it to you."

Olivia stared at him, and he stood up to take his cup to the sink. When he turned around, she saw that his face was still flushed. This time without prompting him, he continued explaining.

"The last day that I saw you, we were at church. I've never forgiven myself for not stepping in to help you."

It was Olivia's turn to blush. "It was one of the worst days of my life," she whispered.

Zachary picked up his things and headed to the door. Before

he left, he leaned toward her and locked onto her eyes. "It never should have happened. None of it should have ever happened."

He turned away and opened the door. Olivia stood there stunned as he walked down the driveway. Before Zach got into his car, he turned around to look at her again. "I'm on duty all night, and I'll be by here again at least two more times. Go to bed. Get some rest. I'm on watch."

She nodded and watched him until he pulled out of her driveway. She didn't think anyone cared about what happened to her in St. Marksville. She certainly hadn't believed she had left any friends behind.

It seemed there was a lot that she didn't know about her hometown. She was going to make it her mission to figure out what had happened after she left as soon as she stopped whoever was trying to scare her and Lucas away.

Chapter Thirty-Three

Olivia stared at the clock beside her bed as it clicked to seven a.m. Then the alarm went off. She rolled her eyes and put her feet on the wooden floor. She'd watched every hour pass, and it was time to get Lucas' breakfast and take him to school.

She woke him up, and he complained about a sore throat and said his head hurt. She placed her hand on his forehead, and although it was warm, she knew he always felt warm when he woke up. They headed to the kitchen to search for the thermometer but couldn't find it.

"Are you sure, buddy? Wouldn't you like to meet the kids in your class?

He shook his head. "Too sick," he moaned.

Olivia was exhausted too. What difference would one day make?

"Okay, kiddo. Let's climb back into my bed and get some extra rest this morning." She watched him slip back to sleep and wondered if he had first-day-of-school nerves that constantly plagued her as a child. He'd never been that way before, but he hadn't seemed keen on the idea of going yesterday.

It was her duty as his mother to make him comfortable, and

her hang-ups about being in St. Marksville had to stop. Could he sense her apprehension? She double-checked that he was sound asleep before getting up to make herself some coffee.

It had been a long time since she'd stayed up all night worrying, but she knew it was a waste of time to lay there and wish for sleep. Her brain wouldn't slow down, and until her body shut down, she would have to drudge through insomnia.

She thought about the intruder. If Zachary hadn't driven by when he did, would the burglar have gotten to her and Lucas?

She held her warm coffee cup, trying to soothe her trembling body. It was up to her to defend Lucas. She considered what Zachary had said and whether he could be right. Was it simply some local kids fooling around? Of course, Officer Bowman didn't know about the men from New Orleans. Those bad guys hadn't followed her across the lake to Maisonville, so she had a hard time believing they would make the effort to travel to St. Marksville.

Whoever it was, ran when they saw Zachary's blue lights. They were afraid of the police. She knew there were flood lights on the corners of her house because her father had installed them years ago. She would head back to the hardware store and buy the replacement bulbs. If the prowler came back, then perhaps it would deter him? She had to try.

Finishing her first cup of coffee, Olivia looked around the house and all that she and Lucas had done. The fresh paint and clean drapes had made an enormous difference.

She'd even polished some of the wood furniture and removed the excess, making the place look larger. Her mother had a terrible habit of collecting useless things like porcelain figurines and straw baskets. She either hung things up or had them placed on shelves and counters. It had always seemed odd that her mother left them behind. If those items were so important, and she insisted they were, why wouldn't she take them with her?

Olivia didn't like the porcelain figurines. When she was a kid, her mother scolded her if she dared to pick one up. They were an odd collection of animals, bells, and odd-shaped pieces that had collected loads of dust and grime.

It took less than half an hour to remove them all. Olivia kept one white marble heart she'd given her mother for her birthday and then threw the rest away. She kept busy washing the windows and sweeping and mopping the floors.

Once she finished, she went out back and cut some greenery from the bushes and placed the arrangement in a vase on the kitchen counter. It was the final touch to making the house her home.

When Lucas got up, he looked around and smiled at his mother. "Looks good. Doesn't it, kiddo?"

Lucas nodded, and Olivia hugged him. "We are an awesome team. Let's get some breakfast and eat out back on the patio. You could bring your remote-controlled car and play with it after eating."

Lucas hadn't played with his car since they'd arrived in St. Marksville. Olivia had noticed he hadn't really played with anything, and it was time for him to resume his seven-year-old life.

They had breakfast, and Miss Goings next door stuck her head out to speak to them. Lucas showed her his car and then asked if she could come over for lunch later.

Olivia watched as the older woman's face lit up when she saw Lucas and especially when he'd asked her over for lunch. She couldn't remember Miss Goings ever coming over. What would it hurt to act friendly? It certainly was what Lucas had wanted, and Olivia took her lead from his generous heart.

They planned to have lunch at one, but before lunchtime, Olivia and Lucas returned to the hardware store. Mr. Robichaux volunteered his son Mark to help Olivia and Lucas with their floodlights and wouldn't take no for an answer.

Back at the house, Mark explained from the top of his ladder how Olivia shouldn't replace the lights on her own. She smiled sweetly to his face and then rolled her eyes behind his back.

She tried to appreciate his help and kept her thoughts to

herself, although, deep down, she wanted to say that in the real-world women did things like change outside lightbulbs all the time. She stifled a giggle because the horror of women doing men's work might make Mark fall off the ladder.

When he finished, he checked all the switches and then took a look at her breaker box. He then went inside and changed two filters for the air conditioner and offered to take out the stack of garbage and boxes she had stacked in the laundry room.

Thankfully, Miss Goings arrived for their luncheon before he could do anything else. Both women stood in the carport and waved to him as he left. It seemed like he was disappointed for not being invited to lunch, and when he drove off, Miss Goings patted Olivia's arm.

"That was a close one," she said before turning and walking into the house with her strawberry pie.

Olivia followed behind and pulled out the chicken salad she'd made for lunch. Lucas helped set the table outside and put ice in the glasses for their tea and lemonade.

It was apparent that he enjoyed having someone other than just his mother to entertain, and no one listened like Miss Goings. She seemed to love his storytelling, never looking away from him as he spoke. It was similar to how Miss Lynn treated Lucas, and Olivia's eyes watered when she thought about how much she missed her dear friend.

Lucas pulled out his remote control and showed Miss Goings how to work it. She laughed when he let her control the car and then handed it back so she could coo at his skilled maneuvers.

Olivia offered to cut everyone some strawberry pie, and when she returned outside, Lucas was happily chasing after his car in the backyard.

"Thank you, dear," Miss Goings said as she accepted the dessert plate.

"Thank you for coming over today," Olivia responded.

Miss Goings sat her fork down and smiled at Olivia. "It's about time we became friends, young lady."

It was clear the older woman had a lot to say as she turned her chair around so she could look at Olivia.

"What did you mean by, that was a close one, after Mark Robichaux left?"

Miss Goings' eyes warmed. "A lot has happened in the time since you left town. One of those being that Mark Robichaux's wife had an affair with the preacher."

"What?"

Miss Going's nodded. "If I'm correct, Theresa Miller was a Junior when you were a senior."

Olivia nodded. She remembered the flirtatious young girl. Theresa Miller always acted appalled when Olivia said something inappropriate and would pretend to faint to get attention. Olivia didn't like Theresa but didn't care if she manipulated the idiot men in town.

Miss Goings took a bite of her pie and then continued. "It was one in a long string of affairs. Theresa also slept with that weasel coach that tormented you while at the same time she was also sleeping with a couple of her friends' fathers." Miss Goings smiled. "That little Miller girl liked to kiss and tell. She burned them all with her diary, and when they tried to silence her, Theresa made copies of her journal that gave explicit information on the affairs, dates, and times. It included a rating system on how she scored each man's performance. It was perfect."

Olivia's eyes were saucers as she listened to Miss Goings. "I can't believe I missed all of that."

"You definitely missed out. Mark married Theresa the year after you left. The entire town was there. They had a horse-drawn carriage deliver her to the church in her snow-white wedding gown like a princess in a fairytale. Everyone talked about the wedding and how she'd saved herself for marriage. It was completely over the top and inappropriate." Miss Goings snickered as she reached over to hold Olivia's hand. "Six months later, she gave birth to a full-term nine-pound baby boy with red hair and green eyes."

Olivia shook her head. Mark Robichaux had dark hair and eyes, and so did Theresa. The only people in town with red hair were Coach and the Preacher.

Without saying it, both women were on the same page. Miss Goings leaned in as she smiled and said, "Exactly."

Olivia was speechless as she stared at Miss Goings, who was about to burst with more gossip. "Theresa tried to tell everyone that she got pregnant on her honeymoon and then when she went into labor, exclaimed it was a premature birth. Can you imagine an almost ten-pound baby, ha!

"Finally, dumb Mark came to his senses. He refused to lie for her any longer, and they had it out after church during the Wednesday Night spaghetti dinner."

"You are kidding me?"

Just then, Lucas came up to eat his strawberry pie. It was so delicious that he ate the entire thing while standing, one slow bite after another. Olivia didn't want to gossip in front of him, and it took all her willpower to wait for the rest of the story.

Finally, when Lucas finished eating, he hugged Miss Goings telling her it was the best Strawberry Pie he'd ever had in his entire life.

Olivia laughed. "All seven years of his life," she said and watched Miss Goings' sincere face thank him for the compliment.

He went back out in the yard and set up an obstacle course for his car to drive through, and when he was sufficiently preoccupied, Miss Goings began talking again. "I'm not exaggerating when I say it was spectacular." She remembered the event like it was yesterday. The unhappy couple sat at a large table beside his parents and hers. Her mother was holding the newborn baby as the young couple seemed to disagree. Suddenly, Mark stood up, causing his chair to hit the floor. Theresa stood up too, and her chair hit the floor. The entire room went quiet. He admitted to being a virgin on their wedding night, and she admitted that she could tell. After every revelation, the room "oohed" and "aahed."

Her mother ran out of there in shame as Theresa said she'd

been sexually active since she was fifteen and then named names. She then yelled that she couldn't possibly be expected to have one sexual partner for the rest of her life.

"When she told her tale and strutted out of the room, you could have heard a pin drop. Of course, all the men denied it. Even the coach and preacher were shaking their heads, but you could tell they were both terrified over which one of them was the baby's father."

"So, what happened?" Olivia was biting on her fingernails. A habit she hadn't indulged since she was a teenager.

"Well, you know this town. Gossip traveled far and wide that Theresa Miller was a siren. A true-to-life Jezebel sent to temp the good men of our town by the devil. But for once, the women didn't sit idly by and let it happen. Theresa made copies of her diary and handed them out by the hundreds at the grocery store, library, and then in the church's sanctuary before Sunday service.

"When the preacher tried to stop her, her mother and several older women stood up and insisted she be allowed to explain herself. After all, she was underage when it began, and it was not only immoral but also illegal." Miss Goings had a sparkle in her eye as she continued.

"The men involved were marched out of town in shame. Theresa stayed another year but then decided she needed big city lights to make her happy. She left the baby to be raised by her parents.

"Zachary Bowman moved back to town and helped get rid of the preacher who would not leave without a fight. That young man then stood in front of the entire church congregation and told them that if they had listened to Olivia Dufrene when she was in high school, then most of the town's trouble could have been avoided.

"It was a big day for the women of this town. A few more girls came forward, and eventually, the coach and preacher were arrested."

"Zachary stood up for me?"

"He wasn't the only one. I stood up, and so did three of your teachers, Mr. Robichaux, Mark, and a handful of other young people from your high school."

Olivia wiped the tears that filled her eyes. Her own parents hadn't stood up for her, and she'd felt alone in the world until she moved to Maisonville and met Miss Lynn. She certainly didn't think anyone from St. Marksville cared at all. She had told herself it hadn't mattered. That none of them or what they thought of her mattered. But as Miss Goings admitted how wrong they had all been for not believing and protecting her, she felt a part of her heart melting. All the emotion she'd shut down inside was bubbling to the top, and she wasn't sure what to do.

She stood up and hugged Miss Goings. "I need a moment. Do you mind watching Lucas for a few minutes?"

Miss Goings nodded in understanding as Olivia told Lucas she'd be right back. She barely got out of the backyard gate before tears poured down her face.

She swiped at them and kept walking past Miss Goings' house and then two blocks over until she reached the park. A levee overlooked the water, and she sat there and watched several large pelicans as they flew above the waterline.

Moving back to St. Marksville had been the last thing she'd wanted to do. Even cleaning and painting the house hadn't made it feel like home to her. Maisonville was home. But learning what had happened meant everything, and she wanted to scream, "I told you so," at the top of her lungs. If only her parents had been there when Zachary and the others stood up and defended her. If only they'd believed her.

It took half an hour for Olivia to cry all the tears she had left from what had happened to her in St. Marksville. Those events and the people responsible didn't deserve any more power from her. She'd won. She had been genuinely free after moving away and had a fantastic kid. The misery she'd felt slowly melted away. Taking a deep breath, she felt stronger than before and headed back toward her house. When she turned onto her block, she suddenly realized someone was following her. Trying not to seem alarmed, she walked faster and then across a yard or two. When the car sped up, she broke into a full-on run until she got to her house.

The car stopped in the street, but the windows were dark, and she couldn't tell who was inside. Turning around to face the vehicle and driver, Olivia felt braver as she stood in her driveway. She must have intimidated him because the car sped off. When she turned around, Lucas and Miss Goings were staring at her. "Sorry. I thought someone was following me."

She smiled at Lucas. "It's fine. Nothing to worry about."

Lucas didn't look so sure but headed to his room anyway to get a few books to read to Miss Goings. Before he could return, Miss Goings pulled out a simple-looking cell phone with large buttons and dialed a number. "Hello, this is Madge Goings. I need you to send Zachary or the Sheriff over to my neighbor's house." She went on to explain what had happened and, when she got off the phone, grinned at Olivia.

"I knew I saw police lights last night, and that bar across the bottom of your glass doors looks exactly like the one Sheriff Bowman gave me years ago."

Olivia nodded and admitted what had happened the night before and that she believed it was the same person that had been in her house earlier that day. Miss Goings listened carefully and then held Olivia's hand.

"Zachary is a good young man. He will know what to do. I know he had a bit of a crush on you when you were younger, but he's all business now. He'll be the sheriff when his father retires."

Olivia nodded and told her that she did trust Zachary.

"Now that Mark Robichaux is another story. He has chased every single woman in town, and he was here changing light bulbs and taking out the trash because he has ulterior motives."

Olivia laughed at Miss Goings. She had zero filter and said

precisely what she thought about everything. It was probably the reason Lucas, and she got along so well. Kids and the elderly could get away with saying anything.

Chapter Thirty-Four

Officer Zachary Bowman showed up in ten minutes and wrote down everything that Olivia told him. He was off duty but insisted on driving around the neighborhood to see if anyone suspicious was still around.

When he returned, Miss Goings told them she was ordering pizza, and they all hung out in the living room to eat. Afterward, Lucas told them a few campfire stories and included his trademark sound effects. Miss Goings and Zach laughed at everything Lucas said and did. They were big fans of his already, and when Olivia announced it was his bedtime Lucas, Miss Goings, and Zachary all jeered.

Olivia had to scold the adults and ushered Lucas down the hallway as she laughed. When she returned, Zachary had washed the dishes, and Miss Goings had put away the extra pizza.

"It is past my bedtime," Miss Goings announced. She refused to let Zach walk her home until he promised he would return to Olivia's house afterward.

"I'll be fine, Miss Goings," Olivia insisted.

"Nonsense, child. Here." She handed over her cell phone. "I have a landline, and you don't have either. You keep this until we can get you one tomorrow." She insisted, and Olivia didn't argue.

When Zachary returned, he seemed a little shy. "She's a character," he said, and Olivia agreed.

"How did I not know how wonderful she was?" Olivia said, almost whispering.

"She's a tough one. My dad told me when she was in her early twenties, she lost both parents and her only brother in a car accident."

"That's terrible."

"Dad said she and Mr. Goings had only been married a year. She was pregnant and lost the baby too."

"My mother always said Miss Goings couldn't have children."

"She couldn't have them after the accident."

Olivia's eyes watered, and so did Zachary's. He leaned his shoulder into hers, and they both smiled at each other. There was no spark between them, but the friendship was genuine.

"I'm sorry you're having trouble with someone here, Olivia. I promise I will not stop until I catch him or them. Whoever is responsible will not get away with this."

Olivia nodded. "I need to tell you something, Zach. Something that may change your mind about me."

Zachary sat at her kitchen counter and listened to every word she said about Brent, his gambling addiction, his debt to the mob, and the mobsters that said they would go after her and Lucas to teach him a lesson. "I'm afraid they found us here and are trying to scare us."

He let her explain how happy she was in Maisonville and how she and Lucas left to hide at her old house.

There was an awkward silence while he drank from his water bottle. "If they wanted to teach your ex a lesson, wouldn't they have already done something to you or Lucas? I mean, Brent isn't here with you, so what would be the point of scaring you?"

Olivia shrugged. She hadn't thought about it that way. "Maybe they think I'll call him?"

"You normally call him when you need something?"

Olivia laughed. "Never." She thought about it harder. "I was sort of seeing someone or at least talking to someone for a few months." She looked at her hands and then back at Zachary before admitting, "Alexavier Regalia, the mayor of New Orleans."

"Alexavier Regalia?" Zachary whistled.

Rolling her eyes, Olivia punched him in the shoulder. "He's a sweet man."

"And famous and popular and wealthy," Zach added.

"Maybe. But Alexavier comes from a regular family and doesn't flaunt his money."

"Doesn't matter. Those thugs know he has money, making you a target not only for Brent's behavior but for Regalia's public position. At least that's the way I'd figure it."

"Yeah. That's why I took Lucas and ran."

"You didn't tell anyone where you were going?"

She shook her head.

"Where's your cell phone and computer."

"I don't have either. Electronics can be tracked, right?"

Zachary stood up and paced the room. "Then how did they find you, Livvie?"

No one had called her that since she was a kid in school. The nickname made her heart hurt a little. "I don't know. I never told anyone where I was from, and I never talked about this place. So, it could be kids, right? Like you said before."

Zachary sat back down and leveled his eyes at her. "Here's the thing, teenagers have the attention span of a gnat. I would be surprised if it were kids again last night after they'd broken in earlier in the day. And I don't think they'd follow you in a car like that either. Everyone here knows everyone, and secrets aren't kept for long. I think this is more serious."

Olivia didn't respond to him. She simply walked down the hallway to check on Lucas.

He was asleep with his covers pulled up to his neck. Olivia double-checked Lucas' window and then dumped a few of his Legos onto the windowsill and the floor directly under it. She'd stepped on those plastic pieces from hell enough to know they would slow anyone down.

When she stepped out of the room, Zach was standing there. "I've already called the station and told two officers on duty to patrol your house and this neighborhood extra tonight. I can stay for a while longer if that will make you feel more comfortable."

Olivia wanted to say she was strong enough to handle things by herself. The truth of the matter was that she had dealt with a lot on her own. But Lucas was also in danger, and she would swallow her pride or do anything else to keep him safe.

She made some coffee and poured him a cup. She was running on fumes and wasn't sure the caffeine would be enough to keep her going, but she had to try.

They settled into the living room, but before he got comfortable, he walked around the house one more time and checked all the windows and doors. Zachary also turned on her outside lights in the carport, the back patio, and the one at the front door.

"I didn't think about turning those on. Thanks." Why was she feeling so helpless?

"You would be surprised how many intruders avoid houses simply because of the outside lights. I bet your dad kept them on all the time with a beautiful cheerleader daughter that was also the most popular girl in school."

"I was more infamous than popular."

"Not in the beginning. And we've already established that none of that was your fault."

Olivia smiled at Zachary and picked up her coffee cup. "Two daughters," she said before she took a drink.

"What?"

"My dad has two daughters. My older sister, Beth. Remember."

"That's right. I had forgotten. She was a lot older than us, and honestly, so many people have moved away now that it seems more normal than not."

Olivia was surprised to hear more news of how the town had changed. She'd never believed it could happen.

Zachary finished his coffee as he explained how the town elders mostly had retired and that their childhood friends were stepping in to become the school principal, the town council, the librarian, the mayor, and every other position.

"Miss Goings said you're going to be the sheriff one day?"

He looked into her eyes, and she suddenly knew he had a different story. "My dad has advanced COPD. He has smoked like a chimney his entire life. No one knows he's on oxygen, and the old man won't stay away from the cigarettes even when he's hooked up to a tank."

"I'm sorry."

Zach shook his head. "He needs me. I'll be here until he doesn't. But when he's gone, I plan to leave St. Marksville for good."

Olivia nodded. She understood that sentiment more than just about anyone that lived in the damned little town.

He stood and took his coffee cup to the sink. He hadn't planned to tell anyone about his father or his secret plan to leave town. It would upset a lot of people. "You won't tell anyone, Olivia, will you?"

She shook her head and then crossed her heart with her fingers. She wouldn't say anything, and he knew it.

It was late. They'd said too much. Both were exhausted, and Olivia let Zachary off the hook.

"I'll be fine. The patrol cars will come by, and I will fall asleep when my head hits the pillow."

Zachary felt guilty leaving her, but he knew she wouldn't let him sleep on the couch. Their town had changed, but in some ways, it was still the same. People still gossiped all the time. The news that he spent the night with Olivia would explode by morning, and he wouldn't put her through more negative talk.

"I could stay in my car out front tonight."

Olivia hugged him, and then shook her head. "You know better."

He nodded. "We'd be on the front page of the prayer list."

"They still do that?"

"Every week."

"So that's a big fat no-way you cannot stay here another minute. Go home. I've got this."

Zachary winked at her and headed out the front door. "I left my number and the department number on the fridge. I don't think you can program it into that phone Miss Goings gave you but keep the numbers handy."

"Nothing is going to happen to me tonight. Besides, if it does, I'll be in a sleep coma and won't find out about it until tomorrow afternoon."

"Don't joke like that, Olivia, or I'm staying."

She shoved him out the door and locked it behind him.

It made her feel confident knowing she had friends on her side, but she wasn't kidding. She was suffering from brain fog, and the only way to clear it was to sleep.

She headed to her bedroom and changed her clothes, but before turning out her bedside lamp, she heard someone outside her window.

Chapter Thirty-Five

Olivia jumped out of bed. It sounded like someone had pushed through the old, rotted fence in the backyard.

She grabbed her mace and crept down the hallway with the phone Miss Goings had lent her. She saw the outside motion lights turn on and immediately called Zach. He would respond faster than 911.

The prowler was in the backyard and had unlocked the sliding glass doors again, but the rod held firm, and the door wouldn't open.

Her hands were trembling as she dialed Zach's number. As soon as he answered, he said her name.

"Olivia?"

"Yes. He's here. He's breaking in the back door."

"I'm on my way. Do you have your mace?"

"Yes," she cried. "Please, hurry."

"Listen to me, Livvie. I need to call the station. I'm going to hang up, but I'm coming. The steel rod will hold, and that glass door is a lot harder to break than you think. But if he gets through, you spray that entire can into his face."

"Okay," she said, trying to sound strong.

You're not going down like this. Olivia told herself as she ran into the kitchen and searched the cabinets for something she could use as a weapon. She found her mother's old iron skillet, the one she used for cornbread. It wasn't huge, but it was heavy, and Olivia could wield it on someone if she needed to.

She heard the door rattle harder like he was shaking it off its track, and then she screamed. "The police are on their way. You'd better get out of here!"

She needed to get to Lucas, but suddenly the noise out back stopped.

Standing still, she listened and thought she heard footsteps in the carport. How did he get there so fast? What if there was more than one intruder? There were noises from the front of the house, and her heart pounded harder in her chest. Suddenly the light on the front corner of the house turned on, and she crept to stand between the front door and the window to look out. She tried not to move as she listened, but her knees were shaking. That was when someone knocked loudly on the front door, and a scream erupted from her chest.

The next thing she knew, the door was knocked off its hinges, and Alexavier, along with three huge men, came barreling into her house.

"Alex?" Olivia launched herself into his arms, and he held her tightly.

"I heard you screaming. Baby, are you okay?"

She nodded her head, but her body was trembling, and she couldn't stop. Suddenly blue lights filled the street. Zachary Bowman and two police officers entered the house with their guns drawn.

As soon as Zach saw Alexavier, he lowered his gun. The other officers followed his lead, and after a few minutes, they sorted out introductions.

Zachary and the officers walked around the house and confirmed that the fence was partially down. Someone had been in the backyard, and the glass doors partly were off the tracks.

Alexavier and his men saw the motion lights turning on and

then heard Olivia scream. He looked around the room before asking, "Where's Lucas?"

Olivia's heart sunk. All the noise would have woken Lucas up. Right? She ran down the hallway to his room with Alexavier right behind her. When she got to Lucas' bedroom and saw the Legos piled up and his bed empty, she fell to her knees.

Alexavier searched the closet and underneath his bed, while Officer Zachary Bowman looked in the bathroom and then searched the rest of the house. As soon as Olivia saw the plastic pieces stacked away from the window, she knew he was gone.

The sobs that wracked her body came from her soul, and Alexavier picked her crumbled body up off the floor.

"Olivia. We will find him. He's going to be okay," he said as he held her close.

Everyone gathered around the long kitchen counter while Alexavier texted a recent picture of Lucas so they could send it out to all the officers.

Rex and his team split up outside the house, tracking the unknown suspect. They hoped that with a small boy in tow, it would slow the abduction progress down.

In all the mayhem that was Olivia's house, Miss Goings walked in and straight over to the young woman. She wrapped a blanket around her and handed her a glass of straight whiskey. "Drink it, child," she said and then watched to ensure Olivia followed her instructions.

"I'm Madge Goings from next door," she said to Alexavier. When he began to introduce himself to her, she nodded. "I know who you are. Who all have you called about this tonight?"

She gently took the cell phone Olivia was gripping and dialed the sheriff's home number. She then made a couple more calls, and whoever answered, she told them what had happened and that they had better get everyone moving immediately. Within a half-hour, Miss Goings had two hundred townspeople there with flashlights and hunting dogs ready to take directions on where to search.

Miss Goings sat next to Olivia and wrapped an arm around her as she looked expectantly at Alexavier. "You're the big talker around here, right? The Mayor of New Orleans? Go out there and rally the troops. I've got our girl."

"Yes, Ma'am," he said before kissing Olivia on top of her forehead as he stepped outside to mobilize the search.

Rex, Reaper, and Cage had tracked the suspect to the woods past the park, and that was where they suggested everyone start. The crowd immediately headed that way, and the intense searching began without a single bit of success.

Olivia was silent for hours as she watched Alexavier, Zachary, Miss Goings, and Rex answer questions, direct strangers, and run the entire operation.

Before dawn, a helicopter landed in the lot two doors down, and when Olivia saw Miss Lynn and Ryan Gentry walk into her front door, she sobbed uncontrollably again. "I lost him. I should have protected him, but I left him in his room alone. I lost our boy," she cried, and Miss Lynn cried with her.

Ryan Gentry had been special ops in the army, and it was his friend's helicopter outside. He brought a few ex-rangers with him, and they joined the search. Several went into the air using heat sensors, and Ryan took a few others who were going to the waterfront to begin diving.

Miss Lynn and Miss Goings gently talked to Olivia, trying to console her. When Miss Goings reached out to hold Olivia's hand, she was freezing cold. Both older women gently encouraged her to sit down, but it wasn't until Olivia almost blacked out that they became frantic.

Alexavier rushed over and laid Olivia on the couch. Miss Lynn elevated her feet and ran to the bedroom to get a comforter to place over her.

Whispering in Alexavier's ear, Miss Lynn told him that Olivia was going into shock. He tried to discuss going to the hospital, but she became hysterical.

Miss Goings gave Olivia that confident nod she needed to

patent when she was going to get something taken care of and then turned around to use her cell phone.

Olivia felt like a corpse, and her lips were turning a grayish blue. Alexavier climbed under the blanket with her to warm her up as he whispered calming words to her. "Olivia, take a deep breath with me," he said, then he took an exaggerated breath so she would follow him. "That's good. One more time. That's good. Now, let's count backward from fifty. Ready? 50, 49, 48—" he had Olivia distracted until Dr. Kinsman, an ER doctor, came in to examine her.

Miss Lynn held Olivia's hand as the doctor explained what was happening and how important it was that she let him check her blood pressure and then give her some fluids and medication.

"I guess this is your doing?" Alexavier asked Miss Goings, who only winked at him. He really liked the older woman and her no-nonsense approach to things.

Once Dr. Kinsman set up intravenous fluids to hydrate Olivia, she slept for several hours. She had been awake for forty-eight hours, and with the mild sedative, her body shut down.

While the doctor was taking care of Olivia, the divers returned, thankful that they didn't find anything, but unfortunately, neither did the helicopter search. The volunteers finished looking through the woods too. There hadn't been one sign of Lucas or his abductor.

Zachary checked the red-light cameras, and there wasn't anything suspicious or anyone driving out of town with Lucas in the car. There was only one road in and out of St. Marksville.

Ryan insisted that was great news because whoever the bastard was, he was still in town. "I like those odds," he said. "We have a perimeter, we have the tools, and we have the know-how."

He and his men set out to search the other side of town, and Rex took his men and some volunteers to begin going door to door to show everyone Lucas' picture.

When Olivia woke, her house was quieter, and it was dark outside. She slowly sat up to test her balance before she stood. She still had the I.V. in her arm, but she felt much better than she had earlier.

Dr. Kinsman was half asleep in a chair near her, and he was startled when she moved. He was kind and gentle as he checked her vitals and then agreed to remove the intravenous fluid needle from her arm. He reassured her, "Most of the time, this type of distress will ease up after a few hours."

Olivia felt like half a person with her son missing. There had never been a time in his seven-year life that she didn't know where he was or with whom. The weight of it felt like she was carrying a ton of bricks on her back. But that wasn't going to bring Lucas home.

She walked into the kitchen, which had turned into a makeshift command center. Miss Lynn was making sandwiches for people, and Alexavier was pointing out something on a map to some men agreeing with him. Alexavier looked up to see Olivia and, in two giant steps, was in front of her pulling her into his arms.

"Thank you, Alex," she whispered.

"We're going to find him," he said firmly.

He held her hand as he answered his phone and then directed another group of people to an area of town.

It was late, and she felt helpless as she watched people come and go. She declined to eat, but Miss Lynn made her a sandwich and wrapped it up for her anyway.

Miss Goings had opened her house to Miss Lynn and any men who needed to rest or shower. The older women worked until midnight when Alexavier insisted they get some rest for a while.

The searching continued through the night, but Olivia's house fell silent in the early hours of the morning. Lucas had been missing for hours, and the quiet made things feel hopeless.

Alexavier drank coffee, and she sat in a chair next to him silently. She hadn't spoken in several hours while kind strangers came in to get directions.

She surprised Alexavier when she cleared her throat and wiped tears from her eyes.

"I should have never brought Lucas here."

Before he could tell her not to blame herself, Olivia shook her head. "You don't understand. This isn't a good place. Good things don't happen here."

Chapter Thirty-Six

Alexavier grabbed a sweater and wrapped it around Olivia. She hadn't eaten, and she still looked pale.

"I didn't want to leave Maisonville. Lucas and I were happy there. It gave us the new start we'd needed. You know it's nicknamed Renaissance Lake because everyone believes something special happens for people when they begin something new there.

"This place, though, St. Marksville, it takes something from people." Olivia wiped her eyes again, and her tears stopped.

"I thought if I came here, then I could protect Lucas. It always felt like St. Marksville was another planet, and I didn't think anyone would find us."

"I would have protected you and Lucas. Didn't you know?"

Kindness was her undoing, and she chanted in her head, don't cry, don't cry, don't cry. "It's more complicated than you know, Alexavier. I couldn't put those burdens on you. I needed to come here."

"Is that because of your parents' accident?"

"Accident?"

He froze, and she watched him take a deep breath, in and then out.

What was going on? Why did it feel like everyone knew something she didn't about her parents?

"You don't know, do you?" He reached over and held both of her hands.

"I'm sorry to tell you, baby—" he paused, and she suddenly understood what people in St. Marksville were saying to her about her parents. They were trying to give their condolences. Her parents were gone.

"When? How?" she asked without emotion.

Alexavier was angry with himself. She didn't need to deal with another tragedy. But he would always be honest with her. "A month ago, they were heading back to Florida from a long road trip and fell asleep at the wheel. The truck and camper they pulled rolled several times, and they died on impact."

Olivia nodded and then stood up and walked across the room to look out the window. They'd abandoned her while she was still in high school. She was like the items they'd collected but left behind to gather dust. Useless. Worthless.

She felt Alexavier as he stood behind her. He didn't touch her, although his body heat surrounded her. Comforting her was his nature, but she didn't know how to accept it.

"I'm fine, Alexavier. Really. You may as well know they didn't love me."

He wrapped his arms around her and pulled her back against his front. He kissed the top of her head and whispered in her ear. "I do, Olivia. I love you and Lucas."

Silent tears rolled down her cheeks. She wasn't crying for her parents. They were strangers to her that she never did and never would understand. Those tears were for Alexavier because she wasn't sure she was worthy of such love.

He gently guided her back to the sofa, but Olivia curled up away from him. She pulled her legs up close to her body and then pulled the old quilt she dragged everywhere over her bare feet.

"Talk to me?" he asked, locking eyes with her.

"You always asked me where I was from, and I always avoided

talking about this place. Six hundred residents, give or take. One school, kindergarten through high school, in two buildings. One church that everyone attends. People are born here and die here. Strangers rarely wander in, and residents rarely leave."

"You did."

"Yes, but I was kicked out." Olivia stared into his eyes when she admitted she was kicked out of town, but Alexavier didn't flinch. Instead, the stalwart man lifted his chin, encouraging her to continue. As if she'd said the sun set in the west or something equally as normal.

"St. Marksville is like a cult town where you're brainwashed into thinking you can't make it in the outside world. You're taught as a kid that the rest of the world is full of sinners trying to take your soul. Girls are expected to be pure and pretty. They're taught to save themselves for marriage which the parents practically arrange for them as children. Otherwise, girls or boys would leave to find a mate, messing up the whole ecosystem.

"It sounds awful, right? But when you grow up here, it feels wonderful and safe. I loved being a kid here, and my family was happy. My older sister and I walked to school together with lots of the neighborhood kids. We all went to church together on Sunday mornings, Sunday nights, and Wednesday nights whenever there was an event. Our families ate together at church, and it felt perfect."

"When did it not feel perfect?" Alexavier knew there was no such thing as a perfect life but especially one that didn't accept change. Life was difficult, but you could make it better by getting through those difficult situations. He'd always handled them straight on with no holding back.

"The first time I questioned any of it was when my sister, Beth, went away to college. It was odd for our community. She was ten years older than me, and I don't know what happened, but most of her friends stayed in town and married shortly after graduating high school. I never heard her argue with my parents, and she didn't have some big meltdown where she later ran away.

She simply packed up and kissed us all goodbye. I only saw her one time after that. She called me maybe once a year and still calls me about every other year around my birthday, but I haven't seen her since I was a kid. I never understood why that happened, and my parents never would take me to see her or even see her themselves. It was like she didn't exist, and I wasn't supposed to talk about her."

Alexavier reached a hand out to touch her cheek. She looked into his eyes and found encouragement there. "It was weird for Beth to be gone from my life like that, and sometimes I felt like I'd made her up like an imaginary friend. She'd always been sweet to me and braided my hair for school or allowed me to tag along with her when she had a movie date.

"After she left, my parents had the house painted and made her bedroom a home office. They even took down our family pictures in the hallway. There was one picture in my bedroom, and they also had one with Beth in it, but that was it. Life went on without her. I grew older and hung out with my friends and did my chores at home or church. I forgot how painful it was after she'd left, and life was pretty wonderful again. Then I hit puberty at twelve and started looking more like Beth, and I think I understood what the problem was for her and then suddenly for me."

Alexavier didn't have any sisters, but he had plenty of female cousins. It was hard to hear what she went through next.

"All the girls wore the same modest uniform for school; plaid skirts hemmed to the knee, white button-up blouses with a red or navy sweater or navy blazer. I wore the exact same thing everyone else wore, but suddenly I began to get into trouble every day for calling attention to myself. I didn't wear makeup, but my dark eyelashes made it look like I did, and they would make me scrub my face in the office to prove I didn't have on mascara or eyeliner. It was like a flipped switch, suddenly turning a spotlight on me. It happened overnight, and I didn't understand. I was upset every day when I went home from school because I felt ashamed. I thought I must be doing something wrong. My parents would get a note from the teacher that said the school counseled me, and my parents would punish me.

"When I got to high school, it was a little better because girls were allowed to wear a small amount of makeup. My mother still didn't let me, but at least they didn't call me out of class to make me scrub my face every day at school. The skirt issue hadn't gotten any better, so my mother began making all of my skirts. She would make them longer, like a poodle skirt from the fifties, and at least I couldn't get into trouble for them being too short. It started a trend, and most of the girls in 9th and 10th grades began to wear their skirts the same. I had a few boys that would flirt with me, but I made sure to act shy and not pay attention to it, which worked for a while. Then I made varsity cheerleader my junior year, and that was the beginning of the end." Olivia tried to slow down, but it was no use. Once she'd decided to tell Alexavier her story, she couldn't get the words out fast enough.

"This is where I should tell you that we had the most modest cheer uniforms in the district, and when we went to other schools and saw the girls, it was shocking. Our shirts were sleeveless but covered our abdomen, and our skirts were fingertip length so mid-thigh. But I had a tiny waist and was a curvy girl. I got a lot of attention at the games and not from only the boys. One of the coaches told the cheer coach that I was causing a distraction, and they suspended me from the football game the following week. My parents wouldn't stand up for me, and my father even told me he was embarrassed at the school board meetings because my name was always brought up.

"My mother would pray for me to be plain. She and her women's group would have meetings at my house with my friends and me, explaining the importance of being modest. They would act like it was for all of us girls, but then they would have me stand up and try to correct my walk so my hips wouldn't sway so much. They even padded the waistline of my skirts, so I looked less curvy. It was embarrassing, and at sixteen, I felt insecure because everyone was disappointed in me." As Olivia admitted feeling inadequate as a young girl, her old insecurities slammed into her.

She paused awkwardly.

Alexavier got on his knees before her to look into her eyes. "You are the most beautiful woman I've ever known. On the inside as well as the outside. They were wrong for making you feel ashamed of how you looked." He leaned over and kissed her forehead, nose, and then lips.

Olivia slid off the couch into his arms, and he held her close. She wasn't sure if he could handle the rest of what she had to tell him.

Chapter Thirty-Seven

Olivia wrapped her hands in Alexavier's shirt to hold him tight, and he responded by kissing her deeply. He cared about her. He wanted her, and he wouldn't let her think for one minute that her past could change the way he felt.

They sat on the floor together for a few minutes before she began again. "It was winter of my junior year, and it was colder than usual. I wore oversized jackets and tried to cover up my figure. I pulled my long hair up into a messy bun and didn't even wear chapstick on my lips. It didn't help, but it made me feel better. After Christmas break, my math teacher had surgery, and the coach complaining about me at the football game became the substitute for the rest of the year.

"Coach Pratt was still pretty young. He'd been there for ten years, and all the guys loved him. Every adult in town thought the coach was fantastic. He was in his early thirties and still single. He volunteered for everything at church and even taught Sunday School to the teen boys. But he was in our class for less than two weeks when he began picking on me.

"At first, he would call on me to give answers and go up to the board and work problems. Math wasn't my best subject, but I worked hard. He loved to embarrass me and would tell me to take off my oversized coat or sweatshirt in class. He would say it wasn't part of our uniform, and he was right, but no one else made me remove it. I would get embarrassed and turn red all over. He seemed to get off on that, you know.

"I was still naive and didn't understand. Then one day before class started, he saw me in the hallway, and he decided my skirt was too short. I had stopped wearing them long, but my mother still made them by hand, and they were past my knees. But still, he called me into the classroom and made me kneel on the floor. He ran his hand over my head before removing my ponytail holder. Then he ran his hand through my long hair before anyone came into class. He made a grunting noise, and I started shaking. He loved that I was scared of him. Of course, my skirt was so long that it tucked under my knees, but he made me stay down there all through class. Walking in front of me where I could see the front of his pants bulging.

"I went home that day and cried myself to sleep. I had to give my parents the note he sent home about reprimanding me. I told my mother in private what he'd done to me, and she slapped my face. She told me that he was a wonderful man and that I had better not disrespect an adult from our church like that again. She told my father, and that night they threatened to pull me out of school if I caused more trouble for Coach Pratt. They said he had proven he was a respectful man because he was dating a girl from my high school with her parents' permission. She was a senior, and he would go to her house and sit in the living room with her and her parents. They told me I should be so lucky to find someone that wonderful for my husband, especially since whoever they had lined up for me had backed out because of my reputation. Then they made me write an apology letter to Coach Pratt, and my mother walked me into his classroom the next morning to make sure I personally gave it to him." Olivia's jaw was tense as she talked about the coach.

"He acted like a rockstar after my parents made me apologize because he knew he could get away with anything. Strangely, a few of the boys in the class were nicer. They felt sorry for what he was putting me through, but almost all the girls were mad. They all had crushes on the coach or the boys who defended me. Most girls stopped talking to me and said I was acting out to get his attention.

"He didn't do anything huge for a few weeks. He would call me up to the board every day, but I was ready and worked the problems he gave me perfectly. Then around mid-March, right before Easter break, he called me up to the board for a problem, and while I was working it, he walked up close behind me. I couldn't tell what he was doing, but apparently, the padding in the waistband of my skirt had slipped, and he was pointing it out to the other kids. The whole class laughed at me. He pulled a piece off my skirt and asked, 'What is this, Miss Dufrene?' I tried to put it back, but he grabbed my hands. He said it wasn't part of the uniform and then actually reached inside my skirt and pulled the rest of them loose. My skirt fell to the ground in front of the whole class, and I was mortified. He acted mad and dismissed the class. I tried to pull my skirt back up, but he wouldn't let go of my hands until everyone left. Then he walked over to the door and closed it. He stared at my plain white cotton underwear, and all I could think was how my mother bought me those ugly panties as part of my modest ensemble. There was nothing sexy about them, and yet, there he was, this respected adult teacher drooling over me, a sixteen-year-old student. I got so angry. How could every one of those students leave me there with him? I had grown up with them. I stepped back, and I wasn't scared anymore. That jerk had humiliated me in every possible way, and I lost it. I yelled at him. Do you like what you see? What are you going to do, rape me now? In school? In your classroom? Don't think I won't scream my freaking head off. One of the female teachers next door heard me screaming and came into the room. He then acted relieved, as if she saved him from me, but for the first time, someone acted like I might be the victim there. She helped me back into my skirt, and I held it up while she walked me out of his classroom.

"She took me to the office and stapled my skirt together so it would stay up. She then questioned me there in front of the secretary. I told them what had happened, and then they called the principal into the office. He called some of the kids from my math class. The girls told him I had been flirting with Coach Pratt since day one, and they felt like I padded my skirt to trick him into pulling the lining out and exposing myself. Some of them were on the squad with me, so I quit. Two of the older senior boys said they thought Coach Pratt had been inappropriate with me from the beginning. They said they couldn't believe what he did that day, and they felt terrible for not defending me.

All in all, there were only two of them out of twenty. It came down to my word against the coach's, and he was a beloved teacher. The female teacher filed a complaint against him and the principal because she felt the principal should have called the police. Shortly after the incident, she was forced to transfer from our district to another school. She'd grown up in St. Marksville but never married, so no one seemed to care. Coach Pratt was allowed to continue to teach the class, and they made me take a self-monitored online course.

My parents freaked out that I embarrassed them in front of everyone with my promiscuous behavior. I hoped they would home school me as they'd threatened. But they didn't want to be around me. My dad quit his school board position, and he and my mother made me sit away from them at church. They made me eat dinner in my room and stopped talking to me.

"I was so hurt and angry at how I had been cast aside. I felt like someone had sewn a scarlet letter on my clothes. The female teacher that left filed a formal complaint against Coach Pratt, and there was an official investigation. Since I was only sixteen, they couldn't interview me without my parent's consent. My parents wouldn't let me do it. But because I was named in the file and he'd come close to getting into trouble, Coach Pratt didn't come near me, nor did the principal.

"I lost everything. I had no friends. My parents wouldn't talk to me. Everywhere I went in town, people gossiped about me. I finally accepted that I couldn't make anyone else happy no matter what I did, but I could try and make myself happy. Once I decided I deserved that, things changed. I woke up and started wearing skirts that were actually in my size. I took all my old uniforms, placed them in a metal can in my backyard, and to my parents' horror, I set fire to them. I felt like I burned away all the old guilt and remorse for not being good enough. Screw them if they believed all the gossip and didn't like me for me. I was a decent human, and I decided I didn't care what anyone else thought about me.

I got a job that summer working at the hamburger stand in town. I was surprised when they said they would hire me, but I worked hard, and they had me at the counter waiting on customers. Their sales doubled that summer. I wore tight clothes and smiled a lot. I made a fortune in tips. It turned out that a lot of the happily married men that had been set up with their wives since they were in school weren't really happily married after all. A few minutes of flirting was what they needed. I learned how to wield my womanly powers and returned to school with a brand new attitude. I nicknamed Coach Pratt, Coach Prick. When I called him that the first time, I felt invincible. I swished my hips around that school my senior year and didn't care who the hell thought I was wrong.

"I got a couple of the boys to teach me how to cuss properly, and I began to curse around Coach Prick, shocking and embarrassing him because he couldn't do anything about it. I loved every minute of it. He hated me. But he didn't mess with me or any other young girl in school while I was around. He started walking the line and acting like an upstanding community member. I wasn't sure he would keep it up when I wasn't around, but I gave him something to worry about as often as possible. He knew he couldn't write me up or make a complaint against me again because that would cause another investigation, and it would come from outside the area. He couldn't control the outcome if that happened.

"Unfortunately, my newfound independence had a price. My father retired in November of my senior year, and he and my mother announced they were moving to Florida. They were gone before Christmas. In January, my father called to tell me that I could stay in the house because it was paid for, but I had to pay for everything else. They never spoke to me again.

"No one knew they'd left me. It took a few weeks before someone asked, and I made excuses that they went on vacation, then I told them they were visiting my sister. It was tough learning to care for myself with the bit of money I made from Johnnie's hamburger place but even harder to act like I was okay.

"I graduated and earned enough money to make it here but not enough to move away. Honestly, I didn't have the nerve to move away. I'd never been anywhere.

"Coach Prick ended up marrying the girl he'd dated from school. No one acknowledged that it was odd for an educator to marry one of his students. Especially since he'd had her in his classes since she was fourteen."

Olivia shook her head. She'd watched Coach Pratt after the wedding because he looked miserable. It was exactly what he deserved.

"Unfortunately, he was on his best behavior, and I was on my worst. He couldn't do anything to me while I was in school, but late that summer, he got me kicked out of the church. I had been baptized there and been a member since I was born. Besides, I always figured that church was the one place everyone was accepted. You know, because of redemption and all that forgiveness stuff. But apparently, I was wrong again. The preacher stood before the entire congregation that particular Sunday and told them that a seductress was amongst them. He said that a teenage siren was tempting their sons and their husbands. No man was safe as long as she was around them. I couldn't believe he was saying that about someone in our town. He then pointed at me. I was sitting alone in the middle pew, wearing a simple blue dress with flats and a white cardigan sweater. My hair was pulled back, and I probably looked like I was twelve. He had two of my classmates' dads pick me up and physically drag me down the aisle and out the front doors in front of the whole town.

"You should have heard the gasps and the mutterings as everyone watched. Some women fainted, and others were overcome with shock at being in the same building as someone as awful as me.

"Then I was fired because no one would go to Johnnie's Hamburger anymore since the preacher denounced me. I could barely survive, but then a check came in the mail with enough money for me to move."

Chapter Thirty-Eight

Alexavier wanted to explode over the way the townspeople treated Olivia. However, she didn't need him to get angry. Not yet. He reached for her hand, and she let him hold it. "That's when you moved to New Orleans?"

She nodded. "I packed my clothes and filled up my car." Olivia shrugged. "The same car I have now. I didn't stop until I got to New Orleans. Found a job the day I arrived and never looked back."

He moved into her space, and she stared into his eyes. "Olivia, you didn't have to return to this place."

She looked away as she said, "I did."

"Did you think I couldn't handle the truth?"

"I didn't want you to have to handle it. I mean, what happened to people just fooling around and enjoying each other's company?"

He laughed because that was the first thing she'd said to him when they'd met.

"None of the stuff that happened to you here was your fault. And I don't care what anyone else thinks about it except for you."

"I didn't want to embarrass you. I was kicked out of a church.

Dragged down the aisle and thrown down the steps out the front door. And I didn't want your family to know."

"Sweetheart, my family would defend you as much as I would. They don't expect perfection, and they don't judge. Besides, my family isn't perfect. I'm not perfect. We live and we learn."

"But you're the Mayor of New Orleans. I would hate it if I messed that up for you."

"That's what I do. Not who I am, Olivia. I want you to know I'm not worried about an image. I want a life."

"You deserve a great life, Alex. But I'm afraid it can't be with me."

He could see how much it pained her to say that. So, he used humor to try and get through to her. It was part of his charm. "Getting ahead of yourself there, aren't you? I haven't asked you to spend your life with me yet, Olivia Dufrene."

She looked up at him and saw the gleam in his eyes. Things had been great between them, and she'd never had a relationship like it before. It was one of the reasons she'd run as fast as she could away from Maisonville and him.

"You've worked so hard, and you've been a great mayor. I can't put your career or even your reputation in jeopardy because of me. Brent told me he was gambling and borrowed money again. Lots of money. That man that followed us at the park and then showed up on my street was there for me. They've threatened me before, and I think that he's the one who took Lucas."

"I'm not so sure, Olivia."

She stared at him and then stood up. She couldn't sit down and talk about Lucas. She wrung her hands and walked to the back sliding glass doors to look out into the dark yard. Her son in danger was her worst nightmare. "You don't understand. Brent told me they were the ones who showed him the picture of Lucas in the paper with you. The mob knows you and I are connected, and they implied they would use Lucas or me to blackmail you for money or power. Whatever it is, my son is gone. Everything I did, from running away from New Orleans to leaving you so you wouldn't be involved and even moving here, was for nothing. They have him, and I don't know if he's cold or hungry or scared."

Alexavier turned her around to stare into her eyes. He loved how fiercely she wanted to protect those she loved. Olivia had never experienced that kind of love, the kind that would always protect her and be there. Unconditionally.

"There is nothing I won't give for you or Lucas. But while you were here, we questioned those men. Or at least the local mob, and what Brent has told you isn't true. He grew up with Joey Giordano. They're friends. He's loaned money to Brent, but he's never collected by sending people after you or Lucas."

"I was there. They came after me when I was pregnant and then again when Lucas was a baby. I could have fallen climbing out the bedroom window onto the fire escape with my baby to get away."

Alexavier kissed her hard on the mouth. The idea of her going through all of that tore him up. "I believe you. It's just that maybe Brent was behind it?"

He explained how the NOPD and local FBI had raided Joey Giordano's businesses, and they ended up questioning him. Joey had never really been much of a mobster and had let the fantasy of that life go since his father passed away. He was angry over anyone thinking he would hurt a kid.

When Alexavier finished, Olivia seemed even more confused. "Why? What would be the reason Brent would send someone after me? We were never a couple, and the pregnancy was an accident. I don't have anything. No family, no money. What could he want? There's nothing."

"You," Alexavier said. "I think he did it all because he wanted and still wants you for himself."

Olivia laughed and shook her head. "No. That's silly."

Alexavier pulled her into his body. "You don't see yourself the way everyone else does. Men go to war over women like you, Olivia."

She laughed painfully. "Not a chance."

He could see how hard the information was for her, and she struggled with the idea that Brent could be behind it.

"What did Brent say when the police questioned him?"

"That's the thing that is so confusing. No one could find him. In fact, before questioning Joey, we thought maybe he'd done something to Brent."

Olivia was still in denial. "No. He told me he was working on two or three different job sites. He's in construction and probably sleeping there too."

Shaking his head, Alexavier explained how the arson fires from a few weeks earlier were Brent's work sites. "There is nothing left at those addresses except for empty lots."

"Are you sure?"

"I'm sure."

"You don't think something happened to him, do you?"

Alexavier answered her the only way he knew how. "I hope not for Lucas' sake."

"But you think Brent could be behind whoever broke in and took Lucas?"

"I think it's a real possibility."

"None of this makes sense. But if Brent were behind it, then he wouldn't let them hurt Lucas. Right? He never was close to him, but he couldn't let anything happen to his own son." She began to wring her hands again and, watching her suffer, took a piece out of Alexavier's soul. He would like to get Brent alone and beat the hell out of him for tormenting Olivia. And if Brent was behind Lucas' abduction, then he'd do more than take a piece of him.

He had to get Olivia to think more about getting Lucas back and less about whether Brent could harm him. "Olivia, what does Brent know about St. Marksville? Did you show him around town or introduce him to anyone? We need to think of where he might hide with Lucas."

Tears filled her eyes. She couldn't help in the investigation at all. "I never told Brent about St. Marksville. I certainly never brought him here."

Alexavier kissed her forehead, but before he could do anything else, his phone rang. It was Ryan Gentry.

"We found him!" he said loud enough for them both to hear, and Olivia went to her knees.

Chapter Thirty-Nine

Ryan's words vibrated through the quiet house. He'd found Lucas. Olivia was down on her knees with her hands clasped, waiting to hear if her child was okay.

Alexavier knelt in front of her as Ryan explained the situation.

"Their barricaded inside the church. He's demanding we send Olivia inside."

"Not going to happen, Ryan," Alexavier said, but Olivia pulled away from him so she could put on her shoes.

"They have my son," she said, and he knew she wouldn't be stopped. He could only try and contain the situation.

"We're on our way," he told Ryan and then hung up the phone.

He waited until he had Olivia in the car before he tried to reason with her. "We don't know who or how many people are there with Lucas. I can't let you go in there without regard for your safety."

She ignored him, and he tried again. "I love you, Olivia. Lucas loves you too. We both need you. You can't put yourself in jeopardy without trying to negotiate a safe outcome."

She gasped as they pulled near the church. The whole place was lit up like daylight, with spotlights on every corner. A swat team truck was parked out front, and armed police officers surrounded the building, including Rex, Cage, Reaper, Zachary, Sheriff Bowman, and Ryan Gentry with his team.

Chaos surrounded the church building. The biggest disgrace to hit St. Marksville had been Olivia Dufrene until Theresa Miller tried to outdo her. Now Olivia had returned with her only son and would reclaim her spot on the top of the scandal chart.

Rex met them at the SUV. "He won't give us a name, and he says he won't talk to anyone but Olivia. Ryan has tried to reason with him. I tried to talk him into letting Lucas go and giving himself up. He yelled that he would wait as long as it took for Olivia to show up."

Olivia ran toward the church, and Ryan Gentry grabbed her around the waist and hauled her back. When she began to fight with him, Ryan put her down. Alexavier was by her side as Ryan tried to explain. "We've been friends a long time, Olivia. You know I love that kid. You cannot go in there half-cocked. Do you understand me?"

She glared at him but nodded. If it was the mob and they had already hurt her son, she didn't care what they did to her.

Zachary Bowman and his father walked over with a young preacher she'd never met. "This is preacher Mobley. He's been head of the church for almost two years," Zach said. "He slipped out the back when he heard the ruckus outside. He said there is an opening in the bell tower that someone might be able to get through." He looked directly at Ryan, who smiled.

Ryan was a fearless ex-army ranger, and if his wife, Sydney, or his sister, Reagan, were there, they would kill him for volunteering. There were others that could go in through the roof, but Ryan cared about Lucas, and he'd be damned before he'd let anyone else do it.

Rex agreed that having Ryan inside was a great idea, but he picked up the phone and dialed the church number. "Let's see what we are working with first?"

He handed the ringing phone to Olivia, and all eyes were on

her. "Hello?" she said, waiting on whoever had answered the phone to speak to her.

"Olivia?"

When she heard her name, her jaw tightened. "Yes, it's me. Let me speak to my son now!" she demanded.

"You're not making the rules, Olivia."

"And you are? You planned this craziness, Brent?"

Ryan and Alexavier both exhaled at the same time.

"I didn't do this. You did this. This was all your choice," Brent said, and she could hear the wildness in his voice. He was crazy. Or at least, he was losing it.

Zachary stepped up and whispered. "Calm down, Livvie. You have to take control of this situation. Calm him down."

She looked at him and then Alexavier, who nodded her way.

"I'm sorry, Brent. I didn't know you were here. I didn't know you wanted to be with us."

He smirked, and she thought she'd said the wrong thing, but then his voice cracked when he spoke. "I'm not much of a dad. I know that, but I could work on it. You could show me. I need you, Olivia."

Her stomach twisted. Where was Lucas? Was he okay? "I'm here, Brent. What do you want me to do? I'll do anything you want."

"What about Regalia? You're dating him. I know he's in town. Don't lie," he warned.

"We did go out. But I didn't invite him to St. Marksville. I left Maisonville to get away from him." She looked away from Alexavier as she spoke.

There was some truth to what she'd said. Alexavier knew her well enough to know that. It didn't matter as long as they rescued Lucas. Whatever she had to do to save her kid and come out of the situation okay, he could handle. He'd already told her there was nothing he wouldn't do to get Lucas back, and if she thought being away from him was better for them, he would find a way to live with her decision.

He would never love again like he loved Olivia and Lucas, though. He'd wanted them to be his family. He would make sure their happiness and safety came before his.

"Come inside with me, Olivia. Show me that you choose me."

"I will. I swear I will, Brent. Please, let me speak to Lucas first. They won't let me come inside unless they know he's safe."

"Damn it. You tell them I said to let you go, or I'm going to burn this building down with us inside."

"Please don't, Brent. W-We can't be a family if you get hurt," saying those words made her tremble, but she bit her lip to keep it from quivering. "Just hold the phone and let Lucas say hello."

The next thing she heard was Lucas saying, "Hello, mom. It's me, Lucas."

"Hey, baby—" was all Lucas heard because Brent grabbed the phone back and said, "There. You heard him. I know they're listening. Get inside now."

"I'm coming, Brent. Hold on. I'll be in there in a minute. Let me talk to the police chief, and it'll all be okay."

He hung up on her without a word, and Olivia closed her eyes. When she opened them again, she was ready.

Ryan stepped up and told them he was heading to the top of the church to get inside. "I'll be there, Olivia. Don't you worry. If he tries anything, I'm going to shut him down." He gave her a chin nod and then disappeared.

Alexavier didn't want her anywhere near Brent, but he didn't get a vote. He tempered his anger at the situation as Ryan climbed the building like a parkour expert and the rest of the men spread out around the outside windows and doors.

He locked onto her eyes and said, "Go get Lucas."

It took everything in him to let her go in there without him.

She turned away, and he felt the words that were left unsaid between them. Then he watched as her friend Zachary escorted her to the church doors.

As Olivia stood outside the chapel, she knew the only way she would have ever gone back inside that church was for her son.

Otherwise, wild horses couldn't have driven her back across that threshold.

Reaper opened the heavy wooden door on the right and winked at her. Olivia gave him a determined look before heading down the aisle she'd last been dragged across by two men from the congregation.

The door closed behind her and made a louder bump than she'd expected. She jumped. Then she saw Brent step out from behind the pulpit.

He looked around to verify she was alone.

"Where is he?" she asked. Then she called his name, "Lucas?"

Lucas was on the floor, hidden by the podium, but he poked his head out so she could see him. He looked smaller than his seven years, and she ran toward him, but Brent yelled at her. "Stop! Don't come any closer."

Olivia froze. "I-I thought you wanted to be together?"

He took two steps away from Lucas toward Olivia. "Stay, Lucas," he growled and then took another step toward her. "Come to me, Olivia, not him."

She never noticed he was jealous of Lucas before. He was her son and his son too. "I'm coming to you, Brent."

She pulled her shoulders back and walked down the aisle toward Brent. She stopped two feet away and stared at him. He hardly looked like the man she used to know, but he wore the same clothes he'd worn the day he'd pushed his way into Miss Lynn's diner. Had he ever gone home? In his right hand, he clutched the knife he'd had that day too.

Brent pulled her body into his before kissing her hard on the mouth. It meant nothing, but she tried to put feeling into it.

"Brent. Why didn't you tell me how you felt?" she whispered intimately.

"I-I thought you knew. I was afraid you were going to leave me over the gambling when you were pregnant. That's the only reason I paid those guys to scare you."

"And when Lucas was a baby, you sent those guys again? It was never the mob?"

He shook his head and his eyes filled with tears. "I could tell you were fed up when I lost the rent money. I thought, I mean, I assumed it would work again if they showed up and you could see that I could save you by paying them off."

Olivia vibrated with anger, and it took everything she had to keep control. She didn't trust her words, so she hugged him instead of speaking. Brent sobbed as he crushed her body into his.

Lucas slid out from behind the podium and threw a book at Brent. "She doesn't like you," he said, and she could see how upset little Lucas was at Brent.

She shook her head at Lucas and pleaded with her eyes for him to stop. But Lucas had been alone with angry Brent for over twenty-four hours, and he'd had enough.

Brent yelled at him like he was an adult and not his son. "You shut the fuck up, kid. She belongs to me. She was mine before she was yours. You got that?"

Lucas stood up and threw a vase at Brent. It hit him in the leg. Brent warned him to stop, but Lucas was his mother's son, and he was only getting started. He found two more hymn books and chunked them, one right after the other, at Brent's head.

The vein in Brent's neck popped out, and he gritted his teeth as he lunged at Lucas. "I'm going to beat your ass, kid."

Before Olivia could run between them, Ryan Gentry stepped out of the shadows and told Brent to stop. When Ryan yelled, "Stop!" everyone froze.

Ryan had a red dot pointed at Brent's chest, and Brent froze as he stared at it in disbelief.

"Move to the door, Olivia. Lucas, go around to the outside aisle and meet her at the front door. Hurry."

"Hey, Ryan," Lucas said before running the entire way to his mother. Olivia picked him up and held him tight. Suddenly the church's front doors opened, and Reaper scooped up Olivia and Lucas as law enforcement filled the church.

Officer Zachary Bowman was the one that handcuffed Brent and then read him his rights. Olivia and Lucas missed the aftermath because she couldn't stop kissing him and checking him out to make sure he was okay.

She didn't know where Alexavier had gone, but Ryan took her home. They were greeted at the front door of her house by Miss Lynn and Miss Goings. They had made dinner for Lucas and reheated it while Olivia helped him get a bath.

Always the storyteller, Lucas barely ate his chicken and macaroni and cheese before he began explaining what had happened.

Olivia tried to tell him he didn't have to talk about it, but he couldn't wait to explain his kidnapping.

"I heard Mom yell that the police were coming, and that's when he opened my window. I tried to hide under my bed, but when he stepped on the Legos, he said a bad word. You know, the 'Sh' word, and I stuck my head out to look at him."

Lucas made an exaggerated expression of surprise, which made them laugh while he finished eating his chicken. Then he picked the story back up, "He said we were going on an adventure, and I'd never climbed out a window before, so I didn't think it was a big deal until I heard that loud crash inside the house and mom screamed."

"That was the front door being kicked open by Alexavier," Olivia said.

"I told you he was coming, Mom."

She nodded and held back tears at her funny, precious boy. "You sure did, Lucas."

She didn't know why Alexavier hadn't returned to the house or even if he was coming back. They'd said a lot to each other over the last twenty-four hours, and most people would need some time to contemplate what had happened. Still, she'd thought he would want to see Lucas.

"When I heard you yell, I yelled for you, Mom. But we were already outside, and he put his hand over my mouth like this,"

Lucas used his own hand to cover his mouth and then talked through it, "And he carried me into the dark."

Miss Goings patted his hand. "You are a very brave boy," she said and then gave him another chicken leg.

He smiled, and Miss Lynn added, "Yes, the bravest boy we know." Then she gave him more mac and cheese.

"I cried once," Lucas whispered, and Olivia teared up.

"I cried some too, buddy. It's okay."

"He told me I would never see you again if I didn't listen to him, so I listened. He made me walk through the woods all night, and then he had a truck. Remember that truck that followed us when we were riding bikes, Mom?"

Olivia didn't think Lucas saw that truck. "Yes, baby."

"It was that truck. He made me lay down on the floor behind his seat. I think he drove a long time because I fell asleep. When I woke up, we were inside the green dumpster behind the church. I heard a helicopter and a lot of cars, but we stayed there all day."

"I'm glad you're clean now," Miss Lynn teased.

Lucas held his nose for effect and agreed. "Me too."

The older women laughed before they brought out the pie they had made Lucas for dessert. Lucas' eyes got heavier with every bite he took.

Miss Lynn and Miss Goings both kissed Lucas and Olivia before they went next door for the night. Olivia took Lucas to her room so they could sleep there together. She told him it would be a while before she could sleep alone again. Lucas patted her on the arm like she usually did to soothe him.

As his head hit the pillow, Lucas fell asleep, but Olivia lay there for hours. She didn't want to miss a moment of him sleeping peacefully. Knowing he was safe, warm, and happy was everything. She prayed for the first time in years that she could keep him that way.

Chapter Forty

Early the next morning, Olivia woke to someone knocking on her front door. She quietly crept from her room so she wouldn't wake up Lucas. She peeked out the side window and then finger-combed her hair when she saw Alexavier standing there.

He wore dark slacks and a red polo shirt that accentuated his athletic build. Olivia admired how he always looked put together no matter the hour of the day.

She was his complete opposite, wearing rumpled pajama shorts and a long sleeve t-shirt. She smoothed her shirt down as she opened the door and smiled at him.

"Hi. Come in," Olivia said, watching his body language. After everything that had happened the day before, he hadn't stopped by, and she understood it was a lot to handle.

He'd said sweet things throughout the ordeal, but perhaps it was the stress talking? He now knew all her secrets, and after Brent's arrest, she could understand if it was all just over the top. It wouldn't be anything new to her. She'd been too much for a lot of people.

He leaned in and kissed her cheek. There was no heat behind it, and she knew for sure now that things between them had cooled.

"Good morning," she said. "Can I get you some coffee?"

Without waiting on him to answer, she hurried to the kitchen and began pulling out the French press. He didn't have a seat but stood in the doorway, watching her heat water and pull out some ground coffee beans.

The silence made the room colder, and Olivia had goosebumps as she poured the hot water over the coffee and let it steep.

"Excuse me for a minute." She ducked out of the room to grab her robe and returned wearing it and a pair of worn slippers.

She felt his eyes assessing her when she stepped back into the room, but he still hadn't moved from his spot in the doorway.

It wasn't until she pulled two cups out of the cabinet that he finally spoke up. "I really can't stay, Olivia."

She froze stock still for a moment which was the only tell that she was affected by his leaving. She nodded and then put the extra coffee cup back into the cabinet. She poured herself a mug and added sugar and cream before she turned around and faced him.

She avoided his eyes. "Thanks for everything. Lucas and I appreciate you coming."

Her voice was flat, and her face expressionless. It was a dagger to his heart. The we-appreciate-you-coming was only missing the bless-your-heart to seal how she really felt. Obviously, it wasn't the same way he loved her. They'd gotten so close, and he didn't know if he'd ever be able to get over her or Lucas. His almost family.

He had to get back to the city and to work, but he was going to leave Rex, Reaper, and Cage behind to help Olivia. She shook her head when Alexavier told her they were staying.

"No need."

"You're not staying here in St. Marksville?"

Olivia shook her head. She and Lucas didn't belong in St. Marksville. She never really did. Her parents were gone, and her sister who used to call around Olivia's birthday hadn't made the effort in several years. They'd never honestly considered her a single day even before leaving her behind. Olivia wouldn't spend any more time carrying guilt or burdens over them.

"No. Maisonville is our home. We have a few loose ends, and then we're heading back."

The old house she and Lucas had painted looked better than it had in years. Perhaps she could sell it and save half the money for her sister. Olivia would use the rest to help her get on her feet. She wouldn't have to worry about putting food on the table for Lucas or buying him winter coats and shoes. It was a relief that she hadn't seen coming.

She watched Alexavier's eyes and didn't understand why he looked sad. He'd left her before even knocking on her front door that morning. "Have a safe trip back to NOLA," she said as she followed him to the front door.

He turned and locked onto her eyes. She thought he was going to say something more, but he leaned in and kissed her cheek again before whispering, "Goodbye, Olivia."

THE REST OF THE DAY, Olivia felt like she had a hangover. Her head was foggy as she dragged through every task she'd written down. First, her parents' attorney confirmed that the house had been left to Olivia in their will years ago, and they'd never changed it. Next, Miss Lynn and Miss Goings helped her straighten things before the realtor arrived. He walked through the house, and she signed a contract with him.

Officer Zachary Bowman stopped in to take an official statement from Olivia and Lucas. He then helped her load her suitcases into the car before he hugged her and then Lucas goodbye. "Maybe I'll see you in Maisonville someday," he said, and Olivia told him it was the perfect place to start over when he was ready.

Ryan checked in to make sure Olivia and Lucas had everything they needed, and then he promised to get Miss Lynn home safely.

Miss Lynn hugged Olivia at least four times and Lucas at least eight. "You two are getting on the road soon. Promise?"

"Yes, ma'am. We'll be right behind you and Ryan," Olivia promised.

It didn't take long for Olivia to take one last look around at the house that built her, tore her down, and then rebuilt her again to know that she was ready to leave for good. She might have to come back to sign papers when it sold, but it would be for an afternoon at a closing attorney's office.

Miss Goings packed lunch for Olivia and Lucas before hugging them both fiercely. She'd been the most refreshing thing about St. Marksville, and neither Olivia nor Lucas wanted to leave her behind.

"Oh, stop that frowning," she scolded them. "This isn't good-bye. Lynn and I have already discussed me visiting, and who knows, I might find myself a little place in Maisonville too."

Olivia wiped tears from her eyes and nodded. "That would be so great. But you know you can always stay with us anytime. R-right, Lucas?"

Lucas nodded and hugged the elderly lady again.

She handed him his brown-bagged lunch and then one to Olivia with an envelope. "Now, don't open that until you pass the city limits. You hear me?"

Bossy as ever, Olivia had grown to love that woman in a short amount of time. She hugged Miss Goings once more and then hustled Lucas into the car to begin their trip back home to Maisonville.

As soon as Lucas saw the half-harvested sugar cane fields, he squealed. "Mom. It's time. Open the envelope."

Olivia laughed at her son. He always loved surprises. She found a spot to pull over and then turned halfway in her seat so he could watch her as she revealed what was inside.

What she found was a handmade pop-up card with a three-dimensional hummingbird. As she carefully pulled a tab on the side, a handwritten note was attached to a paperclip that also held five one-hundred-dollar bills. It was the exact amount that she'd received when she'd left St. Marksville the first time.

The note was written in Miss Going's beautiful cursive handwriting. Olivia read the first part aloud to Lucas. 'My dearest Olivia and Lucas. I have treasured the time we've had together and know that it is only the beginning.'

Then she read the rest silently to herself.

'Precious girl, this is simply a little pocket money to ensure you have enough to make your way home. The last time I had to give it to you anonymously, but now I am old and get to say whatever I want. You have done a fine job with that darling boy. I knew you were special when you were simply a little girl and loved watching you play in the backyard and sneak treats to my dogs. I have always rooted for you, and although you probably don't need to hear it from me, I want you to know that I am proud of you and the amazing mother you have become. I knew you had it in you all the time.'

Olivia couldn't hold back the tears that filled her eyes.

"I like her a lot. Don't you, Mom?" Lucas said as he watched out his window as the large tractors harvested the sugar cane fields.

"A lot, a lot," Olivia agreed and then wiped her eyes before pulling back onto the two-lane highway that would carry them most of the way home.

She'd felt alone for so long and couldn't believe how many people had actually been in her corner. She wanted to regret running away from Alexavier and her life in Maisonville. However, if she'd never gone back to St. Marksville, she would never have known about Miss Goings or Zachary Bowman. Even Mr. Robichaux and his son, Mark, had stood up for her.

She'd practically had an army of people from the town rushing to help search for Lucas. She hadn't been alone at all.

Chapter Forty-One

Olivia stood behind the counter at the diner, drinking her cup of coffee and listening to the new waitress, Daisy, tell her and Miss Lynn about her encounter with the man named Reaper.

Reaper had waited in St. Marksville so he could follow Olivia and Lucas home. He even sat outside of their duplex for a couple of hours to make sure everything remained quiet. Although his parents were together, when Reaper was young his father had worked offshore leaving his mother to look after everyone and everything. It was a huge job, so he made it his personal mission to always keep an extra eye out for young mothers and their children.

Afterward, he showed up at the diner near closing and ordered a full meal, dessert, and coffee. He was the only customer left in the restaurant, and according to Daisy, he ate slower than any human she'd ever met.

Daisy had always been on the quiet side, but she nervously explained what had happened. "The guys in the kitchen were getting so mad and every time I walked in there, they grumbled about me refilling the man's coffee cup."

She finally told the kitchen employees they could go home while she stayed an extra hour and a half waiting on Reaper to finish.

He then lectured her on how unsafe it was for her to wait with a complete stranger alone in the restaurant.

Miss Lynn smiled at the pretty young waitress. She didn't want to admit to Daisy that she agreed with Reaper.

"So, what did you say?" Olivia asked.

Daisy was still rattled. But Miss Lynn had told Daisy to expect one or all three of the mayor's security team to stop in because she'd insisted on giving them a hot meal for all that they had done for Olivia and Lucas. "I looked him square in the eyes and asked him if he was a serial killer. When he said no, then I told him that apparently, I knew what I was doing, and he shouldn't try and tell me what to do."

Olivia stifled a laugh. Reaper was one of the biggest men she'd ever met in person, and he looked like he could rip someone apart with his bare hands. Miss Lynn had told Daisy how great Rex, Cage, and Reaper were, but still it was hard to believe she was that brave in front of such a massive guy.

Miss Lynn and Olivia glanced over at each other, then watched as Daisy walked off to unlock the front door so they could serve breakfast. Miss Lynn hadn't scheduled Daisy until the afternoon, but they were her only friends, and she obviously needed to talk to someone about him. She was clearly still frustrated at the handsome man that made her work extra late and then insisted on seeing her home to the boarding house where she was staying.

Things were always entertaining in Maisonville.

Olivia and Lucas had only been back one night, but it didn't take long for them to settle in as if they'd never left. It was a sign, even though she didn't need one, that said they belonged there.

As soon as they got in, Olivia spent her time cleaning the little duplex. However, first thing this morning, Lucas was ready for school as if he hadn't missed one lesson, and so she was ready to work at the diner. The only thing that had really changed was that she no longer heard from Alexavier.

Of course, when she'd moved to St. Marksville without a

phone, she couldn't text him at night. But she didn't think that was enough to end the habit they had developed over the last six months.

She was wrong.

She missed him terribly, and his absence was magnified at home. Lucas asked if he was coming over for dinner last night and this morning before he caught the school bus, but she didn't have the heart to tell him that Alex wasn't coming back. She'd tried to hint at it over story time, but Lucas shook his head and told her she'd said that in St. Marksville too. "Trust me, mom. He told me before that he really likes us. Really, really likes us."

She had to tell Lucas the truth, but she needed a little more time to accept it too.

It was really difficult when Lucas refused to eat her spaghetti for dinner because it wasn't as good as Alexavier's mom made. He insisted that he could wait until she made him some again and then made himself a peanut butter and jelly sandwich.

It was the first time Olivia had gotten really upset about missing Alexavier, and she cried in the shower so Lucas wouldn't hear her. She'd put him to bed and was lying on the couch watching television when Ryan and Sydney stopped by to check on them. Sydney had explained that they both simply wanted to lay eyes on Lucas. She let them peek in on him while he slept and hugged them both for being such great friends.

Ryan told her how much he liked Alexavier and when she teared up, Sydney hugged her tightly.

"What do you mean it's over?" Ryan asked, confused.

"He stopped by the day after Brent was arrested, and I think he was relieved to get back home and away from me and all that drama."

Ryan shook his head. Then, he explained that Alexavier was the one who'd called him when Lucas went missing. He'd also paid a ton of money for the helicopter expenses, and even though Ryan's friends volunteered their services, Alex insisted on paying them for their time since they had to miss work. "Regalia was ruined over Lucas being gone, and he moved heaven and earth to get boots on the ground searching for him."

After Ryan and Sydney left, Olivia couldn't sleep. Alexavier's behavior didn't make sense, and she had to agree with Ryan and Sydney that it wasn't the behavior of someone that could walk away so easily. But he had.

The breakfast crowd was light and talkative, but the lunch rush was extra-long as Olivia's sleepless night caught up to her. Things were slowing down, and she stepped in the back to drink a diet coke while Daisy worked her station for a few minutes.

Suddenly, Miss Lynn came bustling in to get her. "Breaks over," she said. Olivia rolled her eyes. She knew Miss Lynn was up to something. But when she stepped back into the restaurant, she was enveloped in warm hugs from Marie Regalia and Auntie Francesca.

"Bellissima. You shouldn't be at work so soon. You needed some time off to rest and recuperate from all you've been through," Marie said.

Auntie Francesca pushed her into a booth. "Come sit down with us."

Olivia tried not to laugh at the pushy women, but when she looked over at Miss Lynn, smiling so large that all her dentures were showing, she couldn't help it.

"What are y'all doing here?" Olivia asked.

"We had to make sure you were okay with our very own eyes," Marie said.

Francesca finished the thought with, "Alexavier doesn't give enough details, and he immediately went back to work and stayed up at his office overnight. Now, what is good here to eat."

Olivia helped them order, and then the two older Italian women turned and stared at her.

Marie leaned in. "Now tell us what is going on with you and my son?"

Olivia shook her head, and Auntie Francesca reached over and gently held her face. "He's hurting too."

"What? Then why?"

Marie rolled her eyes and shook her head. "I'm afraid his deceased wife did a number on him." Marie made the sign of the cross and then said, "God rest her soul, but she wasn't meant for him. She pushed him away so many times that I'm afraid he wouldn't know the real thing if it hit upside the head."

Olivia nodded and whispered, "I don't want to hit him, but I-I do love him."

Auntie Francesca patted Olivia's hand. "Don't you worry. We truthfully needed to make sure you still felt the same."

"I guess I'm scared too."

Marie's eyes watered, and she nodded at Olivia. "I know, Bellissima. Forgive us because we might stretch the truth a bit. Just go with it?"

Olivia hugged the sweet woman who gave the best mom hugs in the world next to Miss Lynn. "I'll do anything," she said, and then they ate lunch and talked about Lucas the rest of the time.

It was less than an hour after Alexavier's mom and auntie left that he rushed through the diner's front door.

Miss Lynn had made a fresh pot of coffee and stopped what she was doing to sit down and watch the mayor, full of concern, grab Olivia and make sure she was okay.

Daisy walked over and stood beside Miss Lynn as they watched the swoon-worthy mayor, who was always put together, come unraveled.

"What happened, Olivia? Are you hurt? Sick? Did something happen to Lucas? Where is he?"

He was borderline freaking out, and Olivia couldn't answer a single question as he didn't stop and take a breath.

Finally, she stepped away from him and straightened her clothes and apron. "What are you talking about, Alex? I'm fine. We're fine." She suddenly knew what the little Italian women meant when they said they 'might stretch the truth.'

She fixed her eyes on him. "But you wouldn't know that because you haven't freaking bothered to call or come by to see for yourself. So what? The going gets a little tough, and I guess you're over us now?"

Alexavier took a step back. His overall demeanor visibly calmed. "My mother said you—" he stopped mid-sentence. As soon as he began to explain his concern, he realized his mother and auntie had interfered.

He began apologizing for storming in there, and then Olivia's words seemed to hit him. "— the going gets a little tough? Over you?"

Olivia pointed her finger into his chest. "I'm glad your hearing is still good. I didn't stutter. How dare you act like you care. You bolted out of St. Marksville like the hounds of hell were after you."

"Like the hounds of hell were after me?" Alexavier stared at her. "You told Brent you left Maisonville because of me. You said you didn't want me there." He ran his hands in his hair, and it stuck up all over his head, which admittedly she thought was hot but totally messy and nothing like the way Alexavier typically looked. "Then you and Lucas left with Ryan. When I came by the next morning, you practically dismissed me. You thanked me for coming and said you appreciated me like I was, like I was, I don't know, a customer from the diner."

"I. Did. Not!" Olivia poked his chest with her finger for each word.

Alexavier's whole face was red, and he stepped into her space as she put both her hands on his chest.

"You opened the front door for me to leave."

She continued poking him, "I offered you coffee, and you said you couldn't stay!"

He lowered his voice, and she felt the emotion in his words. "You wouldn't even look at me."

It had been the worst moment of her life, and he'd been there by her side the entire time. She felt flayed and exposed in front of him and couldn't explain how the vulnerability scared the bejeezus out of her. She would admit that to him one day, but at that moment, he was vulnerable too. The only relationship he'd ever had other than her had ended tragically. But before that, his wife had shut him out over and over again. Olivia couldn't have him thinking that she was the same as Victoria.

She put her hands on his face and stared into his eyes. "There were a hundred reasons why I couldn't look at you. One, because after being up for twenty-four hours and orchestrating a manhunt like no law enforcement officer had ever seen, you showed up in your pressed slacks and perfect red polo like you'd stepped off the cover of a GQ magazine."

Olivia held up her fingers as she counted. "Two, I stood there with my mismatched pajamas and tangled hair, looking like a hot mess. Three, I was embarrassed over everything that had happened and how I looked and felt."

He pulled her into his arms and kissed her hard on the mouth. It had all the heat she'd missed and then some. She didn't care where they were, and she sure didn't care when Miss Lynn jokingly said, "PDA should be outlawed."

"There are a million reasons why I love you. One, the way you look when you first wake up."

"Love?"

He leaned his forehead against hers. "Love, Olivia Dufrene."

"I love you too," she whispered.

Miss Lynn cleared her throat. "Speak up, Olivia."

Olivia rolled her eyes at her shameless sweet older friend. "I said, I love him too."

Miss Lynn gave her an approving nod, and then they heard Lucas set down his book bag. "You love Alex, mom?"

Chapter Forty-Two

Alexavier pointed at Lucas and said, "Two, that amazing kid right there." Olivia barely could catch her breath but forced herself to turn around and look at her son. "Yes, buddy. I do love Alexavier."

"Me too!" Lucas said as he pulled a picture he'd drawn at school out of his book bag. It was a picture of the three of them together holding hands. Alexavier's eyes watered as he picked Lucas up and hugged him.

"What's that picture, Lucas?" he asked as he sat the little boy back on his feet.

"A family," he said and then headed to the counter to see Miss Lynn.

Alexavier held another finger up as he pointed at the picture Lucas drew and mouthed the word, "three."

Olivia wiped her eyes with her apron, and then she sat down with her son. "You know, you and I are a family, Lucas. Right?"

"Of course." He picked up his grilled cheese sandwich and took a big bite. "Alex, if you're my mom's boyfriend, then what are you to me?"

"Your friend," Olivia answered, giving Lucas her serious mom eyes.

It didn't slow him down. "But if you marry my mom, then what?"

Miss Lynn and Daisy both put their hands over their mouths. It was the most exciting conversation that had ever happened in the diner. At least so far that afternoon.

"Lucas Henry Dufrene!" Olivia said, but Lucas shrugged his shoulder and took another bite of his sandwich.

"I'd be her husband and your dad," he said, avoiding Olivia's stare. "We'd be a family. Do you want that to happen, Lucas?"

The sweet young boy smiled so big his eyes lit up. Alexavier leaned in and whispered into his ear, "Me too."

"Then we could do everything together like a family," Lucas said as he finished his sandwich. "Like build ramps or a tree house or go trick or treating."

Alexavier couldn't think of anything he'd like better than to be with them all the time. "We can do all of those things, Lucas. In fact, this Saturday is the big Halloween Parade."

Lucas looked at his mom, who usually told him she had to think about those sorts of big things. She'd been quietly watching the exchange between Alexavier and Lucas, not knowing what to say to either of them. They hadn't asked Olivia what she thought about them becoming a family. She hadn't let herself even dream of marriage, but her guys both clearly had.

"Please, mom," Lucas waited anxiously, and she realized he was talking about the parade and not marriage.

She half laughed and then nodded. "We can go, buddy."

"Go? I can do better than that. I'm the Grand Marshal this year. We're riding on a float."

"What?" Olivia asked.

Alexavier was ready for that life he'd talked about, and he was done hiding. It was time everyone saw them together.

"This Saturday? Together, in public?"

"You can't hide me forever, Olivia."

Alexavier knew he should feel guilty putting her on the spot, especially in front of Lucas. But he didn't feel an ounce of guilt.

He was ready for the world to know she was his, and he was hers, and Lucas was going to be theirs.

The entire diner seemed to be holding its collective breath while Olivia weighed the consequences of being photographed in public with Alexavier.

She tilted her head back and forth while she bit her bottom lip. Finally, she took a deep breath and let it out. "Okay."

While he secretly hoped she would be proud to do it, he understood what a big step it was for her to agree. It made him, and more importantly, Lucas, very happy.

"Yahoo," Lucas exclaimed, throwing his fist in the air triumphantly. Everyone in the diner clapped, and Olivia realized for the first time that they'd all been listening.

"Stop," she said nervously, laughing. "It's only a parade, not a wedding."

"Yet," Alexavier said and kissed her again in front of everyone as they clapped louder.

Miss Lynn told the happy couple they should take the rest of the night off and gathered Olivia's purse and sweatshirt from behind the counter.

Alexavier picked up Lucas' school bag while the little boy stopped to look at him curiously. "Where would you live, Alex? At our house or still in N'orleans?"

Olivia looked mortified over her son discussing marriage again. Then she corrected him. "New Orleans, Lucas. You know he's The Mayor of New Orleans."

Lucas shrugged. "Why can't you be the mayor of Maisonville instead?"

"Would you like for me to be the mayor of Maisonville?"

Lucas nodded excitedly again.

"It's not a bad idea, kiddo. When I finish my job in New Orleans, I plan to buy a house in Maisonville."

Olivia stared at Alexavier while Lucas smiled proudly.

Miss Lynn was pretty sure she was happier than all three of

them put together. She sweetly wrapped her arms around Alexavier and Olivia as she shooed them out the front door.

They heard her laugh and loudly announce to everyone in the diner that they'd all heard the campaign announcement there first. Then she told everyone to tell all their friends.

It would just be another new beginning in Maisonville.

THE END

The Pursuit

BY LISA HERRINGTON

Book Four of the suspenseful, romantic Renaissance Lake series, Coming Soon!

Something is coming to Maisonville, and it will stir up everything in our quaint little water town!

TENILLE ONLY HAD ONE CHANCE to leave. She was in the most romantic place she had ever been, The Four Seasons Resort in Lanai City, Hawaii, and approximately 3, 857 miles from her home in Texas. She and Peter had arrived only two days ago, but he had reminded her no less than eight times how ungrateful she was and how he was a sucker to spoil her. She didn't make his coffee the way he wanted, and she didn't wear the clothes he expected even though he'd picked out every single item in her suitcase, including the shoes. The list of things she wasn't, went on and on.

She'd met him after her aunt died and moved in with him after only one week. The rest had been unbearable. When she learned who he really was and how he made his money, she understood her life would never be the same.

Peter was in the middle of telling an inappropriate joke as she quietly excused herself from the large dining table. Six Middle Eastern men stood when she did, but Peter just stared at her.

"Going to the ladies' room," she whispered as his jaw clenched. He was angry. Mad at her for interrupting his story or because she took attention off him. Honestly, it could have been because she was human and needed to use the restroom. She had no idea what went on inside his crazy head. She just knew this was her only opportunity and she needed to act as casual as possible if she was going to make it out alive.

She smiled at the guests surrounding the table and smoothed down her blue silk dress before she slowly walked across the opulent room. Softly clicking her four-inch heels like she didn't have a care in the world, when she gently pushed open the door and stepped inside the restroom.

The waitress, Nalani, waiting on their table had been in the parking lot when she and Peter had arrived. Nalani saw Peter grab Tenille's face, slam her head against a window and threaten her before they walked inside the restaurant.

Tenille caught Nalani's concerned eyes as she wiped tears from her face, careful not to smudge her makeup and upset him again. The slight nod and understanding in her expression were almost more than Tenille could take.

Nalani had signaled for Tenille to meet her in the restroom. She waited there with a pair of flip-flop sandals and then hugged Tenille harder than she'd been hugged in a long time.

Nalani led her outside to a pickup truck and introduced Tenille to her cousins, a young woman and man who were twins. "I'll refill the drinks at the table and when he notices you're still gone, I'll stall him by saying you're not well but will be out of the restroom soon. Good luck."

Tenille reached for Nalani's arm. "You can't let him know you helped me. Understand?"

The look in Nalani's eyes told her that she did.

"Mahola," Tenille whispered before she hurried out of there with the cousins and onto a two-lane road. In fifteen minutes, Tenille was on a small boat and heading away from the town of Lanai and the scariest person she'd ever known.

About the Author

LISA HERRINGTON is a Women's fiction and YA novelist, and blogger. A former medical sales rep, she currently manages the largest Meet-Up writing group in the New Orleans area, The Bayou Writer's Club. She was born and raised in Louisiana, attended college at Ole Miss in Oxford, Mississippi and accepts that in New Orleans we never hide our crazy but instead parade it around on the front porch and give it a cocktail. It's certainly why she has so many stories to tell today. When she's not writing, and spending time with her husband and three children, she spends time reading, watching old movies or planning something new and exciting with her writers' group.

Connect with Lisa, find out about new releases, and get free books at lisaherrington.com

Made in the USA
Coppell, TX
23 January 2023

11574398R00164